THE
FAVOURITE

Rosemary Hennigan is an Irish author who lives in Dublin. She studied Law at Trinity College Dublin, as well as the University of Pennsylvania, and is a Fulbright Scholar. She practised as a solicitor, first in corporate law, before moving into the NGO sector. She has worked in advocacy for a number of charities focused on asylum and homelessness. She was shortlisted for the Benedict Kiely Short Story Competition and longlisted for the Colm Toibin Short Story Competition. *The Favourite* is her second novel.

Also by *Rosemary Hennigan*

The Truth Will Out

THE
FAVOURITE

ROSEMARY HENNIGAN

ORION

An Orion paperback
First published in Great Britain in 2024 by Orion Fiction,
an imprint of The Orion Publishing Group Ltd,
Carmelite House, 50 Victoria Embankment
London EC4Y 0DZ

An Hachette UK Company

3 5 7 9 10 8 6 4

A CIP catalogue record for this book is
available from the British Library.

ISBN (Trade Paperback) 978 1 3987 1844 9
ISBN (Mass Market Paperback) 978 1 3987 0485 5
ISBN (eBook) 978 1 3987 0486 2

Typeset by Input Data Services Ltd, Somerset

Printed and bound in Great Britain by Clays Ltd, Elcograf S.p.A.

MIX
Paper from
responsible sources
FSC® C104740

www.orionbooks.co.uk

For David

Why does tragedy exist?
Because you are full of rage.
Why are you are full of rage?
Because you are full of grief.

Anne Carson, *Grief Lessons: Four Plays by Euripides*

Chapter One

He was standing with my sister the first time I saw him, in the Trinity Arts Block after class. He had a crooked nose, sharp brown eyes, and greying stubble that coated the lower half of his cheeks, his jaw, and that part of his neck visible above his black polo-neck jumper. Physically nondescript, nothing unusual in his bearing. Just a shiny American smile and the confidence of a man with no reason to question his position in life.

They had a short and seemingly awkward exchange that I couldn't hear at a distance. Audrey's fingers were playing with the strap of her handbag, her weight shifting from one foot to the other. I wandered over, but he turned to leave before I reached her. All I caught were his parting words. 'See you around, kid,' he said, with a small wave of a large hand.

Arriving next to her, I angled my head in his direction. 'Who was that?' He was already disappearing into the crowds pouring out of different lecture halls. They milled around us, a noisy and bustling mess of bodies, through which he cut like a knife. His stride was purposeful, his gaze deliberately pitched above the heads of students, who parted at his approach.

'Him? Jay Crane. He's one of my professors,' Audrey replied before setting off down the steps, in the opposite direction.

She didn't elaborate, and, at the time, I took her at her word.

I hadn't the faintest suspicion of how much he would come to mean to her, or how much he already meant.

I exited the Arts Block through the swinging doors and stepped outside to Fellows' Square. Trinity's campus struck me as it always did. The grey walls wept in the October rain, the points of Alexander Calder's cactus sculpture made sharp by the dusk light. The long summer days in Dublin were over, the nights closing in again. Together, we made our way to the train station, heading home to Malahide, my older sister walking slightly in front.

It seems so obvious now, so hard to imagine events unfolding in any other way. But, back then, there was ignorance. There was bliss. I didn't know it yet, but we would never be the same, not once Professor Jay Crane entered our lives.

What chance did Audrey have against him? Nobody had ever told her that the word of a man like Crane was not gospel, that he was no god, that his influence could be dangerous, that he could hurt her. Nobody ever told her to be careful of men who dazzle and then withdraw, leaving a wasteland of human wreckage in their wake. Nobody told her of the darkness that can lurk behind an easy smile and a few kind words, and by the time she learned it for herself, the damage was done.

There's no fixing it now.

I should say that what follows is not a confession. It's not an exercise in atonement or motivated by guilt. If I consulted a lawyer, she would tell me not to write it down at all. It could be used against me. Sometimes, my finger hovers over the backspace key, ready to let the cursor chase these words away into nothingness. But always in that moment, just before I give into that compulsion, I think of Audrey again, and I hesitate.

It was her story first, before I made it mine.

When you came seeking answers, I didn't know what to say, because the truth is not an easy thing. I don't even know if I can tell the right and the wrong of it anymore. Every day, more women are speaking up and, as they do, my silence weighs more heavily on me. There have been so many lies that telling the truth now feels like an act of bravery, a leap of faith. Sunlight burning away the haze. So here it is: an honest history of what happened.

Insofar as certain events *may* have followed from my decision to enrol at Franklin University, I can hardly be held responsible for that. The only guilty mind involved was Crane's. What happened to him was his own fault, but I don't need to tell you that. You'll see for yourself.

Chapter Two

On the morning of my first day at Franklin University, I sat in the courtyard of the law school, my notes spread on the round, metal table in front of me, a pen in my hand, and premeditated intention in my heart. It was late August in Philadelphia, the city a swamp, the sun raging down relentlessly. Even in the shade, the heat was audacious, and I had been sweating into my jean shorts for forty minutes. I was about to meet Professor Jay Crane face to face for the first time and I felt far from ready.

There had been a time in my life when Jay Crane was not at the centre of every thought, but that time felt distant now, like a half-remembered dream. He had become a waypoint that I used to direct me, Polaris in the night sky, and I had travelled thousands of miles to find him here, securing a place in his prestigious Law and Literature class at Franklin's law school. All final-year and master's students completing an LLM, like me, were eligible to apply and, every year, only six were chosen. It was a long way to come for such a niche course, but I had my reasons.

A mystique hung over the class, as if secret knowledge was shared behind the closed doors of room 1.04B, and over the professor, whose ideas could be found in newspaper columns and podcast interviews, on bookshelves, and in the law journals we studied. He had a high public profile, at least among the sort of people who pay attention to law professors.

In the baking heat of the courtyard, I was using what little time I had before my first class to read, for the fourth time, the article Crane had assigned us. There were crumbs on my T-shirt, grains of sugar from the doughnut I had just eaten. My foot tapped against the leg of my chair, my hand scratching subconsciously at the mosquito bites along my calves. My T-shirt was the same pale pink as my skin, caused by an unintended nap in the sun the afternoon before. I was beginning to think I might be allergic to the weather here, hot girl summer not an Irish phenomenon.

Right from the beginning, I would need to impress Crane. I had to catch his eye, just as Audrey had done that term at Trinity. My purpose here depended on it.

I needed Crane to notice me, but I had never possessed the conventional, easy attractiveness of my sister. We looked nothing alike – a difference so notable that people felt free to comment on it. My sister and I were direct physical opposites in most respects, as if our genes had been selected to produce the starkest contrast. My face was long, eyes deep-set, hair dark, thick and unruly. Audrey's face was round, eyes bright and blue, hair blonde and sleek.

Even when we were young – too young – men would notice her. She would point them out to me when she caught them looking and I would meander their way, to 'accidentally' step on their feet, or spill a drink on their laps, or – on one particularly egregious occasion – run a key along the paintwork of his car.

But it wasn't just the bare physicality that made us so different. There were other qualities Audrey possessed that set us apart. She had an openness, a way of smiling out at the world, that I lacked completely. Something in her movements, in her habits, drew people's attention. It felt good to be around her. I know this because I felt it in her presence too. The deep peace she had in herself, an unguardedness in the way she met the world – something Crane took from her, an unforgivable theft.

I don't think it was Audrey's looks alone that attracted Crane. But if her beauty had ever caught his eye in a crowded lecture hall, I doubted I would stand out the same way. I would not have the luxury of such an easy appeal to base instincts. I would have to rely on rat wit and fox cunning, on animal chicanery, instead of feminine wiles.

'Jessie?'

A man's voice shook me out of my thoughts. I squinted up at him, his face framed by a sun so bright it seemed to scorch my eyes.

'It is *Jessie*, right?'

He was tall, with dark hair and small brown eyes behind Henry Kissinger glasses, wearing a black T-shirt with '*Hillary 2016*' printed in white. I dimly remembered a conversation we'd had the previous night at a dorm party on the floor below mine about the upcoming presidential election. I had gone to hoover up what intel I could get on Crane before I would face him in class. But, preoccupied by this hunt for information, I had managed to forget this guy's name.

'Yeah,' I said, eyes blinking back the sunlight. 'Hi . . . I'm sorry, I'm useless at names?'

'Right . . . ha! It's Joshua. We spoke last night? You were arguing with me about Bernie Sanders.' He pushed his glasses up his nose, still smiling.

'Oh, yeah. That rings a bell.' I shaded my eyes so I could better see him. 'He should be the candidate.'

'Yeah . . . yeah, you said that last night.' He shifted his backpack on his shoulder, grinning broadly. There was something deeply appealing about that grin, something soothing in its simplicity. 'So, you said you're also in Crane's Law and Lit class, right? I'm on my way there now.'

'Yes!' I sat up straighter. Joshua – of course. He was the first of the other Law and Lit students I had met, and I was curious to learn who Crane had chosen, these students who would, unknowingly, witness my plan unfold. 'Yes, I am . . . I'll just grab my bag and I can come with you?'

I bundled my papers into the backpack at my feet and wrapped a plaid shirt around my waist to hide the presence of any unfortunate sweat patches.

'I wanted to ask you, last night, about our professor – Crane,' I said, trying to sound casual. 'What's he like?'

Joshua was glancing behind him at the group playing cornhole on the grass, a game involving tossing beanbags through a hole cut in a wooden board. I recognised a few of them as fellow international students from my master's course.

Turning back to me, he smiled. 'Crane's cool.' I could tell that Joshua was trying to downplay his enthusiasm. But he spoke with something of the same exhilaration I was accustomed to hearing in Audrey's voice when she talked about Crane. 'I haven't had a class with him before, so I'm excited to see him in action.'

'I heard he's a bit of a character though, right?' I lifted my backpack onto my shoulder and walked with Joshua across the red-bricked path.

The law school was built around this central courtyard, classrooms, a library, and faculty offices all contained within the complex. A few streets over from the main campus, it was its own little world.

The door we were headed for looked as if it had been carved into the thick ivy covering the wall, and it was opening and closing continually as people cut through the courtyard to get to the classrooms on the other side. We reached it just as someone successfully punted a bean bag through the cornhole behind us, a cheer sounding from the grass.

Joshua held the door open for me and I slipped inside, the cold, filtered air immediately soothing my hot skin. 'Yeah, like, he's known as this, like, radical law professor with big political ideas.' He gesticulated while he spoke, his hands sweeping the air. 'When he published his book, he said we should rip up the Constitution and start again, and that got picked up by Fox, and then made into this whole, you know, *thing* . . .' I had seen some of that controversy when I first researched Crane online. A polarising figure, by all accounts.

'I'm looking forward to meeting him,' I said, pulling on the sleeves of the plaid shirt and tightening it around my waist. 'There's a lot of hype.'

'Yeah, I guess there is. I'm a little nervous, honestly. I think Crane keeps the class small so there's nowhere to hide from him.' Joshua laughed. 'All that effort to get into the class and now I'm scared to actually go . . .'

To get into the class, we had to write a short discussion paper on a topic of our choice. I'm sure the other students had worked hard on theirs, but not like me. Arriving in Franklin, it was my first priority. I had flung myself into the writing of that essay as if my life depended on it. I bedded down in the library, absorbing every piece of academic research Crane had written in the previous decade. It was not always the focus of his work, but in almost everything Crane wrote, there was a deep scepticism of the legal system as the formal arbiter for justice. And it seemed as if he was angry about it, angry at the law's own mythologising, angry at the self-serving story it told itself. From his journalistic work, I had noticed an interest in the classics; the foundational Greek texts; the myths and rhetoric; the dramas and tragedies.

Drawing this all together, I wrote an essay designed specifically to appeal to him, a piece about the tragedy of Antigone and the nature of justice. Personal conscience clashing with legal obligation, duties owed to the state versus those owed to higher principles, such as the gods, or even family.

But, to me, Antigone also spoke to something else, the story of the love between two sisters, and a loyalty that persisted, despite a gulf of miscomprehension between them.

For four days, I worked on that essay. The first at the library door in the morning, the last to leave at night, sustaining myself on processed snacks and strong coffee. The other students were propelled by ambition, by competitive zeal, maybe even by the enormity of their student loans, but I had something more powerful behind me. White-hot anger.

On the corridor, feet moved briskly around me, heading towards classrooms and lecture halls, the floors of the law school shining with fresh polish. To my right, light poured into the corridor from the floor-to-ceiling windows facing the courtyard, through which I could see the game of cornhole coming to an end. Beanbags scattered across the grass, lying crumpled where they had landed. I turned my eyes away and followed Joshua towards the library, at the back of which was Crane's classroom, room 1.04B.

'What did you write about?' he asked me. 'To get into the class, I mean.'

'Justice,' I said, after a long pause. 'How we make it for ourselves. Rough justice, I guess.'

Joshua laughed. 'Is that what you're into, Jessie?!'

'Maybe.'

A set of steps led up to the library, the doors of which were panelled in glass. 'That's kind of Crane's thing too – law as power. I think he's going to like you,' he said as we climbed, his hand on the brass railing nailed to the wall beside him.

'Well, that's the goal. Isn't it?' I replied. 'That's what everyone wants . . . to be Crane's favourite student.'

His head jerked, and he watched me over his shoulder as he pushed the door open, holding it for me as I walked inside. 'So you've heard about all that?'

Audrey had been his favourite once, recipient of special care, and particular attention. But it was in Philadelphia that I learned this was not a one-off sort of thing. A girl named Kyra, whose dorm room was three doors down from my own, had told me Crane was known for playing favourites with his students. If you found yourself chosen, all manner of advantages flowed your way: your pick of internships, clerkships, or an introduction to any of his many judicial, academic and political contacts – catnip to the overachieving nerds and the legacy surnames filling the halls at Franklin. Rumour had it that he would whisper in the ear of the influential, telling those in power that you were special, a cut above the rest, someone deserving of every opportunity, someone like them.

Scanning my student card at the turnstile, I gave a small shrug. 'Sure . . . I mean, as soon as people hear I'm in Law and Lit, they ask me about it. Seems like a bit of a fixation around here.' The metal spokes turned, making a mechanical sound as I pushed through.

Joshua pulled a face. 'That's probably true. A word of advice, Jessie? Some people are pretty cut-throat about all that favourite stuff. You might not want to get involved.'

I smiled but didn't offer a response as he followed me through the turnstile. The competitive atmosphere at Franklin was more heightened than I was used to. Along the corridors, in the ladies' restrooms, on the courtyard, I would catch snippets of conversations from the other students, the topics almost always of future plans, career ambitions, the summer associateships they were chasing, or the letters of recommendation they planned to collect from particular professors. Introductions needed, grades desired, achievements fuelling hunger for more.

The persistent, weighty sensation of other people's ambitions sat on me from that first day. But my own ambition was made of altogether darker stuff, and I passed through the corridors feeling like a wolf among sheep. Becoming one of Crane's favourites was the obvious way to gain his trust and it would allow me to lure him closer without making him suspicious of my motives. He wouldn't notice how I bent him to my will, how I tugged on a string and made his limbs rise, marionette-style, at my command.

In front of the librarian's desk, I glanced at my watch. We were nearly at the hour. In a matter of minutes, Crane would enter my life. Everything depended on this first introduction. If he recognised anything of Audrey in me, my plan would be over before it began. All it would take was something small, my manner of speech, my posture, a turn of phrase, a facial expression we shared. Something subtle that could trigger a memory of my sister and then . . . well.

I had taken the precaution of enrolling as Jessica Mooney, dropping the Flynn from the double-barrel surname our parents had given us. Audrey and I usually went by Mooney-Flynn, or just Flynn for short. And since Crane had known Audrey Mooney-Flynn in Dublin, I had to hope he wouldn't suspect the Jessica Mooney who was about to show up in his class in Philadelphia. I couldn't drop the name entirely, since Mooney was on my passport. It was a common name in Ireland, but it was, nevertheless, a risk I couldn't avoid. I didn't know what Crane might do if forced to protect himself.

With a deep breath, I tried to steel my nerves. All the years, all the planning, and all the effort could come to nothing. And then what would I do? What was left for me?

In the hush of the library, Joshua and I fell silent, the carpet underfoot muffling our steps. Fear was wrapped, like a metal cable, around my chest, squeezing ever tighter. Room 1.04B was just ahead, hidden away at the back of the library, on the other side of the bookshelves.

The moment had finally come. It was time to meet Crane.

Chapter Three

I let Joshua lead the way past the students ensconced in their individual neat, wooden kiosks. A few heads bobbed up from books and laptop screens, some eyes meeting mine briefly, then dropping again. They were wearing the same branded merchandise from the university bookstore, a uniform of sweats and shorts, hoodies and hats. Bodies emblazoned with the loud public message that we were part of a club, a higher echelon, specially chosen from all the others.

The door was plain and unassuming, a small metal plaque, the size of a business card, confirming it was room 1.04B. Without Joshua, I might have walked right past it, taking it for a store-room, or part of the library stacks.

'After you,' Joshua said, opening the door for me.

Inside, the room was narrow, with a whiteboard on the wall and a long, oval table occupying most of the floorspace. There was a chair for Crane at the head and a window behind it, look-ing onto Chestnut Street, down which cars rolled in waves with the turning of the traffic lights. Bookshelves lined the walls, a collection of old textbooks, decades out of date, the laws they contained long since changed, though nobody had bothered to throw them out, as if the concerns and travails of the past were still worth preserving, despite its calcifying effect on the present. So here they sat, next to the surplus marble busts of distinguished people now forgotten.

I chose an empty seat halfway down the table, pulled my laptop out of my bag, and arranged my handwritten notes on Crane's articles next to me. They were extensive, and annotated with a variety of coloured tabs. My restless fingers flicked through the pages.

Taking the seat next to me, Joshua spotted them, his eyes widening. 'You *really* prepared for this class . . . can you just answer for me?!' He was smiling again, but I wasn't so sure he meant it this time.

'Oh, no, this is nothing. It's just that I'm interested,' I replied, as another student joined us in the room. 'I'm guessing Crane is the type to ask questions.'

The other student placed his backpack on the table opposite me. His well-structured face – all stark lines and sharp angles – fit well among the angular marble and the straight, mahogany lines of the bookshelves. Blonde, with the sort of floppy hair they put on Ken dolls, he was obnoxiously, conventionally handsome. Perfect teeth and a confident smile. People like him were made for places like this, the corridors built to accommodate them, the air itself thick with the dust of their ancestors. You know, the kind of guy who never doubted his place in the world.

His eyes were slightly sunken, giving him the look of someone already fatigued by life, over it. 'You slacking off already, Joshua?' he said with a smirk.

Joshua didn't look up from his laptop. 'No, Charlie, that's your thing.'

'I don't slack, Joshua, I'm just efficient,' Charlie said, pointedly eying my notes. 'I prepare exactly what I need and no more.'

I wasn't sure if he intended to insult me, or maybe intimidate me. But my mind was elsewhere. Whenever a shadow crossed the door, my heart thumped against my ribcage. A false alarm, just another student arriving, but I felt a blow to the chest each time, as if my heart might give out before Crane even arrived.

The other students seemed to know each other already. They greeted Charlie and Joshua as they sat down, and cast a curious eye over me. I pretended to be absorbed in my screen, leaning my chin on one hand, stealing occasional glances as the seats around me filled. I knew their names from the enrolment confirmation online: Joshua Reynolds, Charlie Duke, Ronald Harris, Amanda Taylor, and Vera Lin.

It was Vera who addressed me first. 'Who are you?' she asked, smiling in a lopsided way that seemed uncomfortable on her face. Her very straight, very black hair hung close to her full cheeks and something in her smile made me feel as if she were sizing me up unfavourably.

'I'm, eh, Jessica. Jessie. Jessie Mooney.' I cleared my throat, gripped my hands together.

'Is that an accent?' Amanda asked, cocking an ear towards me. 'Where you from, Jessie?'

'Ireland . . . Dublin, actually.'

'Cool, yeah, thought so. I'm from London!'

I could have guessed. Her accent had that Oxbridge clip that made me feel like I should fix my posture. She was wearing a pinstripe blue shirt dress and high-top runners, with the sort of effortless natural style I usually found intimidating. But her face was kind. Her hair was tightly braided, her brown eyes alive with interest.

'We're neighbours,' I said. 'You're on the LLM programme too?' Though we took the same classes, the American students – including Vera, Charlie, Ronald, and Joshua – typically took the three-year Juris Doctorate course, but the international students, like me, were almost all one-year master's students.

Amanda nodded to confirm what I had guessed, but we didn't speak about it further, since Ronald had just leaned across the table to shake my hand and introduce himself. His accent suggested he was from a southern state, though I couldn't tell which one. Vera was about to say something else to me when a presence drew our attention to the door.

We all noticed him at the same moment, a hush descending immediately as he entered the room.

'All right, hello, take your seats.'

Crane's voice was deep and somewhat gravelly, the kind used for voiceovers on advertisements. Steady, reassuring, sturdy. He was wearing a black shirt, and grey, flecked trousers with white tennis shoes. In his arms, he carried two books. He was taller than I remembered, but, other than that, just as he had been in the Arts Block with Audrey that day, nothing particularly striking about him. Just a man, really, and yet the source of so much trouble.

'Welcome to the best class you'll ever take,' Crane said, taking us in for the first time as he sat down. A shy laugh filled the room, and he smiled at the sound. 'Let's get started. You can close your laptops and put your pens down – you won't need any notes. Today's class is not going to be examinable. Instead, I would like to ease you in gently, so that you say nice things about me on the feedback forms at the end of term.' There was another flurry of nervous laughter. 'Oh, you think I'm kidding? I'm not! I'm very susceptible to flattery, so please do feel free to compliment me at any point. It might just get you an A!'

More laughter.

I shut my laptop, shifting in my seat, trying to smile along with everyone else. My lips were dry. I ran my tongue over them, annoyed to find that now, after thinking about this moment for months, I was still so anxious. I focused on calming my breathing. When had the act of breathing become something I had to think about?

'Today, we're going to have an open discussion about Atticus Finch. Not *To Kill a Mockingbird*, and not Harper Lee ... we're going to consider a basic question solely about the character of Atticus himself. That question is this: was he a good lawyer?'

I was vaguely aware of Vera next to me, spluttering on the can of Red Bull clamped to her lips.

'Something funny about that question, Ms ...?' Crane's expression was serious, but humour still danced in his eyes.

'Lin, Vera Lin. And I just ... I just assumed the answer was obvious?' she said, looking from Crane to Amanda, who was sitting opposite her, and then Joshua seated next to me, who gave her a sympathetic smile.

We waited.

Crane's eyebrows rose expectantly. 'Well, does anyone else think it's obvious?'

Joshua slid his shoulders back, then said: 'Yeah ... I'm guessing this is a trick question to teach us something ... but, yes, he's a good lawyer, in my opinion.'

Crane scanned the room. 'Anyone else want to weigh in?'

I took a breath, really packing my lungs with oxygen, readying myself for this first offensive, the first of many. 'I don't believe Atticus Finch is a good lawyer.'

Crane faced me and, briefly, he hesitated. Was it the way I spoke? My emphasis? My accent? Or did he recognise Audrey in my face after all? Fear was rising, and I fought hard to keep it from showing.

'And why do you say that, Ms ...?'

'Mooney.' My eyes held his, alert for the flicker of recognition.

'Mooney ...' I watched his mind working, thoughts churning, and swallowed hard, as if to force my heart out of my mouth and back into my chest. 'You're the one who submitted the essay on Antigone?'

'Yes.'

For a moment, Crane didn't respond, his chin pressed down against his chest. I couldn't tell if that was a good or a bad sign.

'Go on,' he said, when it became clear I was expecting further instruction.

I pulled myself up straighter and continued: 'Atticus Finch doesn't care about whether Tom Robinson's trial is *actually* fair by reference to any sort of real justice. He is interested in a fair *process* and that is what he seeks out. He is entirely devoted to the legal process as it is – to producing the *impression* of a fair trial for Tom Robinson, even if that results in the wrongful conviction of an innocent man.'

There was a brief silence.

'Why?' Crane asked. 'Why would he allow that?'

'Because he's willing to sacrifice the life of an innocent man to uphold the integrity of the legal system. He did the bare minimum for Tom Robinson because his loyalty was to his personal politics and not his client.'

Crane's lips spread into the approximation of a smile. 'So you read my article?'

'I did.'

Vera glanced up, slightly panicked. 'There was an article? Did I miss an article? There was no article on the reading list.'

'No,' Crane replied, amused by the strength of her reaction. 'No, it's old. I wrote it in the early nineties. Ms Mooney must have gone trawling through the archives of the *Harvard Law Review*.'

Their faces flashed to me – all five – as if they were seeing me in a new light, as if I had just announced myself to be their competition.

'Don't look too pleased with yourself, Ms Mooney,' Crane said as I struggled not to smile. 'You won't get extra points for intellectual masochism in my classroom.'

There was a ripple of quiet laughter.

Crane's head cocked to the side, his expression curious as he looked at me. 'So, did you agree with me?'

I didn't want to agree with anything this man had to say, but when I answered him, I didn't have to lie.

'Yes and no. It's almost impossible to judge Atticus Finch properly because we only see him from the point of view of his daughter, Scout. And she's an unreliable narrator. It's an incomplete portrait of the man, filtered through her perception of her father. The picture of him is unfinished.'

Crane frowned, touching his nose briefly. 'So, you're saying the prosecution hasn't presented sufficient evidence to convict Atticus of bad lawyering?'

I nodded. 'Yes, I'm entering a plea of *nolle prosequi* – it's not possible to fully judge Finch on the facts as presented, so the question of whether he's a good lawyer is, for me, undeterminable. Any conclusion relies on our minds filling in the blanks.'

Crane opened it to the rest of the class. 'Any counterpoints?'

My eyes followed his, taking in the faces around the table, weighing up who might present themselves now as my competition.

Ronald raised his hand. 'I think there's more than enough evidence in *Mockingbird* to consider Atticus a racist. He defends the mob to Scout, says they're basically good men but they have a "blind spot".' He shook his head, the movement rueful. 'Seriously, like . . . come on. That "blind spot" he's talking about meant lynching. It meant death for people like me, because of how we look. Seems like more than just a "blind spot" . . . and diminishing it like that, the way Atticus does? It gives these murderers an excuse. It gives them a licence to kill, so long as they're killing the right sort of people. So, yeah, Atticus is definitely a racist. Unquestionably. And, you know, I'd really like to think that makes him a bad lawyer . . .'

'Ms Mooney? How do you defend the charge?' Crane's attention felt hot on my face, a challenge in his eye.

But Ronald had shifted the discussion out of my comfort zone, into places I didn't belong. 'I think . . . I think Ronald makes a very fair point,' I said, scratching at the back of my neck, beating a retreat. 'I, eh, I hadn't considered it that way.' I had been so focused on Crane's theories, on what I thought Crane would want to hear, that I hadn't fully engaged with the idea for myself.

'But, wait, don't we need to know the standard we're using to judge Atticus?' Charlie said. His voice was a little elevated, louder than necessary. 'I mean, I take Ronald's point. By the standards of today, Atticus's innocent client got a life sentence – so not great lawyering. And I totally agree with what Ronald said about the blind spot thing – that's not great, right? But at the time? In Maycomb, Alabama? With two young kids? Seems almost heroic to me that Atticus represented Tom Robinson at all. And he paid a steep price for representing him. He was looked down on by many in the town for it.'

'Looked down on? That's all?' Amanda said, snorting slightly. 'Tom Robinson was wrongly convicted, then shot seventeen times by prison guards while trying to escape. I know where my sympathy lies . . .'

Crane folded his arms, cupping his elbows with his hands. 'That's an interesting question, Mr . . .?'

'Duke, sir. Charlie Duke.'

'Mr Duke . . . any relation to *Senator* Duke of Virginia?'

'My grandfather,' Charlie said. There was a hint of embarrassment in his voice that surprised me.

'I should have guessed ... You know your grandfather's not a fan of mine?' Crane rested his hands on the arms of his chair, a smile on his face now. 'He called me a traitor for saying the Constitution needs updating.'

Charlie shrugged awkwardly. 'He called me a traitor once for beating him at Uno, so I wouldn't take it too personally, Professor.'

Crane's laugh was sudden, like a clap of thunder. My classmates joined in, so I matched the sound, though it was hollow to my ear.

'All right,' Crane said, after a moment. 'Let's get back to our friend, Atticus.' He turned to Ronald. 'Your question isn't the one I asked, Mr ...?'

'Harris. Ronald Harris.'

'Mr Harris, I didn't ask if Atticus was a racist – either by the standards of today or the standards of his time. I asked if he can be considered a "good lawyer".'

'But Charlie is right – how are we supposed to make that judgement?' Vera asked. 'We need a standard to judge him by.'

'I don't think this is difficult.' Amanda glanced around, as if unsure if she were missing something obvious. 'This wasn't ancient times. For me, there's really no debate. Atticus is racist, by the standards of today and he was racist by the standards of the past, too. That racism – that latent bias – motivated the way he defended Tom Robinson.' She flicked her hair behind her ear.

'Amanda and Ronald make a fair point,' Crane said. 'The biases and morality of the lawyer affect their ability to represent their client.' He was smiling now. 'Good,' he said. 'Very good. Anyone have a contrary view?'

He looked around the room expectantly, and though I tried to think of something clever to add, my mind was devoid of ideas.

Joshua coughed. 'Um, well, it's not a contrary view.' His sentence finished with an upward inflection. 'But, isn't it *possible* to be objective? I mean, isn't that the goal of the law? Put yourself aside and represent your client? Otherwise, how do you represent a murderer? A rapist?'

Crane seemed bored by the question, as if it were one he had answered far too many times. 'Do you really think a person can be truly objective? Mr . . .?'

'Reynolds.'

'Mr Reynolds . . . do you think you're an objective person?'

Joshua gave a half-shrug. 'I do, yes, mostly. Certainly, I can be.'

Crane visibly winced. 'Not sure how you snuck into this class.' I caught the stricken look on Joshua's face before he could hide it. 'Let's park that one for another day, Mr Reynolds. But for the purpose of this class, let me assure you that you have never in your life had an objective experience of the world. We are all the products of our influences – good, bad, and indifferent. A good lawyer needs to be aware of that so they can try, always, to adjust their thinking when necessary. To be alive to their biases, their minds open, and their ears listening. The law is a tool and a lawyer uses it for a purpose. It is not an elemental force existing outside of us. You're here in this class to learn how to use it, not to worship it, or laud it, or mythologise it. In this classroom, you will have the opportunity to question things, to break them open. But you can't do that if you still think of the law as something akin to religion. That's not what this class is about.'

The room had fallen very silent, no sound or movement breaking through Joshua's discomfort. I could feel the burn of his humiliation.

Crane sat back in his chair, all eyes on him, and waited as we drank in what he had just said.

'To move us along . . .' His voice had softened when he spoke again. 'Maybe we should agree on a standard for lawyers, shall we? What does it *mean* to be a good lawyer? People are always citing Atticus Finch as the archetypal "good lawyer". But what does it say about our society's conception of the law that we think this man is the best of the best? What does it say of our ambition for the law?'

I wasn't paying attention anymore. While he spoke, I watched Crane's mouth move and thought of the messages I had discovered on Audrey's phone. His first text had come in early October of the Michaelmas term he had spent at Trinity.

Breezy and innocuous.

Jay Crane (16.23):

Hi Audrey, Jay Crane here. I'm excited to be working with you on this research project! Can we push back our meeting today? Apologies – another meeting ran over.

From there followed a series of correspondence, stretching over the weeks and months Crane lived in Dublin. When I had pulled on the thread, their secret unravelled before my eye. The messages began innocently enough, but, gradually, their tone began to change, easing out of formality and into something more furtive, something not meant for other eyes, something intimate. By the end of December, he had broken her into pieces.

In room 1.04B, Crane was still speaking, his words directed at Joshua, who was struggling to answer a question I hadn't heard.

Crane's final text had arrived in early January, about a week before Audrey dropped out of university, withdrawing from me, from our parents, from her friends, and hollowing out her life as it had been.

Jay Crane (18.43):

Audrey. Beautiful Audrey. I don't know what to say. It was such a pleasure to know you and now I have ruined that. I am deeply sorry. You deserved better. Forgive me.

Your J x

Audrey. Beautiful Audrey.

Emotion was roaring up from my stomach, into my ears, and I couldn't hear a word anyone was saying anymore. In the months after that last text, I had witnessed my sister disappear inside herself, squirrelled away in her bedroom, shutting me out, refusing even to speak to me.

Eyes glued to my professor, I could only think of Audrey's words in her last message to him.

You know what you did.

Chapter Four

After Crane left, we walked slowly out of room 1.04B, moving as a small group through the library and towards the exit. It felt as if I were emerging from darkness into light, in something of a daze.

When we reached the steps leading down from the library, Amanda suggested we grab a coffee. 'I feel like I need a debrief after that,' she said, her expression somewhat shell-shocked. 'Am I right?'

Judging from the other faces around me, she was not alone.

'We could go to Joe's?' Ronald said.

'I'm down.' Vera's brown eyes roved over each of us as if she were making calculations. 'In a small class like this, we should probably try co-operation over competition ... unless you guys are all gunners?'

'What's a gunner?' Amanda asked from beside me.

'Oh, right, you're not from here,' Vera said, with a flicker of impatience. 'So, like, a gunner is someone who is, you know, like, *gunning* for the top of the class. Think of the kid at the front with their hand in the air constantly.' She looked at Amanda, and then me. 'You guys don't have gunners where you're from?'

'Oh, God, yeah,' Amanda said, laughing. 'At Cambridge, everyone was a gunner. We just didn't use the term.'

I considered it for a moment. 'We called them mature students at Trinity.'

Amanda laughed, but Vera was just confused. 'I don't know what that means, but I do have my suspicions about you, Jessica,' she said, pointing a finger at me and then wagging it. 'You're a secret gunner, aren't you? Crane's Harvard piece ...? *Who* does their own additional research on a professor's back catalogue?! That's some serious gunner behaviour.'

'I'm just interested,' I said, but it suited me just fine for Vera to think my interest in Crane was the ordinary enthusiasm of an ambitious student.

'Leave the Irish girl alone, Vera,' Charlie said from behind me. 'Jealousy doesn't suit you.'

She snorted. 'I'm not jealous, just ... you know.' Vera raised two fingers towards her eye sockets and then jabbed the air near my face. 'I'm keeping an eye on her.'

'In case it needs to be said,' Charlie remarked, for my benefit, 'Vera is the gunner you need to worry about.'

'It's true.' A mischievous little smile lit Vera's face briefly. 'But I have a recommendation from Professor Grouse for a clerkship next year, so you kids can have Crane. It's fine by me. I'm exempting myself from his games.' She grasped the string of pearls around her neck. 'If you're wise, you would too.'

Charlie smiled at me and Amanda. 'I'm sure it's abundantly clear already, but, with charm like mine, I don't need to suck up to any of the professors. So, you don't need to worry about me either ...' For a man learning to be a lawyer, he was an unconvincing liar.

'*With charm like mine?*' Ronald mimicked. 'You mean a *surname*, right, Duke?'

Charlie raised his middle finger, but had nothing to say to the charge.

'Well, you can probably count me out of the running after *that*,' Joshua said. 'Crane clearly hates me.'

'It *was* a little brutal,' Vera conceded, then prodded his shoulder. 'Come on. Let's just go get coffee and forget it.' She pushed a somewhat reluctant Joshua in front of her, striding forward towards the main lobby of the law school, confident we would follow.

I shifted my backpack onto my other shoulder and walked with Amanda to the exit, pretending to listen while she answered a question from Ronald about Brexit. If my plan was to work, I needed to blend in with the rest of the students, hidden in plain sight, with the face of a girl and the heart of a viper.

Through the window behind us, the courtyard was still crowded with students, beanbags still flying through the air towards the cornhole board. We passed the building's security guard at her desk and a member of the janitorial staff who was emptying a bin in the corner, all the unseen labour on minimum wage that made our elite college experience so picture-perfect. Amanda reached for the door and held it open for me and Ronald, who gave a nod of his head in thanks.

Outside the law school, the smell of rubbish cooking in the black bags of the Irish pub opposite rose into my nose, and the angry sun pricked my skin. My feet felt heavy, as if the rubber soles of my Converse were sticking to the footpath under me. For a moment, I stood still while the others moved on, the sky a deep and endless blue, stretching over my head into a vast, expanding universe that cared not a bit about me, or Crane, or Audrey.

Something about the easy, ordinary patter of my classmates' conversation reminded me of how it had been with my sister when we were both at Trinity. She was two years ahead of me, which made me lean on her when I first arrived, particularly because she found it easier to fit into new environments. In those days, we were such a part of each other's lives, so present in the flow of events, that I would have sworn I knew everything about Audrey. Maybe I did, once. But Crane had changed all that.

'You all right, Jessie?' Amanda asked, from the other side of the road. 'You look miles away.'

'Sorry,' I said, blinking fast to banish the restless, waspish thoughts that kept dragging me back to Audrey. 'Yeah … I'm fine. Just a bit tired.' Pulling my mind firmly into the present, I left my sister in the past and followed my classmates into Joe's.

Across from the law school, with a yellow-painted door and a striped awning, Joe's was a favourite of both the law students and staff. He sold erotic art posters and postcards, imported tobacco, *Charlie Hebdo* magazines, and an impressive array of herbal teas and coffee blends. Joe would change the blend of filter coffee sitting on hotplates by the door daily, and sold library snacks of individually wrapped madeleines and macaroons to students working late. He was either a Francophile or he was actually French – nobody knew which. Despite frequenting his store every day, I never learned anything more about Joe. He barely spoke a word beyond the occasional perfunctory mumble out the side of his mouth. 'Two dollars for the coffee. Five with the Danish.'

When we entered, Charlie was already pouring coffee from the pot into six paper cups. He handed them out to us one by one. 'Coffee for Jessica?' he asked as he saw me, and I nodded, watching while he filled the final cup to the brim.

'Now, I'd Irish it up for you,' he said as he gave it to me. 'But it's a little early in the day. Don't you think?'

I couldn't help but roll my eyes, feeling as if I knew him already. Something about his unseriousness, his playful character, had that effect on me from the start. 'That's really funny, Charlie – and *original* too.'

Charlie chuckled quietly, as if he really did think so. His teeth were visible when he grinned, white against his tan face. He reeked of East Hampton luxury, of the pleasant after-effects of a long summer sipping chilled Californian whites and eating clams.

I swallowed down my distaste. He didn't need Crane's favour. He already knew the language, the customs, and the ways of places like this. He already belonged. And, if I didn't keep an eye on him, it was possible Charlie would slip straight into the role of favourite when the time came, heir apparent waiting for his crown.

I joined the queue behind Vera, then paid a very silent Joe for the coffee and thanked him before we all walked to the exit. The bell tinkled as the door opened again, a wave of hot air washing up against my face. On the street outside, a black cat watched us, absently licking its white-socked paws. Its ears flattened against its head as it saw me, staring in a way that pierced, as if it were reading my thoughts, as if it knew I was the one to monitor, the one who posed the danger.

Vera suggested we take our coffees back to one of the tables in the courtyard, so we crossed to the other side of the street again and climbed the steps to the law school. The rest of the group were engaged in conversation. I could hear snatches of Vera and Joshua's chatter about the election as I brushed the frizz off my damp forehead. Behind them, Ronald and Charlie were asking Amanda to pronounce certain unusual British place names, and then laughing at her accent.

Once inside, I hung back slightly, letting the others drift ahead, taking the sound of their laughter with them, so that, gradually, it faded away. I had other plans for my afternoon.

I was heading for the faculty corridor.

Chapter Five

The law school complex was a warren of interconnected corridors. With the help of a map I had printed from the website, I knew where I was going. But what I might find there was less clear.

I had never expected to be here. Law school had always been Audrey's ambition. I hadn't shared her clear-eyed focus on school and grades, so it came as a shock to my parents when their taciturn daughter – hypercritical, hyper-cynical – chose to study something as straight-laced and respectable as the law. I had chosen it out of a stubborn desire to prove that Audrey wasn't the only one who could, but it was only when my sister dropped out that I found a new interest in it, in the power it gives and restrains. I didn't know then how it would come to define me, how it would shape and distort me, how I would use it.

On the faculty corridor, I tried to move with ease, with the affectless, casual swagger of any other student. To my left, a wall of glass provided a view of the courtyard below, where my classmates were now gathered around a table. And beyond the courtyard, at a distance, I could see the tips of skyscrapers standing tall on the other side of the Schuylkill River.

Each professor had an office on the first floor. I read the names on the doors as I moved past – Professor Hoffman, Professor Alves, Professor Grouse – scanning for Crane's.

I was here because he made it necessary.

It began over Christmas break during Audrey's final year at Trinity. My sister started spending all her time in her bedroom, door closed. It wasn't like Audrey to shut herself away, the sudden shift in her mood baffling both my parents and me. We became concerned when it continued beyond a few days, thinking she might be ill. But Audrey had refused a doctor, a therapist, or help of any form. She just wanted to be alone and, the more we pushed, the further she burrowed into herself, until she had curled so far inward that she was cold and lifeless as an ammonite.

On the day the new term started, Audrey dropped out of university. At the time, I had not known that it was our final train journey into Trinity together, Audrey sitting silently in the seat opposite me, facing the window with a sombre, determined stare that masked her turmoil. She didn't stop there. She dismantled her life with a ruthless efficiency that had my parents spiralling into panic. She drained her Credit Union account, purchased a rucksack, planned a route in secret, and informed us one morning in March that she was leaving for Central America.

On the faculty corridor, I gripped my coffee more tightly and forced my mind back to my present purpose. To my right, portraits hung on the wall between the doors, the painted faces of distinguished former professors watching me as I passed them by. I would make sure Crane's face never joined them up there. When I was done with him, Crane would live in ignominy.

I was still searching for Crane's name when he emerged from an office three doors down. The sudden sight nearly caused me to spill my coffee, and he looked equally startled to see me.

'Oh, hello there,' he said. His face was handsome when he

smiled. 'It's . . . Jessica, right?' There was a book in his hand, the sleeves of his shirt pushed halfway up his arms, which were thick and surprisingly muscular for a man devoted to a life of the mind.

'Yes. Hi Professor Crane,' I said with a smile – shy, reticent, unintimidating. That was how I wanted him to view me.

'Are you looking for anyone? Another professor?' he asked, a slight confusion in the angle of his head. 'Maybe I can help you find them?'

'Oh, no, not looking for someone.' I cast my eyes around. Helpless, even a bit vulnerable, allowing him the illusion of a position of strength. 'I must have taken a wrong turn. I'm still new here.' I smiled again.

'Well, wherever you're going, it's likely to be this way.' He pointed back the way I had just come. 'It's only faculty offices on this corridor, but I can get you back to the main lobby and that should allow you to orient yourself again.'

'Thanks, great, it's . . . all a bit confusing.'

He agreed, to be polite, and I let him lead the way to the stairs. He wasn't a large man, but he was taller than me, his shoulder much higher than mine as we walked along together. It felt somewhat surreal to be walking next to him, as if this were completely ordinary, and not the result of a series of cascading events.

'It was a really interesting class today,' I said, moving my back-pack to my other shoulder. It was stuffed with my notes and, together with the weight of my laptop, sat heavy on my back. 'I learned a lot.'

'Well, good. I'm delighted to hear that,' Crane replied, and he seemed to mean it. 'It sometimes takes a new cohort a little while to warm up, but you guys seemed to get the hang of it quickly.' He glanced at me. 'Your essay was excellent, by the way. One of the best.'

'Oh.' I felt a rush of warm blood fill my cheeks at the compliment, and immediately hated myself for it. 'Thank you. I appreciate it.'

'No, really, I . . . I've been thinking about it a lot since I read it and, well, that doesn't usually happen. After a while, in this job, you start to feel like you've read it all before. It's hard to find anything . . . new.' He paused, brown eyes narrowing as he contemplated her. 'But you managed it, Jessica. That's impressive.'

As we reached the stairs, I realised I had been holding his gaze for slightly longer than normal. 'You can call me Jessie,' I said. 'Or just Jess – whatever you prefer.'

'All right,' he said as we descended the stairs, seeming pleased by the idea. We hovered at the bottom. 'Well, Jessie, I have another class, so this is where I'll have to leave you. But if you walk directly ahead of you, you'll be back at the main entrance. You can ask the security guard for directions. Nina doesn't bite.'

'I think I'll find my way from here. Thank you, Professor.'

'Any time . . .' He took several steps away from me, in the direction of Wilson Hall. But I didn't feel quite ready to lose his attention, not when I was so hungry for progress.

Impulsively, I shouted after him: 'See you on Wednesday morning, Professor!'

Crane flashed a quick smile over his shoulder, and then, quite suddenly, he stopped dead. 'Jessie, actually—' He turned around and, once again, I was standing in the glow of his gravitas. 'Quick question . . .' He scratched at the stubble on his chin, his expression inscrutable. I needed to learn how to read him, to burrow under his skin.

'Yes, Professor?'

'Your accent . . .'

A ripple of nerves, a tightness in my chest. Where was this going?

'You're Irish, right?'

'I am . . .' I replied slowly. 'Why? Are you going to ask me if I know your Irish cousins?'

'No,' he said, laughing. 'No . . . it's just . . .' Another glance my way, another scratch at his chin. 'You remind me of someone.'

The coffee was sloshing inside my cup, a shake coming to my hand. He was looking at me now, really *looking*, in a way that made me want to hide. I rammed a rod through my spine, stiffened, willing myself to withstand that look.

A group of students passed through the empty space between us, chattering, laughing, and distracting Crane enough to break the train of thought I knew would lead to my sister.

'Oh crap,' he said, eyes falling to his wristwatch. 'I need to run, or I'll be late for class.' A small wave, another smile. 'I'll see you around, Jessie.'

I waved back and returned his smile, but it was very much my intention that Crane *wouldn't* see me around. Not unless I allowed it. He wouldn't see me dogging his steps, wouldn't know how I made a study of his whereabouts, his habits, building my case against him. The perfect case, the end justifying my means. What good is knowing the law if you haven't learned how to evade it?

In my dorm room that night, I wrote in a black notebook I had bought from the Franklin Bookstore about my first class with Crane, and about bumping into him afterwards. My entries would be modelled on the sorts of things Audrey had noted in her diary during the term Crane spent in Dublin. It was to be a mirror of her experience, as close a copy as I could manage, threading together her experience and mine, to make a net in which to trap him. I sat on the hard mattress, Audrey's phone by my knee, her laptop on my desk, next to a forgotten cup of tea, and her diary open on my lap. She was charmed by a joke he had made in her first class with him, and planning to meet him after office hours to ask a question about her coursework.

I read the entry from that first private meeting in his office, wanting to scream down at the page to run the other way.

> I didn't expect C to give me so much of his time, but it felt like we could have talked for hours! I've never met anyone like him. He knows exactly what he's doing, like he has life all worked out, with this total lack of self-doubt. But not, like, in an arrogant way. I think he just accepts himself as he is – the good and the bad. God – I'd give anything to feel that way. Just to feel like I'm good enough.

Closing the diary, I leaned my back against the wall behind me and searched for her face on the wall opposite, smiling out from the photographs I had pinned to the corkboard over my desk. But that wasn't the only piece of my sister I had brought with me. Audrey's clothes were hanging in my wardrobe, her shoes lined up next to the door. I had taken them from her bedroom in Malahide, driven by some urge to stay connected, or preserve her presence somehow, as if something of my sister might remain in the fabric, caught in the fibres. The rest of her clothes still hung in her bedroom, which my parents had barely entered in the past two years.

The news came through very early on a Sunday morning in August, a phone call to my parents' house, persistent ringing from the table in the front hall. As she made her way downstairs, my mother's gait was heavy with sleep, her voice groggy as she answered the phone. A silence had followed, during which I had turned over in bed, burrowing deeper into my duvet, eyes closing sleepily in those last few moments of oblivious contentedness, before our world had turned upside down.

An embassy official in Guatemala said they had found Audrey

dead, shattering my mother's heart in an instant. The sound she made shot upstairs to startle me out of sleep, a howling like nothing I've heard before or since, echoing through my mind even now, as if no time has passed at all. There was the life I had before that moment and the life that followed after, my sister's death driving me and my parents into separate, lonely pockets of grief. After Audrey died, we faded from each other, my parents diving deeper into their loss, while I tried to find some path out.

Her death didn't make sense to me, my need for answers propelling me forward. Why hadn't she stayed in university? Why had she left Dublin? What had happened to drive her away from us? Why was my sister dead?

I locked myself away, spending the long nights after her funeral alone in Audrey's bedroom, the lamp dimly lighting a collection of her belongings I had gathered around me. Photos, old diaries and notebooks. Sitting on the floor, I riffled through her things, searching for my sister in the ordinary items of her life. A sentence scribbled on the back of a torn envelope. A Post-it note falling out of a half-read book. A doodle in the corner of a crumpled page. Her absence had turned them into treasure, and I was a dragon guarding my hoard, listening for her voice whispering to me.

It was when the authorities in Guatemala returned Audrey's possessions a week later that the pieces began to fall into place. Of all the possible explanations I had considered for the great change that occurred in my sister, it had never, for a moment, been this, the idea of him never crossing my mind. But here he was, all over Audrey's texts, emails, and diary. Professor Jay Crane.

I combed through it all, every word, every sentence, hunting for answers, for an explanation for my sister's actions in the weeks leading to her death. And I continued to land on the same conclusion: the texts and emails with Crane ended right around the time Audrey had dropped out. The diary pages were blank after that date, silence falling. I could sense that something bad had happened. But the discovery provided no relief, leading only to more questions.

It was Audrey's best friend, Chloe Desmond, who filled in the blanks for me. Months after the funeral, in December, she came to me with what she knew about the night of the Law Ball. But it wasn't the sort of evidence that would hold up in court, not enough to convince a jury of peers – no DNA or CCTV, no witness who was present at the time, no victim still alive to testify. And I could not stand the idea of telling the world what had happened, only for my sister to be branded a liar, while Jay Crane was exonerated. But nor could I ignore what he had done and move on with my life.

I had to take things into my own hands, craft the perfect case. I would recreate Audrey and Crane's relationship, inserting myself in her place, and construct the evidence that had been missing for her. Screenshots with date stamps, a map of our movements on some tracking app or other, a suggestive photograph of the two of us together, credible witnesses. Real life is never evidenced so clearly and that's where the doubt always sneaks in. For my case against Crane, there would be no doubt at all. I would create the evidence myself. A lie told to reveal the greater truth.

And this trove of circumstantial proof would support something bigger when, at the end of term, after months of drawing Crane close, I'd lure him right where I needed him and land the final blow.

But if I'm being honest, it was more than that. Getting close to Crane served another purpose. I needed to get under his skin, to screw with his mind, to erode his confidence little by little.

I needed to make him suffer.

Up to this point in my life, I had been following in my sister's footsteps, my decisions always guided by her, Audrey always leading the way. Now, she was gone, and I was still trying to follow her. The diary and messages she had left behind were a path of crumbs spread behind her, leading to the source of her downfall.

He had destroyed her life. It was his turn now.

Chapter Six

Law and Literature meant that I would see Crane twice a week. The next class was on Wednesday morning, and this time, I planned to make better progress. If I was going to succeed, I needed to find ways and means of being in his company. I could try bumping into him here and there, creating reasons to meet him, and lessening, gradually, over time, the gap between professor and student. But gaining status as his favourite would provide a shortcut through all of that. It was a direct route to Crane. And he found his favourites in the classroom. Always, his brightest students. In room 1.04B, there were six possible candidates and I planned to be the one he chose.

When I arrived to class on Wednesday morning, Charlie was already seated at the table. It was just the two of us, punctuality a trait we seemed to share. There were other traits too, though we didn't know it then.

'Well, well,' he said, looking up from his phone as I entered. His feet were curled around the legs of his chair, jiggling against the metal with excess energy. 'If it isn't the mysterious Jessica Mooney.'

'How have I earned that title?' I opened my bag and pulled out my laptop.

'You disappeared on Monday. Where'd you go?' He placed his

phone on the table and brushed his fringe back from his face to get a better view of me.

'What do you mean?' I asked, avoiding his eye.

'You got your coffee at Joe's with us and then bailed.'

I shrugged. 'So? What's it to you?'

'I saw you wander off towards the faculty offices.'

It surprised me greatly that Charlie was the one who had noticed. I wondered if he was more observant than I'd assumed.

'You're a nosy little fecker, aren't you?' I said.

A laugh sounded from his mouth, robust and fulsome. 'Guess so,' he said. 'So, you're not going to tell me?'

'Nope.' I sat down at the table, watching curiosity light his blue eyes.

He lay his chin on his hand and squinted, as if this would allow a clearer picture of me and my veiled motivations. 'Come on, Mooney,' he persisted. 'What were you doing? Tell me.'

Joshua had just arrived, munching on an apple. He caught the irritated expression on my face, then bore a hole in the back of Charlie's head.

'Is Charlie bothering you?' he asked me.

'Not anymore,' I said as Charlie sat up straight in his chair, reaching for his phone again.

Joshua tossed the last of his apple into the wastepaper basket in the corner. It whooshed as it hit the plastic bin liner. 'Don't mind him, Jessie. None of us do. Charlie Duke gets some weird high from annoying people. You can see why we all ignore him, right?'

'Uh-oh,' Amanda said from the door. 'Who are we ignoring and why?' She took the chair next to Charlie, slipping her arms free from her backpack and laying it on the table in front of her.

'Me, apparently,' Charlie said, as he made more room for her beside him. 'Because Joshua doesn't find me charming.'

'Really?' Amanda said. 'Well, that hardly seems possible.'

I laughed quietly into my hand.

Vera appeared next with a large iced coffee, exhaling a long, 'heeeeeeey' as she slipped into the seat beside mine.

While we waited for Crane, I picked up the copy of Aeschylus' *Oresteia* I had borrowed from the library, leafing through it absently. It must have been on Crane's reading list for some time because this copy was battered, the pages littered with lingering signs of all the other students who had held it before me. They were there in the comments, scrawled along the margins, in the underlining of certain passages, and in notes written in loopy cursive. At the bottom right of page forty-seven, someone had written in red: *Crane is HOT!*

I swallowed the deepest sigh. How many women had sat where I sat, where Audrey had sat, and stared in silent admiration of a man who couldn't be trusted with it? A man who preyed on it, like an insect, a tiny bloodsucker piercing the skin. My hand brushed the bites on my legs, scratching unconsciously.

'Here we go,' Vera mumbled beside me. Glancing up again, I followed the path of her gaze. Crane was walking quickly to his spot at the head of the table and launching into the lecture without so much as a greeting.

'The Furies ... three female deities, representing all the rage and vengeance of Ancient Greece,' Crane said, writing the letters F-U-R-Y in red marker on the whiteboard. I stared at the word next to his head. 'The Furies appear in *The Eumenides*, in another trial we're going to consider – the trial of Orestes. Orestes murdered his mother, Clytemnestra, as revenge for the murder of his father, Agamemnon, whom Clytemnestra killed as revenge for the murder of their daughter, Orestes' sister, Iphigenia.' He mapped this out on the whiteboard with large arrows between their names. 'Blood bringing forth more blood. Tragedy creating more tragedy. And death the final act.' He wrote D-E-A-T-H next to F-U-R-Y.

He looked at each of us in turn, and I couldn't shake the sense that his eyes lingered on me. It took such enormous concentration to keep possession of myself around Crane there were times when I had to remind myself that I was the only person aware of the great deception under way.

I drew a bottle from my bag and gulped some water down, emptying my mind of conspiracy, and focusing on Crane's face again.

'The trial of Orestes is no ordinary trial, of course. The facts are not in question. We know that Orestes killed his mother and her lover, Aegisthus. He doesn't deny it, but he says he did it at the direction of Apollo, who told him that his father's death had to be avenged, even if that meant killing his own mother. Remember, Agamemnon was killed by Clytemnestra because he sacrificed his daughter, Iphigenia, in order to summon a wind to allow him and his ships to sail to Troy. And the only person who seems to see something wrong in Iphigenia's death is Clytemnestra. She alone sees the evil in it, a wrong deserving of the greatest punishment. But Orestes doesn't, and neither does Apollo. A man can kill his daughter with impunity and a man can kill his mother – but a wife cannot kill her husband, no matter what he did.' He scratched at the grey tufts at his temples, his eyes rolling towards the window, through which the hot sun roared. 'That's the view of the Olympian gods, but in Ancient Greece, there were other gods – older gods.' He looked back to us. 'The Furies were much older deities than Zeus, Apollo, and the rest, and they were deeply feared and venerated. The superstitious Greeks wouldn't say their names, calling them the "kindly ones", or the "gracious ones", for fear of drawing their ire.'

Crane paused, his hands now in his pockets, his feet shoulder width apart. He was wearing brown trousers that sat slightly low on his hips so that his white linen shirt kept coming untucked.

'The Furies were the daughters of night, the gods of vengeance who punished guilty men, tormenting them to death. And, according to their old morality, Orestes had committed a terrible wrong – matricide, one of the earliest and most egregious of crimes. They would not let it pass without punishment. Blood needs blood.' He paused again. 'Clytemnestra was dead, but this was not just a crime against her. It was a crime against women, touching on something much more fundamental than the new gods. This was something elemental, foundational, primordial. It was something female. And the Furies would make Orestes answer for it. They would have their justice.'

I watched Crane as he spoke, thinking of my sister, of all the ways he had wronged her, and how I would set that right.

'On Orestes' side, speaking in his defence at the trial, was Apollo – wonder boy, god of the sun, the most beautiful of the gods, personification of the Greek ideals of athletic youth. And, as the audience, we love Apollo, right, so we're primed to be on Orestes' side.' He moved slowly from the whiteboard to the window, standing so that the sun was shining around him, casting him in silhouette, light and shadow crossing his face. 'Remember, there were very likely no women allowed in the theatre, no women on stage when the play was performed. This was a male space, watching a spectacle of female rage. The shrieks and cries of the Furies, the appeals for justice for the women who had been killed, were heard only by male ears.'

Crane walked to the table, drew his chair back, and slowly lowered himself into the seat, cracked red leather squeaking as his weight met it.

'As you'll know if you did the reading . . .' He cocked an eyebrow briefly at us in accusation. I sat back in my chair. I was prepared.

I was ready. 'Orestes is ultimately acquitted by the appointed judge, Athena, and the Furies are – fairly miraculously, I think you'll agree – stripped of their malice. It's Athena – a young, beautiful, female goddess – who placates the old hags, turning them from creatures of nightmare into peaceable, venerable old women, beloved grandmothers of the community. It is Athena who promises the Furies that they will be respected in Athens. They'll be thought of as protectors of the city, if they'll *only* stop their nagging ways.'

'Give me a break,' Amanda muttered into her hand.

Crane laughed. 'Right?' he said. 'It's a happy ending for the men of Athens. No longer faced by the shrill, howling voices of angry women. No longer under threat.'

On his feet again, Crane walked to the whiteboard, and beneath the word 'fury' he added: 'Eumenides – the kindly ones'.

'The final play of *The Oresteia* is *The Eumenides*. That is the happy ending for the audience. It is how they want their women. Venerable and kindly. Unthreatening, calm, passive.' He let a silence fall. 'This is a story of the triumph of law over justice, the triumph of legal process over the violence of axe and sword. The institutions of Athenian democracy deliver a fair trial and a righteous outcome – at least, by the definition of Athenian men. Compare that to our previous class, to our jury in Maycomb, Alabama.' He turned to Ronald, who looked slightly panicked to find himself suddenly beneath the spotlight. 'Those institutions exist to copper-fasten the power of Athenian male citizens, the power of the master over the slave, of the wealthy over the poor, of men over women. Doesn't that sound familiar? And though it is indisputably an end to the cycle of familial violence – Orestes faces no consequence for his mother's murder – is it the right outcome? Has justice been done? Does the law provide the right answer?'

His voice carried the same restrained anger I had found in his article on the topic. It was deeply perplexing. He was angry – no, more than that. He was *furious*. I recognised it in him, vibrating in the tiny muscles around his eyes and lips. Why? Why should *he* be angry?

You know what you did.

'Too many lawyers behave as if the law is a religion,' Crane continued, 'and law school trains you to serve as its priests. But the law is a human institution. It is not handed down from the gods. The law is an empty vessel, neutral as to outcome. It is good, or bad, or middling, depending on what we make of it.'

A part of me wanted to call him out then and there, to put it to him that he was a part of the power systems he was now so nobly admonishing, a direct beneficiary, in fact.

I tuned Crane out and let my gaze lift to the shapes made on the ceiling by the sunbeams shining in through the window. My sister had always been the light to my shadow, filling every room she entered, while I stood to the side and hoped nobody would notice me. But after what Crane did to her, all that changed.

The last time I saw her was in the queue for departures at Dublin Airport, the half-moon of her face appearing briefly as she waved a final goodbye to me and my parents. She looked so lost in the security queue, so tiny in a sea of strangers. And then she was gone.

Shutting my eyes tightly, I gripped the edge of the table, pushing her image from my mind so I could focus on my purpose here, the only useful thing I could still do for her. When I opened my eyes again, back in the present, Charlie's gaze was fixed on me.

'Sorry, I've gone off topic, haven't I?' Crane said, his hand tracing over his brow. 'Where was I?'

'Angry women,' I said at once, brushing my hair off my face

45

and trying to ignore the curiosity in Charlie's stare.

'Ah yes,' Crane replied, with a small laugh. 'Indeed. Ms Mooney, tell us . . . what did you think of Orestes' trial?'

I snatched at my scattered thoughts, gathering them into some sort of order again. All the work, all the preparation was for this reason. 'I thought it was a disgrace.'

'A disgrace?'

'Yes.'

'Why?'

'Its sole purpose was to paint over real human suffering with a varnish of "reason" and "process". Because that's what is valued by the disinterested audience. They want the violence to end – that's the best outcome for them.'

'Go on.' Crane's right hand held his chin. His left arm was folded across his chest. He was giving me space to voice thoughts I had long held, but which Audrey's experience had made much more real to me.

'It just . . . it suggests that justice must always be calm and objective, as if a victim's torment, their *real* pain, has to be cleansed and moderated and made palatable. Because that is civilising. Because anything else is barbarian. It's ludicrous. It's inhuman.'

It was a side of the law I had disliked from my first days at Trinity, the imposition of dispassionate order on human emotion, as if the aim of justice is to give the *impression* of resolution, of a functioning society, of a tidy house. Once the judgement is read, the case is adjourned, and judicial hands are washed clean. But it is not how we experience the world, divorced of any feeling, the human condition reduced to the application of a rulebook, sanitised and sterile.

'So, you would unleash the Furies on Orestes, then?' Crane asked, folding both his arms now, watching me carefully.

'I wouldn't hesitate.'

'Am I seeing a pattern here?' He was referring to my Antigone essay.

'You are.'

'What does justice mean to you, Jessie?'

'It means . . . it means doing right by the victim of a wrong.'

'And how do we do that?'

'We punish the guilty.'

'Isn't that what our legal system does?'

'Absolutely not. It perpetuates power dynamics, which, when it comes to the crimes of men against women, leave us unprotected. It lets Orestes walk free. It has done this for centuries.'

'Why is that?'

'Its origins are deeply patriarchal. The legal system is a male institution – designed by, and for, men.'

He was leaning forward, his excitement palpable. 'But beyond that – not every man is a rapist or abuser of women, right? Most men are as angry as you are about the crimes of such men. I know I am.' I flinched at his words. 'So why does the system still protect them? There's a majority who want to see them punished.'

'Is there? Because that only seems to be the case where there's, like, zero risk of getting it wrong. You know, where there's CCTV, or DNA, or the rapist just – I don't know – admits he did it. If there's anything less . . . if there's *any* room to doubt a woman, she will be doubted. Culturally, we find women less trustworthy, less stable, less believable.'

'Hard agree,' Vera said, dragging my blinkered focus away from Crane to my classmates again.

I had almost forgotten there were other people in the room. Joshua was moving about uncomfortably in his chair. Amanda looked very grave, her head nodding rhythmically. And when I glanced at Charlie, I found him still staring at me with the same rapt attention I was directing towards Crane.

47

'That's quite a claim, but, accepting it for the sake of argument, how should the law address that?' Crane continued. '*Can* the law address it?'

'Yes, by centring the victim,' I said. 'Not blind belief, but giving women the bounce of the ball for once. The accused man should be required to prove his innocence, instead of the other way around. The deck is stacked against women. Let's shuffle it and see what happens.'

Crane was silent for a moment. I observed him, my chest rising and falling. In the beat of my heart, there was anger, there was fury. And in the look in his eye, I could see there was understanding, a gut-wrenching mutuality. Its presence felt like a knife twisting in my gut. Why was he agreeing with me?

He turned away, towards the rest of the class. 'Any other opinions?'

There were plenty, all varieties on the usual theme. Due process. Innocent until proven guilty (him, never her). An appeal for balance, for slow progress over my radical upheaval. I had heard it all before.

My mind drifted, eyes moving to the window while I took a moment to try to calm myself down and restrain the emotions vying for escape. When I began to listen again, it was to catch the end of Charlie's contribution.

'. . . the law is human,' he was saying. 'And humans are, by nature, imperfect.'

'But that's exactly it,' I said, unable to stop myself from jumping straight into the fray again. There was danger in it, in showing my true face to them like this, but I could see encouragement in Crane's expression, as if he were cheering me on, as if he wanted me to display the full courage of my convictions. In hindsight, I can see that he was enjoying the burst of wildness in me, breaking open settled beliefs. 'The law is human,' I continued, 'which means there's nothing sacred about it. Nothing magic. And that means we can *change* it when it's not working – right?! There's this myth that things are the way they are for good reason, as if someone has thought it all out and decided this is best. But it's just the result of centuries of rich, heterosexual, white men deciding how the rest of us should live. And that has produced serious unfairness – for women, for people of colour, for the LGBTQ community, for the poor, for indigenous communities, for, for, for . . .'

'For those without power?' Crane offered.

I looked at him for a moment and wondered if he had ever – even fleetingly – known what that felt like. 'Yeah,' I said quietly, the air leaving my lungs like wind from a sail.

I had lost myself, let my guard drop. Crane had done that to me. He had brought my honest self to the surface. How could I have given him such power over me? Such influence? I gripped the table again and waited for my breathing to calm, for my mind to restore some semblance of control over my emotions.

At the head of the table, Crane sat back and let his eyes flick over us, searching for any signs of drifting attention in the faces gazing back at him, but we were his entirely. 'Law as power,' he said, his delivery professorial again, the beat of the lecture resuming after the discussion, the interlude in which he had permitted our thoughts to breathe. 'Law as protector of the powerful and only occasional ally of the powerless.' His eyes met mine. 'Wherever power sits, there you'll find the law. Take the example set in *The Oresteia*. The only place where we see women's lives in all their complexity, their rage, their grief, and their subordination, is in the Greek tragedies. Ask yourselves why. Why are women always the movers of *tragedy* for the Greeks? Or, let me put the question another way . . . what is it about women that threatens male power?'

49

'The master has always been terrified of the slave,' Amanda said.

'It's sex,' I added quietly. 'Sex is the ultimate female power and men are afraid we'll realise that someday. They're afraid we'll use it against them.' My voice betrayed some of my bitterness, as if stomach acid had risen into my mouth and was now spitting outward from my tongue.

I thought I saw a shadow of fear in Crane then, of hesitation, a wobble running through his body. The balance of power tilted, momentarily, towards me. But I couldn't trust it entirely.

'It makes you wonder, really,' Crane said with a mirthless chuckle, 'why women still follow the law when it doesn't protect them.'

'Who says we do?' I replied, gauging how far I could push him. He was trying to decide if I meant what I had just said, waiting for the joke to hit, and, this time, I am quite sure there was alarm in his eyes. I let my expression soften, and a smile grace my lips, and then I gave a mild laugh, let my eyes shine, and said: 'Just kidding.'

When, at last, our hour together ended, the tension in the room finally broke, seats scraped back along the wooden floor, notebooks were shut, bags packed, and the movement of breath through my lungs became a little less laboured. Crane was gathering his papers together, shuffling them into a pile. He seemed to be loitering, as if for something to happen. As I zipped up my backpack and rose to my feet, he glanced up. 'Ms Mooney, can I speak to you for a moment?'

My eyes caught Vera's at the door before she left, the last student to exit, leaving me alone with the source of my rage. I turned around and faced him, steadying myself against the desk.

What exactly did he want with me?

'Sure,' I said. 'We can talk.'

Chapter Seven

Crane shut the door, the two of us now alone. I sat down again at the table, resting my backpack against my ankles, my eyes travelling to the closed door.

Our conversation on the faculty corridor was still on my mind, Crane's interrupted thought still unresolved. *You remind me of someone.* It seemed, at least, possible that he was about to say who. I tucked my hands under my legs, between the leather chair and the skin of my thighs, bare in shorts.

Coming to Philadelphia had always felt like a long shot, a hopeful grasping at a vaporous justice that kept vanishing the moment my fist tried to close around it, seeping out between my fingers.

But Crane was smiling, the lines at either side of his lips deep and dark. 'Well done today, Jessie. Your contributions really interested me. You've clearly spent some time considering these themes.'

'Thank you ...' I said, cautiously. 'But they're not themes to me, Professor. They're real life.'

Crane nodded, pensive for a few moments. 'Of course. Right. Yeah. Look, the thing is, Jessie, the classroom can be somewhat limited for detailed discussion. I try to cultivate an atmosphere of open debate, but students are so careful these days, afraid to rock the boat.' He seemed put out by this, his expression clouding briefly. 'Jessie, look, there's no obligation to take this on, of course. You shouldn't feel pressured. I know the academic demands are high at Franklin without taking on even more. But sometimes, when I see promise in a student, I like to offer them a position as research assistant.' I tried to keep my shock hidden. I had expected him to call me out, not offer me this position and, though I had hoped it might happen in time, the fact that he saw something in me so soon was unexpected. 'It's a good opportunity. You can use it on your resumé and I'd be happy to write a reference ... you know, if your work is good!' He smiled and then added: 'That's a joke. I'm sure your work will be excellent.'

'Right, yeah, no, I ...' I wasn't sure what to say. Everything I did was so calculated these days that the unexpected had a tendency to knock me sideways. It wasn't quite favourite status, but surely this meant I was getting places with him?

When I continued to dither about an answer, Crane offered more context. 'I'm working on an article, right now, that I think you, in particular, would find interesting. It touches on some of the themes of today's class – and your Antigone article ties in nicely.'

He was writing about democratic rot, about power and authority, about Antigone and the Greek tragedies, about what female justice might look like. How would society be organised if we began again from a starting point of true equality between the sexes, a world in which women had always held the same civic status as men? Wiping out the past and relieving ourselves of the burden of a history in which women were either invisible or irrelevant, where women could be owned and sold.

'Would you be interested?' Crane asked. 'In the position? Research assistant?'

Audrey had been his research assistant too, and though their emails were usually cordial and professional, every so often, either Crane or Audrey would slip, dropping in something casual at the end, something which hinted at another story.

'Yes. Absolutely. It would be an honour to work with you, Professor Crane,' I replied, the lie bitter in my mouth.

'Oh good,' he said, with another short laugh. Crane had a habit of laughing to cover his tension, the source of which must have been . . . me. 'For a minute there, I thought you were going to say no.'

He didn't like hearing that word – no.

Pushing my hair behind my ear, I forced a smile to my face, where it wobbled uncomfortably and threatened to slink away again. 'Not at all,' I said, rising to my feet. 'I'm looking forward to it.'

I lifted my backpack and pulled the straps over my shoulders, then turned towards the door.

Together, we left room 1.04B and walked through the library in silence. At tables and carrels, curiosity sent wandering eyes our way, wondering who it was who was with Professor Crane.

At the exit, Crane promised to send me the current draft of his article once he was back in his office, giving me a short wave before heading off in the direction of the faculty lounge.

I watched him walk away, then checked my wristwatch and set off at a run for my next class. We had talked for so long that I was now quite late. This was the cost of my plan, this need to pretend that I was an ordinary student who cared about this master's, who wanted all the things the other students wanted – the good grades, the letters of recommendation, the professional contacts I'd rely on in later life. All I wanted was justice for Audrey, but I couldn't risk coming to the Dean's attention for skipping class and failing tests. A star student makes a better complainant, and juries like good girls.

Through the window, I could see some of my classmates on the courtyard: Amanda, Ronald, and Vera, sitting on a bench at the far side. They looked relaxed, a picture of collegiality, and it made me think of how we used to be, my sister and me, heading home together from college, on the train to Malahide, catching up at the end of another day. If you had asked me then, I would have told you I knew everything about her, that Audrey and I had no secrets. But I would have been wrong about that.

Late to my Admin Law class, I tried to slip into the back of the lecture hall. Rows of seats were laid out in a crescent shape, two very large chandeliers hanging from the high ceiling, a remnant of a previous era in the law school's past. The lecture had started, the seats mostly filled. Climbing over bags and feet, sliding past knees, I could feel the other students' irritation as I attempted to get past them.

The student next to me sighed pointedly as I settled into an empty seat. I ignored his disgruntled muttering, but from the front of the room, Professor Hoffman's voice boomed in my direction.

'I don't tolerate latecomers,' she called to me, provoking a wave of faces to look back in search of the source of the disruption.

My hands, which had been digging through my backpack for my laptop, froze immediately. I sat up straight again. 'I'm sorry, Professor. I was delayed in another class.'

'Another class . . .' She folded her arms, a frown wrinkling her forehead. 'You're telling me a class ran over by fifteen minutes? Which class is this?'

'Law and Literature, Professor.'

I kept my focus on Professor Hoffman, but I could feel the effect of my words on the room. They were impressed, jealous, curious, or irritated, the outsized influence of Crane's class visible in the ripple of reaction around me. These were the star performers of their high schools and undergraduate colleges. All their lives, they had won scholarships, academic awards, and scholastic prizes. High achievers, whose parents' cars bore bumper stickers declaring them to be honours students. And, of course, the legacy students whose parents' wealth and privilege had bought them their place at Franklin, though they couldn't buy their way into Crane's class. For most of them, Crane's gatekeeping of Law and Lit was the first time they had met real rejection. The class represented a failure for them that was rare, and, for some, it stung, adding to the intrigue of what precisely it was that happened behind the closed doors of room 1.04B.

Professor Hoffman ran her hand through the silver-grey strands of her hair. 'Ah,' she said dully. 'Don't let it go to your head. You're not so special that you can't show up on time for my class like everyone else.'

I mumbled another apology while she cleared her throat, trying to recover her place in the lecture notes in her hand, the class continuing again from there. Though the attention of the other students in the room gradually shifted back to the professor, I remained conspicuous for the rest of the hour, eyes flitting to me occasionally.

I tried to focus on the class, but Crane kept pulling me back to him. Grooves were dug deep into my mind now, their cerebral paths always leading to him.

I had the upper hand. At least for now. Crane was none the wiser about who I was, and I was making progress winning my place as favourite. But hindsight is a funny thing. And, after all that happened, I'm not so sure of that assessment anymore. After all that happened, I find myself wondering. Was I luring Crane closer? Or was he luring me?

Chapter Eight

The rest of my week was spent in the library reading through legal texts to find quotes Crane needed for his article. He had also sent me a list of articles as long as my arm to track down and send to him by Monday, so I shuttled back and forth between my dorm and the law school, sustaining myself on a diet of bananas, salted crackers, and Joe's coffee. As methods of justice went, this one seemed to involve a lot of homework.

On Friday afternoon, Amanda and I were in the library preparing for classes the following week. She had spotted me by the window, and plonked herself down next to me. We were each silently absorbed, but I was glad of the company, a small comfort to break the isolation of my days in Philadelphia, far from friends, family, home. The library was quiet, the librarians chatting at their desk on the floor below while they restocked shelves, their voices floating up the stairs to us every so often.

For the purposes of this research project, Crane and I were exchanging emails every couple of days. Though they were a nascent bridge of communication, a beginning, they were entirely professional, each in the same format. A greeting; a request for some book or article, a quote, or a citation; then a sign-off. Always his full name, always formal, always perfunctory, always blunt.

I knew from Crane's exchanges with my sister that the deepening of their relationship was reflected in the way he wrote his emails. The closer they grew, the more informal he became with her, moving from *Jay Crane*, to *Jay*, to *J*, to *J x*. If I were to make it to the stage of using initials, I had considerable work to do. I needed to loosen him up, bring his guard down.

Opening a new email, I typed Crane's name, and gazed at the empty white text box, the flashing cursor, while I considered what to say, which words could, like a spell, summon his worst self to the surface.

Jessica Mooney (15.52):

Dear Professor Crane,

I was able to track down that Eisenstein critique of Mac-Kinnon's Toward a Feminist Theory of the State, *as requested.*

My fingers hesitated over the keyboard. How could I steer the conversation away from feminist theory to something a little less dry? Something more casual, maybe even a little flirty?

I stole a look over at Amanda, who was making notes for her Public Corruption class, and paying no attention to my screen.

I hope you have more exciting plans for Friday night than sitting around reading feminist theory?

Too much?

I read it again. No, the tone was fine. Friendly, slightly humorous, but not disrespectful.

I added my name to the bottom. Soon, I would have to find a way to break the wall between professor and student, the boundary protecting the person without power, status, or influence from the person who had it in spades. I was hunting for his weakest spot, the point where a well-delivered blow would cause the most destruction, bringing the edifice of his respectable life crashing down around him. This email would be a first proper strike.

'Did you see Charlie's message?'

I jumped at the sound of Amanda's hushed voice next to me. She was leaning my way now. My finger sprang forward, hitting the send button before she could see the email.

I turned towards her. 'What message?'

Amanda slid her phone along the table, the screen of which contained an invitation to drinks at Charlie's apartment before Bar Review that evening. I checked my own phone and found an identical text. He was inviting the whole Law and Literature class.

'What do you think?' Amanda asked. 'Should we go?'

'What's Bar Review?'

Amanda didn't know either, so I texted Joshua, who said it was a weekly night out the social committee organised, and a pretty lame pun on the Bar exams prep course. He said he would go if I did, adding a winky face emoji to the end of his message.

It was a long time since I had been to an ordinary social gathering. Back in Dublin, everyone I knew thought about my dead sister when they looked at me and it was something of a downer at parties, I tended to find. So, instead of all that, I took to losing myself in rancid clubs and dodgy encounters with strangers. Running from myself, self-medicating, fading away beneath the flashing, coloured lights of a dance floor, where hands reached at me out of the dark, not knowing or caring who I was, or what I was feeling. Reckless, dangerous, and a little dehumanising, but in those first grim months when I could think of nothing but

Audrey, it was how I tried to hide from the grief, from the pain. From the loneliness. Worst of all, the loneliness.

I checked my inbox again, refreshing the page to see if Crane might have replied. *No unread emails.* He probably hadn't seen it yet. I pinched my lower lip between finger and thumb, then refreshed my inbox again. Nothing.

Pulling my hair free of the tortoiseshell claw clip at the back of my head, I fought to stem a rising restlessness. It wasn't that I expected him to drop everything and answer me, it was just that nature abhors a vacuum, and I had a habit of filling silence with anxiety. Had I made a mistake? Had I offended him? Was my tone *too* casual? Presumptuous?

I pushed my laptop away and leaned towards Amanda, tugging on her elbow to get her attention. 'I think we should go tonight,' I whispered. 'It'll be fun, right?'

Fun was obviously the last thing on my mind, but I couldn't just sit around with this apprehension, waiting for Crane's reply. And Charlie's pre-game offered an opportunity, outside of the classroom, to better understand the dynamics around Professor Crane, and how I might become his favourite. My classmates could either prove to be my allies in this, or my enemies. And if there were shifting loyalties and antagonisms among the group, I would need to figure out how that could affect my plan. It was more productive than sitting around refreshing my inbox, at least.

I made a plan to meet Amanda later, then left the library, unable to sit still. There was no particular reason to think that Crane's office might be empty, except that it was a Friday afternoon and the law school was generally quiet, which seemed as good a time as any to check it out.

The clock hit five as I took the stairs, two at a time, from the front lobby to the faculty corridor. There was nobody around, no sign of life. I rapped gently on Crane's office door with my knuckles, and pressed my ear against the wood. No sound came from inside.

Grasping the handle, I turned it gently. The door opened an inch and I slipped inside, closing it behind me with a tight click.

Crane's office was more spacious than I expected. The desk was a towering mess. Papers and textbooks – plucked out, briefly perused, abandoned again – were scattered across available surfaces. A window behind the desk faced onto Sansom Street and, from there, he had a clear view of Joe's. On the wall beside the desk, there was a corkboard and, stuck to it with thumbtacks, a series of quotes. One that caught my eye said, *Sauve qui peut*, with a translation next to it: 'Save himself, whoever can'.

I felt as if I were walking on hallowed ground, my presence profaning his sanctuary, and I hoped the stink of my malice towards him would cling to the upholstery, to the carpet, to the air he breathed.

My eyes swept over his desk. I wasn't looking for anything specific, just something that might help me know him better, or even something I could weaponise against him. With the tips of my fingers, I flicked through the papers on his desk, and the post piled in his in-tray. Letters addressed to him at the law school, but also a bill he must have brought into work with him. His home address stared up at me from the top right of the page.

218 Delagny Street
Old City
Philadelphia,
PA 19106

I took a photograph, thinking quickly how I might use it. Maybe a deliberate run-in near his home some weekend morning, off-campus, where the dichotomy of our student-professor status might appear lesser to him. His guard would be lowered, and then I could pounce.

Just then, something else caught my eye.

Sticking out from under the corner of a textbook.

White paper with black printed text, annotated with hand-written cursive in jet-black ink. I recognised it immediately.

I lifted the book, slid the paper out, and held it up to my eyes. It was *my* essay, the one I wrote to get into Crane's class. He had written a note to himself in the top left-hand corner.

GOOD POTENTIAL – WORTH PURSUING.

Worth pursuing for *what?* For favourite? Is that what he meant? A small shiver of excitement ran down my spine. There was no other essay on his desk, not that I could see. He had told me my work was excellent when he offered me the role of research assistant, so clearly I had impressed him academically. But did this mean something *more?*

Voices outside shook me from my thoughts, my heart leaping into my mouth. I replaced the essay where I had found it and crept back across the room again.

The voices grew closer, two women discussing a meeting they had just attended, something about scheduling clashes next term. I listened for a third voice, for Crane.

He might not have answered my email yet, but he had made me his research assistant, just like my sister before me, and I had every reason to believe that he'd make me favourite next too. In his own words, scrawled across my essay, he had said it. *Worth pursuing.*

On the corridor outside, I heard a door open and then shut again, the voices disappearing behind it. No sign of Crane, no further noise.

Silently, I slipped back out to the corridor, and walked quickly away. But the words he had written were a refrain in my head. *Worth pursuing.*

Chapter Nine

Charlie lived off Rittenhouse Square in an apartment building unlike any student accommodation I had ever seen – mirrored walls, polished chrome, and an abundance of flowers pouring out of overstuffed china urns standing on mahogany tables. A concierge wearing a uniform of white shirt and red velvet bow tie stood at a desk in the lobby as we entered. It was a far cry from the beer-can towers and general stink I had encountered at college parties in Dublin.

It was just after nine when Amanda and I arrived, six bottles of Desperados under my arm and a packet of Doritos in my hand – the best fare available at the local corner shop. In Philadelphia, the heat didn't abate even at night, even for a moment, so I was wearing denim shorts and a striped T-shirt, with a plaid shirt tied around my waist for air-conditioned settings. As it turned out, this was a bad choice and I was completely underdressed. But what did I care? The only person I wanted to impress that night would not be there. It had occurred to me that he might well be at home and, thanks to my trespass in his office, I knew where he lived now. The map on my phone told me Delancey Street was only a thirty-minute walk from Rittenhouse.

We rang the bell at number twenty-three, the muffled sound of voices and music seeping out under the door. I was on something of a high after finding my essay on Crane's desk, buoyed by an optimism that had been long absent in me. I wasn't even bothered by Crane's continued silence towards my email.

'Well, well, well – look who it is!' Charlie said as the door swung open, his smiling face appearing before us. He had slicked his blonde hair back and, even though it is the favoured hairstyle of the biggest assholes in America, I have to concede that it suited him. 'Did you two come together?' he asked, grinning at us from the door. 'How *cute!*'

'I was expecting a frat house until I met your butler at the front door,' I said as I stepped into his apartment.

Charlie laughed, shuffling backwards to make way for Amanda, who floated inside behind me. 'Well, he let *you* in, so clearly he's not much use,' he said with a sly smile, a comment I punished with a quick thump to his upper arm. I tended to forget myself around Charlie. He had a playfulness to him that I found contagious. It provided relief from the burden of my own grief. But it also made it easy to relax in his company, an inclination I needed to watch.

'I like your place.' Amanda looked around her. 'Very mid-century chic.'

'Oh, thanks, yeah,' he replied, closing the door behind us. 'My mom decorated.' He gestured in front of me. 'There's liquor on the table in there, beer in the bucket. Good *American* beer, Mooney. Hope you'll survive.'

I walked towards where he pointed, into a small kitchen with marble surfaces damp already with alcohol. It was cluttered with bottles of various shapes and sizes. Some lemons and a lime sat on a wooden board, next to a knife resting in a pool of citrus juice.

There were about twenty people standing, sitting, and perching around the couches at the other end of the open-plan living space. Some I recognised from my classes, others I recognised as faces frequently seen in Charlie's company on campus.

I scanned the room for the other Law and Lit students, spotting Vera and Ronald on the couch. Amanda had followed Charlie over to the window and was chatting with him and a guy called Kevin, whom I knew from my Administrative Law class.

I took a wet bottle of beer from the bucket of melting ice and flicked the cap off with an American flag bottle opener in the shape of an eagle, as Joshua appeared in the kitchen.

'Beer?' I grabbed another bottle from the bucket of ice and handed it to him. He was wearing his '*Hillary 2016*' T-shirt again, in case anyone in the room might doubt his allegiances. 'You came in the end?'

'Despite my better judgement, I am indeed here,' he said and clinked the neck of his bottle against mine.

Casually, I asked: 'Why do you think Charlie invited us anyway? Like, is he friends with any of you guys outside of class?'

'Not really. I was on *Law Review* with Ronald last year, so we're pretty friendly – and Vera's friends with everyone. Charlie is mostly friends with other bros, so . . . yeah, I don't know why he invited us.'

I considered him for a moment while I took a drink. Out of all the Law and Lit students, Joshua seemed to be struggling the most so far, Crane singling him out in class a couple of times now, while the rest of us sunk into our seats and hoped his antipathy towards Joshua was not contagious. Entry to the class was based on our essays alone and, though Joshua was book smart – smart enough to get into the class – it wasn't enough to claim Crane's good favour. Crane seemed to like a killer instinct, someone quick-witted and good on their feet.

'Maybe there's poison in the beer and this is all an elaborate way of removing the competition for Crane's favourite?'

Joshua's laugh was slightly uneasy. 'Ha, yeah, maybe ...'

I picked at the corner of the label on my beer bottle, as if I were just making conversation. 'Who do you think he'll choose anyway? Like, if you had to bet?'

'Definitely not me,' Joshua said. 'Crane doesn't seem to like me much ...' His head jerked towards me. 'He's ... *intense*, isn't he? It's not like ... like, I was *expecting* it, but ... I don't know ...'

'He is, I guess ... yeah.'

Joshua pondered my question again for a moment, his gaze travelling over the possible candidates, scattered around the room in front of us. 'He could pick Vera, maybe.'

She was chatting animatedly with Ronald, a drink in her hand that looked like it might be a dirty Martini.

'Do you think so?' I said, doubtfully. 'She doesn't speak up much in class. And she said she didn't want it.'

'I don't know if I believe that,' Joshua replied. 'Vera's basically queen of Franklin so she usually gets these things.'

I knew what he meant. Vera Lin was editor of the *Franklin University Law Review*, a board member of the American Constitution Society, and a two-term president of the Franklin Women's Group.

'Maybe Charlie,' Joshua said pensively. 'He has that agent of chaos vibe that Crane seems to like, happy to watch the world burn.' He began to drift in the direction of the window, where Amanda was still in conversation with Kevin and Charlie. 'Or you.'

'Why do you say that?' I asked, carefully nonchalant as I followed him.

'He listens very closely when you speak. It's obvious he likes you.'

'No ...' I said quickly, to hide a flush of triumph. 'I don't think that's true.'

'Of course it is,' Joshua replied, nudging my arm gently with his elbow. 'Who couldn't like you, Jessie?'

His comment surprised me. I hadn't given Joshua a reason to feel so warmly towards me.

We joined Amanda, and I hovered at the edge of the group, sipping my beer while their voices floated over me, debating the upcoming presidential election. Next to Amanda, Kevin was stressing that, while he, personally, didn't *like* the Republican candidate, he made a lot of sense on immigration, while Amanda was endeavouring to calmly and dispassionately argue that Mexico probably wasn't going to pay for a border wall. Every so often, Joshua piped up with some statistics from the ACLU, while Charlie kept interrupting to suggest a game of beer pong, getting no takers.

Vera was sitting on the couch at the far side of the coffee table, and I gave her a wave, which she returned with a funny little look, before lifting her hand limply. Evidently, she did not share Joshua's warmth towards me.

The debate occurring next to me was getting intense and clearly beginning to irritate Charlie. Losing patience, he dropped his head forward, as if he no longer had the strength to hold it up. 'Enough! Please, *God*, stop ... We're here to get boozed before Bar Review. No politics allowed.'

Ronald, who had been chatting to Vera on the couch, snorted loudly. 'Did I just hear Charlie Duke – of all people – policing free speech?'

Charlie made a face, ignoring him. 'Can't everyone just get drunk like normal people? I swear, law students are the fucking worst.'

I retrieved my phone from my pocket, finding no new emails, then took another half-hearted sip of beer, considering my next move.

Amanda had slipped away and was now lighting a cigarette at the open window. 'Did you hear what Kevin was saying to me?' she asked, as I followed her. She aimed a plume of smoke outside, then pinched her thumb and index finger together in front of her face. 'I was *this* close to telling him I'm second-generation Nigerian-British, then tossing my drink over him.'

'It's not too late.' I watched Joshua trying to edge away from Kevin, who was intent on an argument about Clinton's role in the Benghazi attack when she was Secretary of State.

'Ha!' Amanda gave a small shake of her head, her chin dipping downwards. 'What's the point? They don't change their mind.'

Clearing my throat, I angled back towards Amanda. 'I like that about Crane's class. He's more open-minded than I was expecting, you know? Like, he's willing to spend so much time critiquing the law from a feminist angle ... I really wasn't expecting that.'

Amanda considered it. 'Sure, I mean, I guess, but ...' She scratched her nose with the hand holding her cigarette, a wave of smoke trailing in front of her face. 'Don't you find him overwhelming? When he gets going?'

'Joshua said the same thing ...' I noted, avoiding the question. 'He finds Crane intense.'

'That's no surprise.' Amanda brushed her hair off her face. 'I actually got an email from Crane this evening.' My stomach lurched. So he *had* been checking his emails. 'He invited me to dinner in his house.'

No.

    No

        oo

          oo.

        oo

'Dinner?' I said, because other words eluded me. 'At his house?'

An invitation to dinner at his house was generally considered the confirmation that you had been plucked out from the pack, chosen as his favourite. Over rich foods and expensive wine, Crane would plot out and design whole career trajectories, making dreams come true by the time you reached the cheese course. The next generation of lawyers, built in his likeness, grateful to him.

Amanda nodded. 'Yeah. An old friend of his is visiting, a professor from Yale, and he said it would be a good opportunity for me to meet him. He's an expert on carceral policy, which my essay was about, so ... you know, it makes sense. I'm thinking about a PhD next year so ... it could be useful to speak to this professor about my ideas for it.'

She finished the cigarette and stamped it out in the small glass ashtray on the ledge. Was this the invitation that made someone a favourite? Was that what was happening here? And, if so, why was she playing it down? Was it modesty, or did she not need or want Crane's favouritism?

'Wow, that's ...'

She saw me struggle to find a word. 'Yeah ...' Amanda shrugged. 'I don't really know what to make of it either.'

I opened my mouth to say something, something that might dissuade her from going, but there was no opportunity. Charlie had just arrived at the window, another guy behind him.

Amanda's voice tightened as she spotted him. 'It's Reese Bryant from my Criminal Justice class ... the one I told you about on the way here.'

Reese Bryant had perfectly coiffed dark hair, a prominent chin, and a thin sliver of forehead between his eyebrows and hairline. He was the President of Fed Soc – or the Federalist Society to state its full name – a group of conservative and libertarian law students who believed the Constitution still had the same meaning as when it was written in 1787, guns and all. Yes ... really. According to Amanda, he had a lot of loud and unfounded opinions about the causes of crime and had once suggested in class that the phrenologists just might have been onto something.

He nodded at the lighter in Amanda's hand. 'Mind if I bum a light?'

She passed it over, and I saw a red glow appear at the end of his cigarette.

'What are you two talking about?' Charlie asked. He leaned one hand against the wall next to my face, while Reese blew smoke out the window.

'Crane,' I replied quickly, wondering if Amanda would mention the dinner invitation. I was still trying to process what it meant. Had she pipped me to the post? Was Amanda Crane's favourite?

'What about him?' Charlie asked, interest piqued.

Before I could answer, Reese interjected. 'Has he picked a favourite yet? Who is it?'

'Nobody ... *yet*,' Charlie answered, the upward incline at the end of his sentence sending a wave of nerves through me. Next to me, Amanda was silent, gazing resolutely through the window as if she didn't want to be drawn into this discussion. She had mentioned to me before that she planned to return to London after graduation – possibly for that PhD – but I wondered if Crane's favouritism could change her mind, open up a new world of possibility.

'Are you fighting over him yet?' Reese smirked. 'Which of you is going to knife someone in the back?'

'You're not even in the class, Reese,' I snapped. 'So, I don't know why you're talking about knives.' It was stupid to be provoked by him, but I was on edge, rattled by the possible implications of what Amanda had just told me.

'Relax, Mooney, he doesn't mean it like that,' Charlie said. 'Don't get all worked up . . .'

'Yeah, *relax* . . .' Reese parroted, then grimaced at me. 'Why are you so defensive anyway?'

'Leave it, Reese,' Charlie told him.

The sound of elevated voices had attracted Vera's attention, and she rose now from the couch to approach us. 'Can I ask you something, Jessie,' she said, one hand on her hip, the other still holding her glass. I sensed trouble in the way she regarded me down the shaft of her nose, tilted slightly upwards into the air, as if invisible pince-nez perched precariously in front of her eyes. 'What did Crane want with you? When he held you back after class? Come on, now. Why don't you share with the group?'

I tensed up immediately, beginning to feel somewhat hemmed in, my back against the window. 'Why are you asking? What does it matter?'

'Jessie, seriously, why are you being so secretive about it?' Vera replied, with a small laugh that suggested I was being ridiculous. 'Can't you just tell us?'

I didn't like being put on the spot like this and didn't ever respond well to social pressure. It tended to bring out my contrarian side. 'I don't have to tell you anything, Vera,' I said with quiet obstinacy, hoping she would back off.

'Oh, come on, Jessica,' Vera replied. 'We'll find out anyway . . . one way or another. You can't hide yourself from us . . . even though you try.'

For a horrible moment that seemed to drag and drag, I stood silent in the harsh, antiseptic light of their attention. Exposed to them all of a sudden, or so it felt.

But before I had to answer, I felt a hand on my arm. 'Enough, Vera,' Charlie said. 'Stop trying to psych her out.' He turned to me, glancing down at the empty bottle in my hand. 'You need a drink, Mooney. Come with me.'

Grateful, I let him pull me in the direction of the kitchen, relieved to have escaped the scrutiny of Vera Lin, the kind that I had no doubt she would someday use to break a witness on the stand.

In the kitchen, Charlie poured a shot for me, and one for himself. He picked up the knife next to the now-butchered lemon and asked: 'You want salt as well?'

'Sure,' I said. 'Why not?'

Just the smell of the tequila was enough to turn my stomach. Countless nights letting shots like these obliterate my consciousness, waking in the morning with a blank memory where grief might otherwise have sat. A bad habit I had left behind when I came here, but, if this was an opportunity to bond with my competition, then I'd gladly do it.

Keeping my eyes on Charlie, I knocked back the shot, then placed my glass down on the marble countertop next to his and sucked on the lime slice. A humidor was open on the counter, so I picked up a cigar and ran it under my nose, waiting for the tequila to take the edge off.

'Are you going to smoke that?' Charlie asked.

I shook my head, handing it to him, and he stuck it in his mouth. Retrieving a set of long matches from his pocket, he proceeded to light it and puff pompously on the end.

'You couldn't look more like a bourgeois prick if you tried,' I said.

He gave me a wink. 'Don't need to try.'

Charlie rooted in the bucket for another beer, opening it and thrusting it at me. 'It's none of my business, Mooney, but, if I may say, you strike me as someone who needs more fun in your life.'

'You're right, Charlie,' I replied. 'It's none of your business.'

A laugh emerged from his nose. 'You're the one I have my eye on, you know,' Charlie said in a low voice. 'I've seen how Crane responds to you in class. Your answers surprise him. You catch him off guard, like he doesn't quite know what to make of you.'

'Is that a good thing?' I asked.

'Yes,' Charlie said. 'Definitely.'

'And you?' I asked. 'Do you know what to make of me?'

For a moment, he was silent, sizing me up, amusement in his eyes. 'Game recognises game,' he said at last.

I took a step closer, until my breath was on his face, testing how he would respond. Was Charlie going to make trouble for me? 'And what do you know of my game?'

He didn't flinch, just smiled. 'Oh, I *know*, Mooney. I know you.'

Vera had said something similar. They might not have known precisely what but, clearly, they could both tell I was hiding *something*.

A dull ache was settling in my stomach, the optimism of the early evening curdling into frustration, a sour taste filling my mouth. Crane had invited Amanda to dinner. He had seen my email but hadn't responded.

'No, Duke,' I said. 'You really don't . . .'

Charlie's smile was steady as he regarded me. 'Maybe not. Not yet. But I will.'

Chapter Ten

Audrey used to say I was reckless when I started sneaking out of the house at night. She would sit up waiting for me while I was gone, too rule-abiding to come with me but unable to sleep until I stuck my head in her bedroom door and let her know I was home. A teenage girl, wandering alone in the dark, is somewhere she's not meant to be. But those night walks didn't scare me. At night, the world was quiet, the streets empty, the curtains closed, the foxes skulking, the cats prowling, animal eyes shining out at me from the suburban gardens of Malahide. Those walks grounded me. They calmed me down. They let me sleep. For as long as I could remember, I always had been drawn to the darkness.

Counting the numbers next to the doors on Delancey Street, I came to a stop at a three-storey red-brick house with white windowsills and dark blue shutters. It was tasteful, a wooden porch sitting around the black front door, the top of which rose to a point, like the apex of an isosceles triangle. On either side of the door, there were two glass lamps, both of which were lit with a soft white LED electrical bulb. And on top of the doorbell, there were three numbers, painted in an elegant blue to match the shutters: 218.

Only one faint light shone from the second floor, back from

the street, as if a lamp were on in a bedroom at the rear of the house. I was watching for movement inside, for a dark figure visible through the window. For him.

I had made him the centre of my world, a magnetic pole to which I was drawn, building my days around him, and now my nights too. But there was no sign of him here.

Taking several steps backwards, I shut my eyes. The whole evening had been a waste of time. Amanda was probably favourite already, while I was busy drowning in Crane's research project, my email ignored. I cursed under my breath. If I was making any progress at all, it was at such a slow pace that I would find myself in a graduation gown before I could ever get past the awkward hellos, the shy smiles, and the stilted discussions of jurisprudence, with the object of my enmity.

In one of the houses behind me, a dog began to bark, as if it were aware of my sneaking presence, perceiving the threat. But I couldn't make myself turn away. Not yet.

I was thinking of Audrey. Her bedroom door ajar, her body hunched on the bed inside, shaking as she cried in a long, quiet drone. She shrank from me when I had tried to comfort her, unable or unwilling to let me help her, intent on bearing the burden alone. With hindsight, I could see that she was shielding me and my parents from what had happened. She had always been like that. The eldest daughter, with a strong sense of responsibility. The protective big sister.

On Delancey Street, standing opposite Crane's home, my temper began to flare.

At my foot, there was a collection of potted plants in a row, a small figurine of a duck holding an umbrella sitting among them. Next to it, a rock, varnished and painted with the words 'CAPE COD' in white letters. A memento from a holiday.

With a surge of anger that I couldn't restrain, I picked up the rock, held it tightly in my hand and, with several quick steps towards the house, hurled it at the front window of number 218.

Chapter Eleven

When I woke the following morning, there was a notification on my phone. *One unread email.* Rubbing the sleep from my eyes, I sat up on my elbow, my head groggy, the memory of what I had done to Crane's window arriving late.

Jay Crane (08.17):

Good morning, Jessica,

Thank you for sending the article. My Friday night was spent at a faculty dinner. A staid affair, at which I was the youngest person. Hard for you to imagine, I'm sure, but it was quite fun to be the enfant terrible *of the evening. I do hope your Friday night was more exciting. At your age, I expect nothing but wild parties and sleepless nights. It all goes by faster than you can imagine.*

Jay Crane

My breath blew free of my mouth. His email was restrained and cordial, nothing inappropriate in it, but I had successfully moved him out of strict professionalism and into the realm of something a little more friendly. A personal anecdote, a vision of his life.

It was the reply from Crane, and not the smashing of glass, that made me feel powerful. And now, we were edging away from formality and building – dare I say – something of a *rapport*.

He hadn't mentioned the window. I had fled the scene as soon as the glass smashed, not delaying to see what would happen next. I had, it seemed, got away with it.

All morning, relief energised me again, like fresh oxygen in my blood. Dressed in my running clothes, I headed out with a lighter step, taking my usual route down the Schuylkill River, past the boathouse, and along the riverbank, where I could watch the university rowing team glide through the glassy water. A thin haze clung to the banks, making the air feel different: crisp, new, and unpolluted, as if my lungs were the first to inhale it. I could see why the rich and the gifted were so protective of their gilded world, why they poured hundreds of millions of dollars into these institutions. Endowments were like a moat of wealth around elite campuses. Franklin was a shining city, an aristocracy of consciousness, as D. H. Lawrence might have said, surrounded on all sides by a poverty it mostly ignored, by a lack of opportunity that was none of its concern, to which, at best, it paid lip service.

Back at my dorm, I jumped in the shower, and then, when I was good and ready, I stretched out my arms and reached for my laptop.

Jessica Mooney (13.13):

Sorry to report, there were no wild parties last night. Just drinks with your Law and Lit class – you were a popular topic of conversation, Professor!

Jessie

Pacing my room, I waited for his reply, and this time, I *knew* it would come. I had dangled the idea of a room full of people talking about him and I was confident Crane would not be able to resist knowing what was said. He cared about the opinion of students, just as they cared about his. It was a toxic symbiosis at Franklin Law, and a personal weakness in Crane that I could exploit when the time came.

As predicted, his response did not take long.

Jay Crane (13.39):

Is that so? Let me guess . . . you were discussing my dashing good looks? My surprising youthfulness? My mag-netism? My sparkling sense of humour?

Jay

So many questions, inviting me to answer. A light tone, slightly self-mocking, highlighting all his strengths, while pretending to do the opposite. He had even dropped his surname from the sign-off.

I took my laptop down to Chestnut Walk and found a bench next to the quad. Summer was fading, new colour seeping into the treetops, a scattering of yellow and brown swallowing up the green, branch by branch. All around me, the campus was alive, bodies spread out on the grass, enjoying the last of the warm and languid days. Under a chestnut tree, a girl was reading, a boy's head resting on her lap, which she stroked absently with her fingertips every time she turned a page. To my right, a group of students had set up a vot-er registration stand, and a peppy girl with a short ponytail swaying behind her head was handing out leaflets to people passing by.

I wanted to leave Crane in a state of anticipation. Not too

long, but enough to let him grow impatient, just as I had been. I'd give him the impression I had other things in my life.

While I let more time elapse, I contemplated Amanda's dinner invitation, and how it fit with the tone of Crane's latest emails to me. If Amanda was favourite, it complicated matters hugely. I couldn't let her go to that dinner without warning her about Crane, but that would mean revealing how much I knew about him, a difficult thing to explain away. And if I wasn't Crane's favourite, how else would I get close to him?

When enough time had passed, I typed a reply.

Jessica Mooney (14.43):

All of the above, of course, and much more. But, I must confess, I heard something that surprised me . . . Amanda received an invitation to dinner at your home.

Trying to make me jealous?

Jessie

I read and reread the email, my thumb between my teeth, my knee bobbing up and down. It was risky, but then again, this whole plan was an exercise in risk-taking.

I hit send.

And then I waited.

And waited.

Music was blaring from a frat house further up the walk, its faux-classical colonnades adorned with flags bearing a series of Greek letters. A loud cheer sounded as a very peaky-looking pledge finished a large funnel of foamy beer while dressed in a clown costume.

Still I waited, as if for word from a prophet.

By the time Crane's answer came, I had abandoned my bench and was on the steps of Joe's, about to walk inside.

Jay Crane (16.25):

That particular dinner invitation relates to Amanda's research interests. Your research interests would require me to summon the ghost of Sophocles.

Jay

The law school was behind me, his office facing onto the street where I stood. With a glance over my shoulder, I tried to identify which was his. It had to be the window two from the end of the building, looking down at me like a square eye in the red-brick. There was nobody at the glass, but I couldn't quite shake the sense of being observed, a prickle across my skin.

Jessica Mooney (16.28):

Surprised to hear the great Jay Crane couldn't find a way!

I was paying Joe for my coffee when my phone vibrated again in my pocket.

Jay Crane (16.30):

It's true that I'm great, but, sadly, my talents end at necromancy. Besides, you know Sophocles would make a bad dinner party guest . . . you might even say, he'd be tragic.

Back on Sansom Street, I found myself laughing at his joke. And, the thing is, I wasn't pretending – Crane had actually charmed me.

I took a sip of my coffee while the black and white cat, who liked to hang around outside Joe's, glared at me.

Jessica Mooney (16.35):

Well, I must say I'm disappointed that zombie Sophocles isn't an option. However, I would like it known that I am excellent dinner company – just if, for some mysterious reason, Amanda can't make it.

Jessie

I peered back at the law school building. The window was still empty. If Crane had been there at all, he must have stepped back out of view.

On the screen of my phone, another email.

Jay Crane (16.37):

Duly noted.

Chapter Twelve

Crane cancelled the dinner with Amanda. When she told me that his friend from Yale was not able to travel after all, I figured my manoeuvring must have worked. It was true that I had taken away some of the advantages of Crane's favouritism from Amanda but, this way, she would be safe from him. In any case, it didn't seem to faze her much. When I asked if she was disappointed, she shrugged and said that it didn't make much of a difference. She was close to her family back in London, and the likelihood of returning home after graduation seemed to insulate her from the pull Crane had for the most ambitious of the student body at Franklin Law.

Though Crane had cancelled on Amanda, he still hadn't extended an invitation to me, or, to my knowledge, anyone else. Over the weeks that followed, I began to meet him in his office occasionally to check in on progress on the article. Together, we would talk about how the law failed women, how it made the male experience normative, and discounted the trauma this caused for women. Crane was so attentive to what I had to say, so accepting of my anger, so understanding of my frustration, that I could almost, *almost*, forget who it was who was listening to me. And what he had done to the sister I'd lost.

Crane seemed content to keep working on the article with

me, but I started to suspect that he was more cautious by nature than I had anticipated. It must have felt easier with Audrey in Dublin, where he was far from home, far from colleagues, far from real consequences. I needed to change things up, break open the comfortable intellectual space we had begun to inhabit together, so he might see me in a different light. I needed that invitation to dinner.

On the first Wednesday in October, after my Administrative Law class, I left the law school and hurried across to Joe's, hoping to make it before the rush of other students. Crane usually dropped in at lunchtime on Wednesdays to pick up *The Economist*, a tin of breath mints, and a coffee, and I needed to get into position before he arrived.

I knew where he would be because I had been gathering information against Crane, following him around campus, studying his habits. By that point, I had a map of his movements pinned to the corkboard over my desk, a record of where he was likely to be at any given time with a red line along his path, and circles around frequently visited sites.

In my notebook, I kept track.

Fridays - sometimes takes a walk down to the river at lunchtime, usually if the weather is good. Returns in time to teach at 3 pm - Wilson Hall. Leaves earlier than usual most Friday afternoons, sometimes straight after class. Usually gone by 4 or 5 pm. Have seen him call into Whole Foods on the way home twice. Last week, he had a drink alone at the Rittenhouse Hotel.

If I could mention these little details of Crane's whereabouts throughout the week, little things that could be checked against his credit card or phone records, it would help me demonstrate my credibility when the time came.

In Joe's, I hid in an aisle of shelves overloaded with stationery, examining a set of spiralbound notebooks. Once Crane arrived, I would get a read on his mood before faking a run-in. If he didn't seem in a hurry, maybe I could suggest a stroll with our coffees, down to the river. I could try to get him chatting about something other than the law, something lighter, maybe something that would encourage him to flirt back.

While I loitered at a stack of notebooks, the door to Joe's opened behind me, the bell tinkling, followed by the sound of multiple voices in conversation. Hanging back at the far end of the aisle, my view impeded by a glass case containing wooden pipes and related paraphernalia, I caught a glimpse of Crane. He was chatting to two people beside him, whom I couldn't quite see.

'Well, you know, the times being what they are, I don't think we'll have any trouble placing the article.' His voice, loud and assured, carried down the small shop to me. 'If nothing else, there'll be interest in the fact that we have found some common ground, given our differing schools of thought. It'll raise a few eyebrows on both sides.'

I turned my back to him, my fingers absently plucking pens out of a container next to me as I pretended to inspect them, then returned them.

'I do think it's a timely subject,' a woman replied. 'But I worry that the intellectual rot has gotten to the editors of the student law reviews too. I had a piece rejected last year by the *Texas Law Review* for being too polemical – can you believe that?'

A third voice spoke. 'It's the idea of speech as harm. Some of my generation take it too far.'

I could hardly believe it. Charlie fucking Duke.

As subtly as I could, I moved around to the next aisle over, where I could hide, more effectively, behind a stand of postcards. Clearly, this was not a good time to bump into Crane.

The three of them got their coffees. There was a rustle of paper, suggesting Crane was grabbing his magazine from the stand, then a rattle of breath mints inside a tin, the sound of Joe pushing buttons on the cash register. The till opened, then shut again.

They were still talking about law journals and submission dates.

More students entered the shop now, drowning out Crane's voice. I peeked around the edge of the postcard stand, and saw that they were leaving. Charlie was walking between Crane and another professor I recognised as Claire Laurent, an arch-conservative and unlikely company for Crane.

When the coast was clear, I made my way out of Joe's and headed back to the law school. A wasted venture, but I had still managed to discover Charlie's little secret.

As I crossed the courtyard, I spotted Charlie again, alone now, sitting at one of the metal tables. His legs were stretched in front of him, his muscular back hunched over his laptop, but his senses alive to the comings and goings through the courtyard. He called my name loudly several times, attracting irritated looks from the other students at tables around him.

I waved back, pleased by this chance to find out what he had been doing with Crane and Laurent. Charlie pulled over an extra chair, which made a horrible rattling sound against the red-brick pavement, and I wondered if he was deliberately trying to cause a commotion, or if he could possibly be that oblivious to other people. Pretty sure it was the latter.

'You have a confession to make ...' I said, sliding into the chair next to him. 'Come on, out with it!'

'What are you talking about?' A look of guilt crossed his face and a catalogue of potential sins seemed to flash before his eyes.

'What were you doing with Crane and Laurent?' I asked, my elbow dug into the table, my cheek resting on my hand.

'Oh . . . you heard about that?'

'I saw you.'

'God, you're everywhere, aren't you . . .'

'Yes,' I said. 'Omnipresent.' Scooting my chair further towards him, I matched his grin. 'What are you up to, Charlie Duke?'

He leaned in so close that I thought, for a moment, our noses would touch. 'You're not the only candidate for favourite, Mooney,' he said, eyes narrowed. 'Crane asked if I could be his research assistant for an article he's co-writing with Professor Laurent.'

'Seriously? Another article?! Does this man sleep?' I said, sitting back heavily in the chair, so that my spine hit painfully against the metal.

'Bet you didn't see this one coming,' Charlie crowed contentedly.

'It's not a game,' I snapped. 'You don't even need this!'

I realised my mistake almost immediately. Revealing to Charlie, of all people, just how much Crane meant to me was a misstep. I shut my eyes, took some oxygen into my lungs, and tried to steady myself.

When I looked back at him, there was an odd expression on Charlie's face. I had the sensation that he was about to ask me why exactly I cared so much. But, before he could, someone shouted his name from the far side of the courtyard. It was Reese Bryant, who didn't seem pleased that I was with Charlie. Even at this distance, Reese radiated hostile energy.

'I should go,' I said before he reached us, grabbing my backpack and heading towards the door into the law school. Next to it, a squirrel was rooting through a pile of raked leaves, the bristles of his tail visible in the leafy gaps, offering a crunching objection every time he moved. He scarpered as I approached.

'Wait,' Charlie called after me.

'I have a class!' I called back, but Charlie was not deterred.

'Then we should grab a drink some time, Mooney.'

I turned around. Charlie was smiling at me, so perfectly suited to this environment, seated beneath the shedding maple tree, the last of the sun shining off his blonde hair.

'Why?' I asked, moving back towards him, because I honestly didn't know what reason he could have to want a drink with me.

'Because we're friends,' he said.

I caught the look of derision flash over Reese's face.

'Are we?' I said, surprised.

Charlie shrugged, as if resigned to a new and unexpected reality. 'Afraid so.'

I smiled, but didn't answer him, intrigued at the idea that someone like Charlie Duke might consider me a friend. What had I done to give him that impression? But it wasn't the prospect of friendship that had me worried. If Charlie was also Crane's research assistant, didn't that mean Charlie could also be Crane's favourite?

Inside the law school, I grabbed my phone out of my pocket and drafted another email to Crane. I had missed my opportunity that afternoon, and I needed to stay in his thoughts one way or another.

Jessica Mooney (13.51):

Charlie Duke was just telling me about your article with Professor Laurent. Interested to learn I am not the only research assistant in your life – at least, tell me I'm your favourite?

Jessie

I typed it out but didn't send it until I reached the lecture hall where my next class was taking place. A river of movement around me, students criss-crossing the school, beneath the watchful eyes of alumni, a legacy of status, power, wealth. Not for the first time, the unlikeliness of my presence here at Franklin hit me in the chest. Somewhere along the line, Audrey had stumbled off a straight path, and I was still following after her, just not yet at that sharp curve.

Audrey had never caused my parents any trouble, rarely ever pushing boundaries, even as a teenager. The only time I can ever recall her breaking any rules was the one time she snuck over the wall into Malahide Park with me after dark. We drank cans of cider with some boys from the local secondary school, but that was as far as her teenage rebellion stretched.

But it nags at me now, doubt tugging at the back of my mind. These were assumptions I made of my older sister, always taking it for granted that Audrey was content to follow the rules, while I opted to pick and choose. What if that assumption was wrong? What if, by claiming the role of difficult daughter, I had forced my sister even deeper into compliance? She never could disappoint our parents, always pleasing other people. Was that why she didn't ask for help? Was that why she couldn't confide in me?

As I took a seat near the back of the room, my phone vibrated. Him.

Jay Crane (13.58):

Are you trying to get me into trouble, Jessica Mooney? I should really deny the suggestion that I could ever play favourites with my students, but surely you know by now?

Jay

I looked down at the message, the implication clear. I had, like my sister before me, been chosen. Favourites, both of us.

In the lecture hall, class had just begun, the other students settling down.

I suppose I should have felt relief, or even joy. I had pitched myself just right, winning the admiration of the formidably brilliant Jay Crane with my mind, my intellect, my sense of humour, and a strong dose of flattery. Surely, I should have felt proud of what I had accomplished.

The sound of rain caught my ear, falling against the window behind us. The patter of drops growing louder as the sky darkened, the light leaving the room.

No turning back now.

Chapter Thirteen

The invitation arrived the following morning while I was eating breakfast in the canteen off Chestnut Walk. As with most Franklin buildings, this one was at least a century old. It had been a chapel at one point, judging from the stained-glass windows, the high ceilings, and the archways that made the acoustics odd. Morning voices, groggy with sleep, bounced from surface to surface around me, the low chattering of my fellow breakfasters.

Jay Crane (08.18):

Are you free for dinner tomorrow night? I must warn you that my expectations are sky-high. You claimed to be a better dinner guest than Sophocles, so now you have to prove it!

I can promise you a wonderful meal, certainly better than whatever slop they serve you in the Franklin canteen. Send any dietary requirements.

Jay

I dragged myself to class as usual on Thursday but couldn't concentrate on anything, all thoughts coagulating on Crane, on the dinner invitation, on how I could best use the opportunity it gave me. By Friday evening, my nervousness felt like a living thing in my chest. A wasp or a bee, trying to batter its way out through my ribcage.

It had taken me twenty minutes to decide what to wear. When Audrey died, her clothes had, by default, fallen into my hands. Her familiar scent was mostly gone from the fabric now, but if I buried my face deep enough into the fibres of a jumper or hoodie, there was still the faintest whiff. When packing for Philadelphia, I had stuffed some of her clothes into my suitcase, and it was one of her dresses I chose to wear to dinner. Red, with thin straps and a lacy finish around the neckline. It was the type of dress that I hoped Crane might like, and I wondered if Audrey had ever worn it for him.

Tonight, it would just be me and Crane, a chance to figure out where I stood with him. When the door opened, who would I meet? The professional, friendly Crane I knew in the classroom? Or had I brought him far enough along the way to reveal the man I knew him to be, the man willing to cross a line? If the latter, maybe I could even test him, push things further, see how far he might go.

I had already prepared the diary entry in my black notebook, based on Audrey's thoughts from her first night alone in his company in Dublin, when they went to a play together, a production of *Waiting for Godot* in the Abbey Theatre. He had suggested it when she mentioned never having seen a Beckett play, something he considered sacrilegious in a Trinity student. I knew from the diary that she had been nervous about going, still intimidated by how impressive she found him, still wondering what he saw in her. *I get so flustered in his company – what if he thinks I'm stupid?* I copied the same sentiment into my notebook, planning to finish the entry later, depending on what happened at dinner.

The cab pulled up outside number 218. The scene was just as it had been the night I came here after Charlie's party, the same dog barking from the window as the car dropped me at the kerb, and drove away again. I glanced down at the flower pots, spotting the duck figurine with its umbrella. The Cape Cod rock had not been returned, but the pane of glass next to the door had been replaced, as if nothing had ever been broken.

Tugging at the hem of Audrey's dress, I walked the couple of steps up the stoop and rang the doorbell. My feet were uncomfortable in patent red heels, another inheritance from Audrey, the sort of shoes I rarely wore.

'Jessica,' Crane said, opening the door. 'You made it. Come on in.' His tone was welcoming, friendly, as if he was very pleased to see me, his gaze flicking down to my dress only briefly. He stepped back so I could enter, and closed the door behind me.

The first thing I noticed was the distinctive smell of patchouli, as if someone had been burning sticks of incense. It was not the sort of smell I expected to associate with Crane, but then this would be a night of surprises. The lighting was dim, candles glowing on the sideboard, over which a mirror hung, the two of us reflected in it together. In Audrey's heels, the top of my head reached just below Crane's chin. I flicked my hair off my shoulder. It was straighter than usual, thanks to my labour with a hair straightener, but the kinks were re-emerging.

'The living room is just through here,' Crane said, pointing into a space that revealed a taste for maximalist interiors.

There were three floor-to-ceiling mahogany bookcases, so stuffed with books that the shelves seemed to buckle under their weight. A heaving mess of bound paper, slotted in wherever they fit, with no apparent order to them. Other than the bookcases, every inch of wall was covered with paintings of women staring mournfully out from square frames; or antique maps of nebulous landmasses that I couldn't identify at this distance; or framed displays of butterfly species pinned onto white boards. High over the mantlepiece hung a painting of a naked woman lying back on a chaise longue, a languorous and very pale arm cast over her head, as if she had just fainted, and beneath this, dominating the mantlepiece itself, two large busts of the gods Apollo and Athena.

'Let me get you a refreshment,' Crane said. There was a song playing in the background, the sound of strings coming from a speaker somewhere. Philip Glass, I think it was, a discordant tune that I can still hear now, the faintest shimmer at the very edges of my mind.

I turned away from the bookshelves and towards Crane, injecting a playfulness into my voice. 'Nice place you have here, Jay. Now, would you read these books, or are they just for show?'

He laughed, a barking noise. 'Of course they're just for show! They're not even real books. I painted them on.' He seemed more relaxed than he did in class, his voice more fluid.

I walked to the mantelpiece and ran my finger over the marble face of the sun god. I did not feel as if I were in my own body, startling myself with the aura of confidence I was managing to project. Crane wasn't the only one who could pull off a convincing deception, hide dark intentions behind a charismatic facade.

'Apollo?' I said, gesturing towards the bust. 'Really? Despite his defence of Orestes?'

Crane's hand was in his pocket, a small smile rising to his face as he stepped closer to me, leaning against the other end of the mantelpiece, next to Athena. 'Ah, I don't hold it against Orestes. Everyone makes mistakes.'

'He killed his mother!'

'It was the style of the times.'

'He got away with it,' I said.

'Indeed. And whose fault is that?'

'The law?' I replied.

'Or the people?' he suggested.

'A little of column A,' I said, meeting his smile with mine. 'A little of column B.'

There was a pause, music filling the silence between us. I wondered if he might bridge the gap, if he might lean in closer . . .

'Take a seat, Jessica,' Crane interrupted the thought, indicating one of the cracked leather armchairs in front of us, angled to the hearth. 'Make yourself comfortable. You'll have to forgive me, but I need to keep an eye on progress in the kitchen.' He walked through the room to the open double-doors leading to the hallway. 'I'll be back in a minute,' Crane called. 'Help yourself to a drink, if you like. There's wine breathing in the decanter.'

Alone in his living room, I sat, my fingers reaching for the miniature polished wooden globe on the coffee table. I gave it a whirl and watched it spin.

The surrealness of the moment was hitting me. I was really here, in the home of the man who had broken my sister. Her phone was in my handbag. I took it out now, typed her passcode, and calmly opened her texts. I had already read them in the car, but I read them again now, feeding the anger in me, making sure I didn't flinch. It was harder to plot a man's ruin while sitting in his home, observing all the things he stood to lose. It was hard to still fervently wish that loss on him. The human in you always feels the pull of sympathy – and that's why you need the anger.

On the morning of her final Christmas, Crane had sent a text to my sister. He might have sent it from this very room. I imagined the fire lit in the grate, a garland pinned to the mantelpiece. A tree decorated in the corner, scarlet ribbons tied to boughs, lights twinkling at intervals, and some mistletoe hung over the door.

Jay Crane (10.34):

I know you don't want to hear from me right now, but I want you to know that I'm thinking of you today. Happy Christmas, Audrey. You deserve every happiness life can give.

J x

I remember that Christmas vividly. Audrey had spent the day hidden away from us, locked in her room, only coming downstairs to pick at a plate of turkey after Dad had roared in the keyhole that she was making her mother cry. Mum tried to put on a brave face, but she took our dog, Bran, for a long walk on the beach, and didn't return to the house until it was dark. By then, Dad and I were watching *The Great Escape*, passing a box of Quality Street between us, and Audrey was back in her room. She barely spoke to us at all that day, but here, before my eyes, were her words to Crane:

Audrey Mooney-Flynn (22.40):

Please, if you ever cared about me, just leave me alone. You've done enough. I'm broken. Leave me be.

Sitting in Crane's house, I read those words again. *I'm broken. Leave me be.*

The doorbell sounded. My head jerked up, my forehead creasing into the deepest frown.

'I'll get it!' Crane said, hurrying down the hallway, a grey half-apron tied around his waist. The front door opened, an exchange of greetings. I could hear a voice that sounded far too familiar.

Charlie fucking Duke.

Chapter Fourteen

Charlie appeared at the living-room door. 'Mooney, hey, you're here!' he said, brightly. He was wearing beige chinos and a dark suit jacket with a white shirt and tie for the very special occasion of dinner at his professor's house. The tie was made of silk with a pattern which, on closer inspection, bore the letters 'V', 'M', 'I' superimposed on one another. These letters stood for the Virginia Military Institute, where Charlie had earned his undergraduate degree.

'Duke.' I rose to my feet, unable to hide my annoyance. 'I wasn't expecting to see you here.'

'I thought I had mentioned it?' Crane said, clamping a large hand on Charlie's shoulder. He most certainly had not, not in any of the emails I had received from him. 'You both submitted essays that interested me. Both quite similar, actually . . . similar themes. I thought we might talk about them some more.' He took a couple of steps towards the coffee table, reaching for the decanter of wine and pouring a glass for each of us.

'Thanks, Professor,' Charlie said, as he accepted the wine glass Crane handed to him. He swirled the crimson liquid – a pinot noir – and studied the legs stretching down the sides. I watched him lift the wine to his lips. Our dinner would have a chaperone after all.

Crane handed me a glass too. I met his eyes, brown and shining in the candlelight.

'The food is nearly ready if you'd like to take a seat,' Crane said, heading through the open sliding doors to the dining room, where a round table was laid out.

Charlie noticed the look on my face as I slipped past him to follow Crane. 'Are you mad I'm here?' he said, his voice low, his fingers gently gripping the corner of my elbow.

'Not at all,' I replied breezily, pulling my arm clear.

'Liar,' Charlie murmured into my ear with barely concealed mirth. 'You thought you were the only favourite.'

I didn't bother giving him a response. This was the problem with Charlie Duke. He could read me like a book.

Just like the living room, the dining room was cluttered with various antiques. In the corner, next to the window, stood a vintage wooden filing cabinet with several small drawers bearing handwritten labels that said things like 'correspondence' and 'tax'. On the walls were a series of framed *New Yorker* cartoons, and behind these, a wallpaper of pale green leaves patterned on an off-white background. The table was draped in white linen, with a large ceramic vase in the centre, out of which rose puffed pale pink carnations.

'Grab a seat anywhere,' Crane said, disappearing towards the kitchen again. 'I'll be back in a moment.'

'Well, this is nice,' Charlie said as he took in the room. 'The inner sanctum.' As I sat down at one of the carefully laid table settings, I could feel Charlie studying my face. 'Are you really that pissed that I'm here?' he asked.

'No.'

'Don't lie, Mooney. You're being weird.'

'I'm not.'

'Did you want Professor Crane all to yourself?'

'Oh, just stop, Duke.' I hid my face behind my hand. 'You're so annoying.'

He laughed, gleeful at my reaction. 'I'm afraid you're going to have to share him with me, Mooney. We can both be favourites.'

The placemats were of an intricate design with symmetrical, abstracted flowers, leaves, and small birds pecking at fruit. I stared down at them, slipping the linen napkin free of its holder, and laying it across my lap.

'Could you please just drop it, Charlie? I don't want to talk about it.'

'Vera was right about you ... A true gunner.'

'Please ... just *stop?*'

Crane walked in just as I said this, a serving dish in his arms, loaded with strips of steak on a bed of chargrilled courgettes. 'Are you behaving yourself, Mr Duke?'

'You can call me Charlie, Professor, and yes, of course I am. I always do.'

I moved the carafe of water out of the way so Crane could place the steaming dish on the cork mat.

'I somehow doubt that very much, Charlie,' Crane replied.

'He delights in annoying me, Professor,' I said, as he sat down and pushed his seat closer to the table. 'It seems to be a hobby of his.'

'Not at all. I would never behave so childishly, Jessie.' Charlie flashed me a warning look that I ignored. He was on his best behaviour, flattering and fawning as if it came naturally to him.

'You don't need to put on the act for me, Charlie. You're in a safe space here.' Crane took a slice of sourdough bread from the basket at my elbow.

Charlie caught my eye, again, then grinned. 'Oh, I'm not so sure about that, sir. You've seen Mooney in class. You know what it's like when she gets going.'

'Now, now, Charlie,' Crane said. 'Enough of that. You know what happens to snitches around here?'

'Professor?' Charlie's eyebrows rose.

'They get stitches.'

A snort of laughter sounded from my mouth, while shock crossed Charlie's handsome face.

Crane didn't wait for Charlie to recover the power of speech. He gestured towards the food. 'Please, help yourselves. I just need to get the couscous from the kitchen.'

In his absence, Charlie grabbed the wine decanter, filling our glasses again until they were very full.

I watched as my glass reached capacity. 'Easy there, tiger. I'd like to remember this evening.'

'You're the worst Irish person I've ever met,' Charlie said, as if I had truly disappointed him.

His tone irked me enough to raise my glass and gulp down the wine until there was just a dribble left at the bottom. I swallowed a belch as it hit my empty stomach, immediately regretting the rush of national pride that compelled me to prove him wrong, though Charlie seemed delighted at having finally provoked me.

'That's more like it,' he said, refilling my glass as Crane returned with a large bowl of couscous. 'Now we're talking.'

Crane scraped the wooden floorboards as he pulled his chair back. 'Please, do start! Let's eat.'

I helped myself to steak and courgette. 'So, Professor Crane,' I said, eyes carefully fixed on my plate as I moved my food around. 'How long have you been teaching at Franklin?'

'Twenty-five years,' he said, his knife sliding through meat. 'Can you believe that?' His eyes danced. 'You'd never guess from my youthful looks, right?'

I smiled back, but didn't answer and instead reached for my wine. Was this how he had been with my sister? Jokey, a little self-deprecating, charming in a way that felt effortless?

'I did my undergrad at Princeton, majored in Philosophy, then received a Rhodes Scholarship for a PhD in Oxford. That was a fun time. But I knew, after those three years at Oxford, that I was more suited to the law. It's where philosophical principle meets practical reality, so I came back to Yale for law school, then clerked on the DC circuit for a year. After that, I clerked for Anthony Kennedy on the Supreme Court – it must have been 1990, or maybe '91 – and then the job came up at Franklin.' He took a quick sip of wine. 'I've been at Franklin ever since.'

Crane was practically moss on the walls of the law school. No wonder he was so difficult to unseat. Think of the influence he had amassed over that time, the friends he had made, the fa- vours he had done, the loyalty he had won. Think of the students who had passed through his classes, the minds that had opened themselves up to him, the other people sitting, as we were now, around his dinner table. The special few. The anointed ones. The favourites.

'I think you knew my uncle at Yale,' Charlie said. 'Conan Duke?'

'Of course I knew Conan! He used to offer me money for my constitutional law notes.'

'That sounds like Conan ... Did he ever succeed?'

'Oh, sure,' Crane said with a laugh. 'I was waiting tables in my spare time. You think I wasn't going to sell Conan Duke my notes? Easiest money I ever made.'

'You waited tables?' I said, taken aback.

'Oh yeah. I worked in this dingy little dive bar in New Haven right through law school.'

Try as I might, I could not picture it. The man before me looked like he had never darkened the door of a dive bar in his life, let alone worked at one.

'My father was a self-made man,' Crane continued, 'and he thought I needed to be self-made too. He did pay for Princeton, but he thought one degree was enough, right? He could never quite understand why I kept going back for more.' Crane sat back in his chair, his chin in his left hand. 'He'd say to me, "Jay, you know, son, there's a time to put away your childish things and get a real job." He said that to me when I was clerking on the Supreme Court.' He began to laugh, his shoulders shaking. 'I was drafting Justice Kennedy's judgements and my father – Roy Crane of Crane Cement Co – thought I was throwing my life away. Can you believe that? He just couldn't understand the law at all. He was baffled by the whole thing.'

'My father is sort of the same. He has firm views on what I should do with my life,' Charlie said, clearing his throat. 'He'd like me to run for office someday.'

'Is that something you'd like?' Crane asked, the last of his laughter leaving him gradually. 'Your family is obviously very well-connected. It would be easy enough for you?'

'My family would like it, so, um, you know . . . it's certainly a possible career path.' Charlie gave the impression that he was choosing his words very carefully.

'Have they met you?' I said, intending to make a joke, but it sounded a little harsher than I meant.

'I'm not exactly a fan of the idea either.' Charlie's eyes narrowed as he looked back at me. 'But thanks for the support, Mooney. You're a real pal.' He glanced towards Crane, who was paying no attention.

I drank some more of my wine.

'What would you like to do, Charlie?' Crane asked. 'If you had a choice in the matter?'

Charlie took a breath. 'Honestly, I don't know. I've never really had the space to figure that out.'

'But you must.' Crane's expression was suddenly deeply serious. 'It's the most important thing you'll ever do.' He took a sip of water, then sat back in his chair again, contemplating the two of us, eyes drifting back and forth across our faces. 'You know, they say there was an inscription on the portico of the Temple of Apollo in Delphi which read, "Know Thyself" . . . that is advice worth following. Try it sometime.'

'Well,' Charlie remarked. 'It's easier said than done.'

'I don't doubt it,' Crane replied. 'You occupy a strange position in the world, Charlie. A lucky one, but a strange one. You'll almost certainly find yourself with an eyewatering amount of power and influence someday, just because of the family you were born into. You should spend this time figuring out what to do with that.'

I gazed at Charlie across the table. A sombre expression clouded his face. He seemed to physically recoil at the idea of so much responsibility landing on him, his whole body shrinking into itself. Smaller, thinner, more vulnerable. And yet, Crane was right. One day, the door would open, and Charlie would be bundled inside. Even against his will, even if they had to take him in kicking and screaming, he was one of them and always would be. Always on top. Always a favourite.

A flicker of irritation rose through me, my foot striking a beat against the wooden leg of my chair. The more I saw of the world, the more it seemed to work in such breathtakingly stupid ways.

'What about you, Jessica?' I jumped, startled out of my thoughts. Crane was looking at me. 'What do you want to do when you graduate?'

I took another sip of wine to buy myself some time. The truth is, I had no idea what I was going to do when this was all over. I hadn't yet contemplated a life beyond the completion of my vendetta against the man who was asking me the question. Before Audrey died, I'd started to form some plans, ambitions, and ideas. I wanted to work in politics or in the non-governmental sector. Maybe behind the scenes, nudging the law in a better direction through political change. Or else, maybe, I would stay at university, where I had discovered that I could be content, find a place for myself in academia.

I set my wine glass down on the table again. A future free of grief and anger felt so distant at that moment that I could hardly imagine it. 'Well, honestly,' I said slowly, 'I'm not really sure yet either.'

Crane nodded a couple of times. 'It's good to be open to possibilities. It's a very special time in your life, when anything can still happen. Because, the thing is, the older you get, the more doors close to you. You become stuck. It can feel quite stifling, the weight of other people's expectations.'

I tore some sourdough from the slice on my plate and stuffed it into my mouth. My parents had received the news that I was moving to Philadelphia through the veil of their grief, in something of a daze. They helped me pay the fees, and didn't seem to wonder why I had chosen Franklin University, neither of them probing my reasons, so long as I seemed to be coping.

A few weeks after the funeral, when I was ready to be around other people again, I returned to Trinity and devoted the final two years of my law degree to methodically plotting how I would get to Crane. Months of study to get the grades I needed for Franklin, then a long process of applying, waiting, and hoping for acceptance, inching my way to Crane, bit by bit.

But my parents knew nothing of what I was planning. Their focus remained on the daughter they had lost, and it seemed like a kindness to let them think I was fine. There were no expectations on me anymore.

'So, let me ask, instead, what brought you to Franklin? What were you hoping to learn here? What can I teach you?'

I chewed the bread, then swallowed hard. 'I guess I'm interested in the nature of justice. I want to really break it down, you know? Because, honestly, I find myself baffled by the way we live, the assumptions we make constantly, about other people, about everything really.' I scratched at my arm, the skin flaring bright red under my fingers. 'Everyone else appears to just accept things as they are, but I can't seem to do that. I can't seem to do that at all. It's like ... I have this need to question everything, and then, if the answers aren't right, to tear it all down. To start again and make it better.'

I looked down at my plate and wished I hadn't made myself so vulnerable in front of Crane. It was his effect on me, making me want to open up, because, well ... I don't know. It's difficult to admit the truth to you. In our talks about his article, in the emails we shared, it felt as if he understood my alienation from the world. I didn't need to put it into words for him. He got it anyway. Audrey had said it herself. In those early days of that final Michaelmas term, my sister told me I would *like* Professor Crane. She said the two of us had a lot in common. I hadn't thought anything of it at the time, but now I was seeing what she meant.

'I share the same need,' Crane said quietly, 'so I have to admit, I get excited when I see it in a student.'

Cautiously, I lifted my head and met his eye again.

He smiled at me and, I'm ashamed to say, I smiled back.

'You wrote about some of that in your latest assignment,' Crane continued. 'The idea of the moral duties we owe to each other, particularly our families, or those we've pulled into our close circle – the core of all morality stemming from those links, and how thin they can be.' He turned to Charlie. 'It was something I saw in your work too – the weakness of universal claims to morality.'

Charlie, clearly uncomfortable, shrugged this off.

For my benefit, Crane said: 'Charlie wrote about Shakespeare's *Julius Caesar* and compared it to the Republican party's response to the impeachment of Nixon, and then related that back to his own family's relationship to the party. You should consider publishing the piece, Charlie. It was tremendous.'

'No, I . . . no . . . it was a little too personal for all that,' he said quickly, then added, more softly again: 'But thank you, Professor. I, um, appreciate that.'

I eyed him across the table, a frown pulling at my face. The sudden show of humility was distracting me. Just when I thought I knew who Charlie Duke was, he would surprise me.

'You know, I'm really excited to have you both in my class and you're both doing stellar work as research assistants,' Crane said, his head turning from Charlie on his right, to me on his left. 'I wanted to invite you both here tonight because, every so often, extraordinary minds find each other, and it is a beautiful thing to behold. It's the reason I teach.'

My dad would have snorted through his nose at Crane and called it a load of *plamás*, but I didn't exactly hate what Crane had just said. I thought I had buried my ego deep inside me, deep beneath the grief and the anger, but here it was now, fighting for life, pushing its way up through the damp soil. His words felt good. I want you to know that, because you need to understand the effect he had on people – even me.

Crane was looking at me. 'Maybe that's what I can teach you, Jessica. Whatever you end up doing with your career, or your life, I can teach you to play the game. I can show you how to use the tools at your fingertips, to instrumentalise the law and its systems, to reach out and grab the world around you and change it if you can. Not necessarily for the better – I don't know what you would consider *better* – but I can teach you how to change it, if the chance ever arises. I can teach you that.'

We finished the meal, and then the wine, the conversation continuing, but my heart wasn't in it anymore. More than anything, I wanted to speak to my sister, to dissect with her the clashing emotions Crane had stirred up inside me. Because, that evening, for the first time since Audrey died, I had felt slightly hopeful for the future.

Chapter Fifteen

Even though I was sharing the status of favourite with Charlie, I was still growing closer to Crane. We chatted daily now, swapping jokes and observations over emails and texts. He sent me cartoons from the *New Yorker* he thought I'd like, and I hid puns in my messages to make him laugh, using the names of legal philosophers I knew he'd recognise. One day, I sent him a quote I found while researching an Anne Carson translation of *Antigone*. The next day, he sent me a picture of the quote stuck on the wall next to his desk. *We begin in the dark and birth is the death of us.* I knew that line would speak to him, because it spoke to me too.

The topic of our next class was *Paradise Lost*. At the appointed hour, I took a seat at the table in room 1.04B, Amanda to my left, Charlie to my right. Though I replaced her at his dining table, Amanda didn't seem to suspect I was responsible for the cancellation of her dinner with Crane, and I was very glad she was not at any risk from him. One less thing to worry about.

While we waited for Crane, Charlie doodled something in the corner of my notepad. It was a cartoon puppy, with x's for eyes, a downward arch for a mouth, and a speech bubble emerging from it that said: 'I feel ruff.'

'You do this to yourself,' I muttered.

Charlie shrugged, catching my tone, then pushed his fringe to one side. His eyes were red and sleepless. 'Just eking the last few drops out of my wayward youth,' he said. 'Real life is coming for me, Mooney.'

I shook my head. 'Only if you let it.'

Charlie slumped low on the desk while he gazed up at me. 'Don't scold me, Mooney. I'm too broken.'

'No sympathy for the devil.'

Across the table and a few seats over, a scoff sounded from Vera. I looked over at her. She was staring down at her laptop screen, a scowl on her face, fingers tapping furiously across her keyboard. Her eyes didn't turn my way, as if I wasn't worth her attention.

Charlie, ignoring Vera completely, said: 'Have you done the reading?'

'Of course I have.' Always prepared, always ready.

He rubbed his eyes, as if to dislodge the grogginess inside his head. 'So, what do I need to know?'

My head cocked to the side. 'Are you just friends with me so you can copy my homework?'

'Mostly.' He gave me his most devilish smile. 'Come on. Give me a synopsis.'

'Milton. Garden of Eden. Fall of Man. Creation of Satan. God really angry. Lots of punishing.'

There was a slight commotion around me. Charlie sat up straight suddenly, everyone else falling noticeably silent.

Crane stood at the door. 'Sounds like you've got this one covered, Ms Mooney. Should I just go back to my office?'

There was a murmur of laughter, the sound automatic. We laughed at his jokes so he would go easy on us when the interrogation began.

Crane walked to the head of the table, momentarily blocking out the sunlight from the window behind him.

'God no,' I said, flicking my hair over my shoulder, feeling a little emboldened. 'We'd miss your performance, Professor.'

Crane placed a stack of books on the table in front of him, removing an expensive-looking pen from the breast pocket of his chambray shirt and laying it down next to a battered leather notebook. He released a small chuckle and said: 'Then I must try not to disappoint.'

I could feel a ripple of reaction around me, the rise of an eyebrow from Vera, a sideways glance from Joshua.

'All right,' Crane said, addressing the class. 'Laptops and phones away now.' He faced the whiteboard while we complied with this direction, reaching instead for notepads and pens, settling in for the Crane show. 'What kind of being is God?' he asked, as he wrote G-O-D in large, imposing letters on the whiteboard.

I sipped my coffee – a strong Colombian blend from Joe's – and stared at the word in black against the white, contemplating its enormity. *In the beginning was the word.*

'Well?' Crane turned around in search of an answer.

'All-powerful creator, omniscient, all-knowing,' Ronald said, rolling his hand around on its wrist bone, as if to imply there were more adjectives to come, but he seemed to run out of steam.

'OK.' Crane wrote down the words Ronald had offered on the board. 'And what else?'

'Loving, kind, just, father figure,' Vera said in a somewhat bored monotone.

Crane wrote out those words as well. 'Thanks for that, Vera . . .' he said, seemingly unimpressed by her tone. 'These are all Judaeo-Christian notions so far. Any Buddhists or Hindus want to pipe up?' He surveyed the class, meeting silence. 'All right,' he said. 'Well, it was, indeed, the Christian God that Milton set out to justify.' Crane reached for his stack of books and picked up the one sitting on top. '*Paradise Lost*. Now, be honest. Who actually read it? I know you didn't, Mr Duke. You were smart enough to admit it within my earshot.'

If possible, this made Charlie appear even more hungover, the bags under his eyes lengthening, their colour deepening. 'I know the gist. Apple, snake, Satan . . . like Mooney said.'

A flash of irritation crossed Crane's face. 'Anyone else?' he asked, placing the book down on the table again. 'Anyone do the *mandatory* reading for this class?'

I, and a couple others – Amanda and Joshua – raised our hands in non-committal fashion.

'I did *try* to get through it,' Ronald said, looking guilty.

Vera said nothing.

'Well, thank you for your honesty . . . I suppose.' Crane stuck his hands into the pockets of his grey tweed trousers. 'For the benefit of those of you who are clearly feeling cavalier about the grade you'll get in this class, Milton's task in *Paradise Lost* was to explain to a sceptic how the god of Christianity could be an all-loving, omniscient creator, while also doling out severe punishments to those who disobeyed him. How do we reconcile that kind of heartlessness with the notion of God as a forgiving father?'

'You can't,' I said flatly. 'Don't even try.'

'Well, sure,' Crane said, laughing. 'But, for the sake of this class, let's give it a go?'

I made a face suggesting I was unconvinced, which he seemed to find amusing. He tried and failed to hide his smile. Was he flirting with me?

I didn't acknowledge any of the others around the table, be-cause I knew they were looking at me now. Subtle signs of a growing closeness. A smile, a glance, a familiar tone of voice, none of it going unnoticed.

'The God we read about in *Paradise Lost* has immense power, a claim of almost total authority, commands backed by the threat of punishment for failure to obey . . .' Crane's eyes travelled over the faces of his students around the oblong table, pausing slightly longer on me. 'What does that sound like to you? Anyone?'

Nobody else seemed ready to offer an answer, so I did. 'The law.'

'Exactly,' Crane said, clapping his hands together, enthused.

I made eye contact with Charlie and looked away.

'Can everyone see it? It's just a rudimentary form of law. The Book of Genesis, the Garden of Eden – it's describing an early legal system.' Crane surveyed my classmates, assessing whether they understood. 'We are subject to the authority of the State and recipients of certain privileges handed down by it. But if we don't follow the rules, if we stray – if we should sin – we are cast out to the wilderness. Prison, in our system. Or death, if you're in the wrong state.'

'So what does that make Satan, then?' Charlie asked. 'An anarchist?'

Crane smiled. 'A rebel, maybe.'

'Is that supposed to be a good thing?' Joshua asked. 'Are you saying we should sympathise with the devil?'

'Well, it depends on your point of view.'

'And?' I said, eyebrow raised. 'What *is* your point of view, Professor? I can never tell where you stand.'

Crane's eyes flicked my way, then quickly away. 'In case you're getting the wrong idea here . . . I am not, generally speaking, a Satanist.'

We laughed, except Vera, who folded her arms and frowned.

Crane's hands were in his pockets again. He stared down at his feet, thinking for a moment. 'Satan is right to challenge God's authority. He has seen no evidence that God is truly the almighty creator, other than God's claim that he is. And if Satan's challenge to God's power is wrong – if God really is almighty – then Satan will deserve his punishment for rebelling. But being wrong in the end doesn't mean he shouldn't ask the question. In the same way, as lawyers – as citizens – we must question legal consensus, political consensus, moral consensus. And if we are wrong, then we take the consequences. But power must always be met with a question.'

Vera's eyes narrowed. Her blood was up, Crane in her sights. 'You're making it sound like we live in some kind of neutral state. But we all know what's right and wrong. It's not a difficult thing to understand. We have consciences.' She paused, then dropped her voice and added: 'At least, most of us do.'

Crane didn't seem to have heard the slight or, at least, he was choosing not to acknowledge it. He sat down, silent for a moment.

'We all see the world differently – through a glass darkly.' His voice was low, as if he wanted us to strain to hear him. 'It's important we accept that about each other, instead of privileging our own points of view, simply because they are our own.'

He flipped open his copy of *Paradise Lost*, a rustling sound emanating from the contact of fingertip with page.

'Here it is,' he said, and began to read: '*What though the field be lost? All is not lost, the unconquerable will, and study of revenge, immortal hate. And courage never to submit or yield.*'

Crane placed the book down on the table again. 'These are the forces that have shaped our species. An "unconquerable will" that has built whole human civilisations. "Courage never to submit or yield" that has sent us to the moon, to the very edge of the heliosphere.' He looked at us; he looked at me. 'These are the words of the supposed villain of the piece, evil personified, who, perhaps, understands what it is to be human more than our punishing creator. And I put it to you that we need the rebellious zeal of Satan to counterbalance the overwhelming power and authority of God. We need an opposing force to counterbalance the State – rebellion, obstruction, defiance. We need to destroy in order to create. We need wrong in order to know right.'

Across from me, Vera sank lower into her seat, as if she wanted to be anywhere but in that room. I could feel the anger, the bristling of her skin, the tension rippling through her body. But the same hostility was entirely absent in me. I agreed with him. I agreed with Crane completely.

When you talk to someone regularly, when you share your thoughts with them, your observations, or stories from your day, it is difficult to keep seeing them only at their worst. When they share their frustrations, their angsts, their hopes, a joke they heard on a podcast, a meme they knew you'd laugh at, you grow soft. Their human face appears to you. And the thing about humanity is that we always recognise it in each other. It makes us empathetic, open to mercy, to compassion. That was the problem. My capacity for ordinary human emotion was beginning to worry me.

I glanced at Charlie next to me, the other favourite, a niggle at the back of my mind, a nagging worry I had been carrying from dinner. Crane was not someone who acted without deep thought and conviction, and the addition of Charlie as co-favourite could offer a gloss of innocence to his extra-curricular activities with me. Maybe Charlie's presence at dinner was a strategic decision: plausible deniability. With Charlie beside me, Crane could invite the two of us to dinner, or other social events, without setting tongues wagging. He could lure me closer without arousing external suspicion.

Crane had reached the crescendo, enthused and energetic as he concluded. 'If you remember nothing else from this class, remember this – the fall of man is the making of us. To eat of the fruit is to know the difference between good and evil – to be conscious, thinking, questioning humans. So, eat the apple. Ask those questions. See what happens. Be a rebellious force in the world.' He smiled broadly. 'And never unquestioningly do what you're told.'

There were two of us in this game and it was increasingly unclear which of us was the cat, and which the mouse.

Chapter Sixteen

Crane left immediately after class, not waiting, as he sometimes did, for questions. I shoved my notes into my backpack and was heading for the door when I felt a tug on the sleeve of my jumper. 'I need to talk to you,' Vera mumbled, pulling me towards the window, so we wouldn't be overheard.

She was chewing on gum, the quick movement of her jaw mimicking the sharp efficiency of a stapler. 'You and Crane are very friendly now . . .' The chewing became faster, an accusation implied.

'I don't know what you mean,' I said, the muscles of my shoulders tightening. I wanted the other students to take notice of the dynamic, but Vera's dislike of Crane had intensified as the weeks passed, as had her iciness with me. She had vehemently maintained she was uninterested in Crane's favouritism from the start, which meant it wasn't a case of jealousy. So why the iciness? And why would she care about me and Crane? Did she want to get us into trouble? Whatever it was, this felt like a problem.

She rested her hand on the bookshelf next to us and moved her weight between her feet, from left to right, then back again. 'There are rumours about him, you know, and Lord knows I have no desire to impugn the character of a man who has not been formally found guilty of anything, *but* ... Crane's reputation around here isn't exactly *clean*, OK? And now that you're favourite, well ...'

I struggled to command my expression, the rise and fall of my chest, the thud of my heart. No words were coming easily, a kaleidoscope of images spinning inside me, my sister's face, her skin grey from lack of sleep, her eyes red from crying, dark brown circles around them. It was deeply affecting to hear Vera say out loud what had been consuming me for so long. And it was worse than I had thought, not an isolated incident but clearly a pattern of behaviour.

Vera rooted in her bag and withdrew a bottle of energy drink that was an unnatural shade of yellow. She spit her gum into the tissue she kept up her sleeve, then took a long and avaricious drink from the bottle before continuing. 'Professor Grouse is a family friend, and she gave me a warning when I started in the class.' Her voice was a little too loud in the quiet of the library, some heads popping over the tops of their carrels to see who was making the noise. 'Crane insists it's a form of equality to treat his female students the same as his male, inviting them into his home, sharing drinks with them, being all ... friendly.' She paused. 'But there are rumours, Jessie, stories ... about Crane pushing things too far.' She set a hand on my shoulder and said, firmly, 'You should be careful with him, Jessie.'

I blinked several times, taken aback.

It could have made all the difference if a warning had reached Audrey, but I doubted Crane's reputation had tailed him to Trinity, the whisper network not travelling that far.

I bit down hard on the inside of my lip, channelling the pain and concentrating it in one place, so Vera wouldn't see it ripple through me.

'But why has nothing been done about it?' I asked, trying to

steady the anger in my voice so I could extract as much information as possible from Vera without exposing the intensity of my
interest. 'I mean, if everyone knows . . .'

'Oh, Jessie . . .' she said. 'Come on. I don't mean to insult you,
but surely you know how all this works?' She scratched at her
lip, at the corner where her lipstick was congealing. 'Look, if
there was some way of stopping him . . . if there was evidence, I
wouldn't hesitate. I'd gut him like a fish.' The look in her eye left
me in no doubt she was speaking the truth. 'But the rumours
have never been concrete, nothing we can prove. All I can do
is pass on the information,' she said. 'And in case it needs to be
said, I'm here for you if that becomes necessary.' Vera gazed at
me levelly. 'Just don't let it be necessary, Jessie . . .'

She didn't wait around to observe my reaction. From where
I stood by the bookshelves, I watched her push through the
turnstiles and disappear down the steps.

I gave it a few minutes, until the students we had disturbed
– the ones who had been bobbing up like meercats – were absorbed in their work again. Hidden behind the neatly stacked
shelves of books, I turned this new information over in my mind.

Rumours about Crane were useful to me. A blemish on his
reputation, even if unproved, would help boost my credibility
when the time came. But, more than that, it showed I was on the
right track, doing the right thing. Vera said there had never been
concrete evidence of Crane's misbehaviour with his students, the
very problem I had come here to address.

As I left the library, I let the anger boil, fuelling my resolve,
feeding my courage. It wasn't just about Audrey anymore. There
was more at stake than I had realised.

A cycle of pain to break, a villain to expose. Punishment to
inflict, justice to create.

Chapter Seventeen

At the start of November, the law school came together for an American tradition that involved the competitive consumption of pies. Ostensibly pumpkin pies, in reality, they comprised a mountain of whipped cream squeezed out of a pressurised can onto a thin crust of something that somewhat resembled pastry. Ronald had entered the competition to raise money for a local soup kitchen where he volunteered, and the Law and Lit class had gathered to offer support and see if he would puke. I went along in the hopes that Crane might be there, the event an ideal opportunity to be noticed in his company.

Around us, the maple trees were shedding leaves, the crunch of which reminded me of home, and I was surprised to find that the turning of the seasons made me feel a bit homesick. It had been a relief to escape the daily confrontation of my parents' mourning. You might think that's selfish, but I don't know if I could have survived much longer at home, witness to their suffering. Their grief was a well and I risked drowning in the cold waters of their unhappiness. They couldn't look at me without seeing Audrey and all they had lost. I was a reminder of the life they had once, now in ruins, and beneath the weight of their pain, I would be crushed. But how I missed the way we used to be, when there were four of us, when we were whole.

Before a lump could form in my throat, I grounded my feet under me and let a sigh loose through my lips, determined to focus on the present. Next to me, a long, plastic table was laid out with warm apple cider and doughnuts for spectators to enjoy. Another table had been set up for the participants. They were sitting in a row, so we could all get a good view while they jammed synthetic creamy paste into their faces as quickly as humanly possible. This part of the event was not fun to witness, and so I didn't, preferring to observe the audience, letting my eyes flit over their faces while they laughed and grimaced at the scene before them.

The Dean of the law school, Martha Thompson, stood by the courtyard door pretending to enjoy herself, only the straight line of her lips betraying her discomfort. I needed to introduce myself to her soon. I would need Dean Thompson in my corner when the time came.

My eyes moved on, seeking Crane, but there was no sign of him. I could never fully relax in the law school unless I knew where he might be.

I sent a quick text.

Jessica Mooney (12.12):

Not coming to the pie-eating contest? It's for a good cause and all your students would love to see you . . . especially your favourite.

Phone back in my pocket, I clapped along with the others as the clock began to run out, envious of their easy enjoyment. It was Audrey who used to drag me to these sorts of social events at Trinity. I usually gravitated away from noise, crowds, commotions, preferring a few good friends in a quiet corner of a pub.

But Audrey was infectious like that. She had a way of bringing me out of myself, opening my horizons. How was I supposed to navigate life without my sister? At least at university, there was some structure. A class schedule, an academic calendar, and the pressure of exams. What would I do when all this ended? Who would I be then?

By the end of the contest, Ronald was so full of fake pie that he immediately threw up the contents of his stomach in the men's toilets. Despite this unfortunate conclusion, he had raised two hundred dollars for the soup kitchen. We told him it was worth the puke, but he just looked back at us with an expression of misery that strongly suggested he disagreed. He didn't join us in the courtyard afterwards.

We were sitting at one of the tables at the far end, away from the janitorial staff cleaning away the disintegrating paper plates, the cream smeared on the bricks, and the red cups of warm cider discarded around the trees, when Charlie showed up. He pulled an empty chair towards me and sat into it heavily, greeting us with a wordless grunt.

I had never seen him in such a mood and the effect on his face was dramatic. Gone was the playful grin, replaced with the sharp-edged jawline of a man who would, for better or worse, probably stand in a legislative chamber some day and make laws governing the lives of others.

Vera and Amanda ignored him, continuing their chat about what they were going to do for Thanksgiving, while I sat awkwardly wedged between Charlie and Joshua. Joshua was almost as distracted as Charlie. He had been scrolling on his phone all afternoon, flicking through updates on the latest election news and muttering darkly about the latest polls.

'Why the long face, Duke?' I asked with a small smile as he kicked his legs out in front of me. 'Annoyed you missed the pies?'

Unamused, Charlie gave a small shake of his head.

'You should be delighted,' Joshua said, directing his attention across me. He was sitting forward on the edge of his chair so he could get a good look at Charlie. 'I thought you guys were sunk over the whole "grab 'em by the pussy" fiasco, but apparently people care more about how Hillary stores her emails.'

Charlie's shoulders rose, his body already tensed, ready for conflict. 'What do you want me to say? I didn't choose him as candidate, Joshua. I'm not responsible for what he does.'

'But didn't your family endorse Trump?' Joshua surveyed my face for a reaction, while I glanced at Charlie, who sank lower into his seat. 'I thought I read about your dad—'

'Don't fucking start about my dad, Joshua. I don't want to hear about it, I swear . . .'

My phone vibrated in my pocket. Focused on the row brewing between Joshua and Charlie on either side of me, I had almost forgotten my text to Crane.

Jay Crane (14.12):

Don't tell me the brilliant Jessica Mooney was involved in that pie-eating nonsense? And here I was planning to write you a glowing letter of recommendation . . .

J x

Just as it had been in Audrey's texts. The first 'J x'. I stared down at the two letters, feeling the full weight of all that they implied.

Next to me, Joshua was still focused on Charlie. 'Wait, are you *embarrassed* by your family's politics?' He nudged me with his elbow expectantly, as if it was my attention he was seeking. 'Is that it? Seriously?'

'Joshua,' Charlie said quietly. 'I'm not joking right now. Please shut the fuck up.'

Putting my phone into my pocket again, I tried to wrench my thoughts from Crane. Joshua was drinking some of his apple cider while he considered whether to press Charlie further, casting occasional glances my way, as if I were part of his calculations. To my left, beneath the sullen expression on Charlie's face, I perceived some disturbance. A tremor – of what, I don't quite know. But there was an emotion rocking him – maybe more than one – and he was struggling to contain its volume. I knew how that felt. I knew how control could slip so suddenly away, until it was only the very tips of the fingers clinging to a cliff-face.

I placed my hand on Joshua's arm, my eyes containing a warning. 'Don't, Joshua,' I said gently. 'Just leave him alone.'

This was, it turned out, exactly the wrong thing to say, Joshua's face creasing into a frown, as if I had betrayed him somehow. His eyes flashed from Charlie to me and back again.

Eventually, they settled very definitively on Charlie. 'It's just surprising to me,' he said, knowing the effect his words would have. 'I didn't think the Duke family had any shame.'

Immediately, Charlie pushed his chair back with a metallic, grating sound, and hopped to his feet. 'Go fuck yourself, Reynolds,' he said very calmly, before turning abruptly and walking away.

He was heading back towards the entrance to the law school, and I don't know why, precisely, but to Joshua's disgust and my surprise, I rose to my feet and followed.

'Where are you going?!' Joshua called after me, his voice bitter. But I didn't reply.

Chapter Eighteen

I pushed the door open and stepped into the law school, where it was quiet now, classes over for the day. In the lobby, the security guard, Nina, was humming quietly while she flicked through a magazine. Across from her desk, a stack of pumpkins sat against the window, each carved into a different shape by participants in the carving competition the previous week.

Charlie was pacing near the stairs that led down to the lockers and the vending machines. Hurrying after him, my footsteps loud against the tiled floor, I called his name.

He looked around, strands of his blonde hair falling onto his face, until his eyes landed on me. 'What do you want, Mooney?'

My hand grasped the sleeve of his navy jumper as I reached him. 'Are you . . . OK, Charlie?'

His surprise deepened, but he masked it quickly with indifference. 'Yeah . . . yeah, I'm fine, Mooney. Go back outside.'

'You don't seem fine,' I said, letting his sleeve go. My right hand rubbed my left arm awkwardly.

'Nah, I dish it out plenty. Only fair I take it, too.' His glance was so brusque it almost ricocheted off the surface of my face. 'I'm just not in the mood for it today.'

'You want to tell me why? Maybe I can help.'

I watched a frown line his face, a crease forming in the

space between his eyebrows. 'What makes you think you can do that?'

'Because we're friends ... you said it yourself.' I paused. 'I know ... it surprised me too.'

He smiled at that, just a tiny amount, because he didn't want to smile at all. Sticking his hands in his pockets, he leaned back against the wall. 'It's just ... it's not important. It's just ...' He was unpractised at sharing. 'It's just my dad. He wants me to decide what I'm doing after graduation. Politics. Washington. All that bullshit.'

'And you really don't want it?' I asked, tucking my hands into my pockets. 'The power?'

Charlie didn't respond for a minute, his eyes on his shoes. They were brown leather loafers he wore without socks. I can only imagine the blisters his feet endured. 'I don't care about politics. I'm probably not going to vote. I just want to make some money and buy myself a nice house somewhere by the sea. And I know it makes me an asshole, Jessie, but I just want to marry some fucking beautiful, uncomplicated woman – with no hang-ups, or any of that shit.' By some miracle of self-restraint, I managed not to scoff. 'Someone else can take care of the rest. Because I don't care about the fate of the world, or how we fix our problems. Never have! I don't want to make the big decisions. Other people can do it.'

'*Other people?*' My eyebrows rose.

'Yeah!' His hands flew into the air. 'Nobody needs another guy like me in politics anyway. And what does it even matter? We're getting wiped out by climate change in the next few decades one way or another.'

'Honestly,' I said, casting a sideways glance his way. 'You don't exactly have that save-the-world energy we're going to need.'

'Right?! I'm not even insulted – it's true!' Charlie laughed so hard that it made me laugh too. 'I am completely wrong for the job!'

I moved to stand alongside him, my back against the wall, facing the courtyard through the window. 'Well,' I said after a moment. 'Sounds like you know your own mind, Duke. That's a good start. And don't worry about your dad. Parents can surprise you.'

From where I stood, I could see Amanda and Vera laughing about something next to Joshua, who was peering over at us, though I'm not sure we were visible through the glass at this distance.

'How do you mean?' Charlie asked.

'I just mean . . . parents change their mind. My parents used to have ambitions for me, but they don't anymore.'

'Why not? What changed?'

Audrey. Audrey's death. Dad flying out on a dawn flight, returning home with Audrey in a box. The lid closed. The horror implied by the presence of the closed casket, a horror shut out by the wooden cover. My mother's eyes, shot through with blood, from endless days and nights of tears.

'Ah, you know, they just got used to me eventually.'

Charlie was observing me closely.

I pushed my hair out of my eyes and didn't acknowledge the question his expression implied. 'I think they thought all the existential angst would fade, but if you cut me open, it's all you'll find.'

He examined me. 'So, they gave up on you?'

My mother's hand had gripped my arm as we walked up the aisle of the church at Audrey's funeral. She had clung to me so hard I had bruises above my wrist when I undressed for bed later that night, purple marks formed by the sheer weight of her grief. If I could, I would have drawn that grief out of her body. I would have taken it into myself and held it there, right in the centre of my chest, imprisoned in the cage of my ribs, so that it could harm her no more.

'Something like that,' I replied. 'Not in a bad way. It's more like . . . they let me go. I needed them to let me go.'

I could feel Charlie looking at me, contemplating. He was always doing that. In the silence, I felt his hesitation, the obvious question hovering between us – what *do* you want to do with your life? – but he didn't voice it. Instead, he said: 'God, Mooney. You're fucked up. You know that?'

'Oh, I know.' My eyes drifted, first to the tiles at my feet, then back towards the window next to me, through which I could see a scattering of red leaves at the very top of the maple tree in the courtyard.

Movement drew my attention, a door opening. Crane entered the courtyard in a smart tweed jacket, his leather satchel in his left hand. In his right, he held the hand of a woman I didn't recognise. Her long black hair was tied neatly at the back of her head, and she was dressed in a high-waisted trouser suit of understated beige. They were taking a shortcut to the other side of the law school, crossing the courtyard rather than taking the longer route through the corridors.

I voiced the question exploding through my mind. 'Who is that with Crane?!'

Charlie watched them together for a moment. 'I don't know,' he answered, squinting to get a better look. 'His wife, maybe?'

His *wife*.

No. I shook my head slightly, askance. No, that couldn't be right. Nowhere had Audrey mentioned a wife, not once in an email or text. There was no sign of her in his office, or in his home. Or was it just that I hadn't been looking for her? I had searched Crane thoroughly online before I came to Franklin, and a wife had never been noted in any essays or articles or bios. But, then again, his public profile was related to his academic work. It was all about him.

I tried to keep my expression blank, pulling a thick curtain of neutral emotion across my face so Charlie wouldn't sense my confusion. I doubt I succeeded.

Crane leaned down towards the woman, said something that made her laugh enough to throw her head back, face pointed upwards to the sky, her throat vulnerable. He slipped his arm around hers, drawing her closer and steering them both through the tables where Amanda, Vera, and Joshua still sat. There was a brief exchange of greetings, but Crane didn't stop to introduce his companion.

I had studied everything Audrey had left behind, knew her diary practically by heart. If Crane really did have a wife, maybe she was in the things Audrey didn't say? There were occasional gaps in the narrative of their correspondence, and though they had appeared minor to me before, these holes in the story, now I wondered at their significance.

Charlie crossed to the window and turned to face me, temporarily blocking my view of the courtyard. I shifted so I could see over his shoulder, just catching sight of Crane and his companion as they disappeared back inside, through a door that led to the other side of the law school.

'I have to go, Charlie. I'm sorry, I just . . . we'll talk again another time?'

One of his eyebrows rose up his forehead, the other dipped down over his eye. 'Jessie, are you—'

But I didn't have time to hear the end of his sentence, or to better manage the situation. I couldn't let Charlie delay me. Crane had just vanished inside the building, and I needed to follow him.

'I'll see you later, Charlie!' I shouted back to him. Jerking the door open, I stepped onto the red-brick of the courtyard once more. It was much quicker to cross again than negotiate the internal maze of the building.

Joshua called my name from the table where my classmates still sat as I hurried past.

'Can't talk right now, sorry,' I said. 'I'm late for . . . eh, something.' I had the sensation I was hurting him somehow, though I had never given Joshua a reason to like me. Reaching the far end of the courtyard in a few hurried strides, I yanked open the door through which Crane had entered, and stumbled inside.

In front of me, a clock was ticking on the wall of the lounge space nicknamed the Ben. It was furnished with leather couches and convenient plug sockets for laptops. The room was dominated by a very large marble statue of Ben Franklin, the university's founder, and I recognised a couple of international students sitting on a couch next to it. Their laptops were out, a study group, I think. They looked up as I burst in, but didn't know me well enough to say hello, watching instead while I flailed about, trying to figure out where Crane might have gone. I was too slow to catch him here, which meant he had disappeared into the warren of the law school again. From the Ben, he could have turned right to the faculty lounge, or he could have gone left and exited the building through the back door from the Great Hall. I took a guess, turning left.

The vaulted ceilings and marble floors of the Great Hall appeared before me as I entered, a large portrait of Abraham Lincoln on the wall opposite, beneath which a janitor in dark overalls was in the process of buffing the floor. The noise of his electric floor polisher filled the echoey room, just the two of us here.

I had lost Crane and his companion.

Taking a seat on the bottom step of the stone stairs behind me, I wilted, resting my chin on my hand, my mind on all the secrets my sister kept from me, secrets I was still in the process of discovering. I pulled my phone out of my pocket and searched 'Crane' and 'wife', but didn't get any answers. Crane had used the term 'wife' in an academic article on Clytemnestra's vision of justice, which accounted for most of the search results. I flicked through images, but the woman did not appear.

Audrey could not have guessed I would read her diary, so why would she leave his wife out of the story? Was it just that some memories were too painful to view written in words? Too close to the bone? Difficult as it was for me to accept, there were things Audrey never wanted me to know. She had never confided in me about her relationship with Crane, or what he did to her. Why was that? Why hadn't she trusted me? It was the question still tormenting me. Why didn't she want me to know?

Chapter Nineteen

Crane and I were walking along a cliff now, inching ever closer to the edge. There were texts, glances, and laughter, none of which went unnoticed by my classmates. A thread of interest now stretched from me to him, so that when one of us turned this way or that, the other found their gaze following. Before class one morning, I bumped into Crane getting coffee at Joe's, and we arrived for class slightly late, in the middle of a shared laugh. The faces greeting us in room 1.04B, the curious eyes, the slight surprise, or, in Vera's case, slight concern, all told me I was right on track. But now that I had seen Crane holding hands with a woman in the courtyard who appeared to be his wife, it was obvious I was not the only one playing a risky game. Maybe that explained some of his caution with me, why things were moving so much slower than they had with Audrey. I'm quite sure it was my impatience driving this feeling, but I knew from her diary that, by this stage of Audrey's final term at Trinity, she was seeing Crane most nights. Off campus, mainly, and in restaurants and bars that students were unlikely to frequent, while my interactions with Crane were still tied to class, the research project, and to small acts of favouritism like career advice and job postings, which he was sending to Charlie, too.

By November, in her diary, Audrey was beginning to talk about the possibility of studying at Franklin, taking what opportunity she could to stay near him, and Crane was encouraging the idea. He told her he didn't want to leave her when the term ended. I couldn't imagine him saying that to me.

There was a fervour, passion, and intensity of feeling between them that seemed genuine; I would need to catch up.

Election day came, passing with a surprising sense of quiet. There were queues outside some of the polling stations, but mostly it felt as if the city were holding its breath, waiting to banish from its lungs the dead and dusty air of a horrible campaign.

The law school was hosting a watch party for the results. I made my way there in the ombre glow of the setting sun, bumping into Ronald among the other students gathered at the traffic light on the corner. He was heading to the party too. I listened politely while he told me about the afternoon he had just spent poll monitoring, standing outside various stations with a clipboard in his hand, a baby lawyer guarding democracy.

It was a strange quirk of my purpose in Philadelphia that Professor Crane was becoming the person I spoke to the most. These days, I only spoke to my parents rarely, mostly an innocuous text about the election, or asking about our dog, Bran. My father sent me occasional photographs of the beach in Malahide on a sunny day, my mother checking if I needed any money. I preferred it this way, finding it too difficult to mix my life back in Dublin with my lies in Philadelphia, too hard to hear their voices and not break.

It had to be like this, but walking next to Ronald, hearing about his day, the weight of loneliness and of my alienation from all this student experience bore down on me. Relentless separation, but for a good reason, a righteous reason. I had to keep believing that.

The lights of the law school shone between the red-brick walls. We made our way to the appointed room in Wilson Hall, where it seemed the entire law school had gathered. The space was laid out in semi-circular rows of seats facing a podium with a large screen behind it. A table of snacks and some beers had been set up just inside the door. We grabbed a couple of pizza slices from the stack of boxes and I opened two bottles of Sam Adams, handing one to Ronald while I scanned the faces for Crane.

Crane told me he'd be here, and I was practically giddy at the sight of his colleagues, a whole room full of esteemed potential witnesses.

His recent behaviour in class had shown he was ready to be steered further, and this had been the first opportunity to get him alone, the first social event we were both attending where his guard might be down in a way it couldn't be in the classroom. Tonight, there was an opening.

When I spotted him, Crane was sitting in one of the rows of seats near the back. I left Ronald at the snack table and meandered towards my target.

Crane was next to Dean Thompson. There were a few other faculty members scattered around the room, some in the rows in front of Crane, the most ambitious students using this chance to position themselves in proximity. Vera had plopped herself down next to the Dean, and I noted from the sheen of her skin and the slightly crazed look in her eye that she was in full 'gunner' mode.

I joined them, taking the empty seat next to Crane. The sleeves of his white shirt were rolled to the elbow, a beer bottle in his hand. He looked relaxed, at ease, as if we were all gathering to watch a spectacle.

As I sat, I offered around the second slice of pizza on the paper plate. The Dean declined, but Crane thanked me as he took a large bite and struggled for a moment with the strings of melted cheese tying his mouth to the rest of the slice.

I smiled somewhat awkwardly at the Dean, wondering if I should introduce myself. It was Dean Thompson's support I would need when the time came to ruin Crane's life.

But she noticed me first and stretched her hand across Crane. 'We haven't met yet. I'm Dean Thompson.' Her voice was deep, comforting, and full of authority.

'I'm Jessica Mooney,' I said, shaking firmly. 'Nice to meet you.'

'Jessica is one of my Law and Lit students,' Crane said, absently. 'One of my best.'

I glanced over at Vera, expecting an eyeroll, but she was clearly on her best behaviour for the night.

On a large screen at the front of the lecture hall, CNN election coverage flashed a complicated patchwork of blue and red states, most of which had not yet been called for one candidate or the other. A smattering of states in the top right corner of the map were blue and some larger states down south were red.

Virginia went to Clinton, but only barely, lifting a nervous Vera to her feet. 'I think I need some air,' she said, heading for the door so that I found myself alone with the Dean and Crane. Vera returned before too long, but she didn't re-join us at the back, instead flitting through different groups of students spread throughout the auditorium, speaking furtively about the unexpected turn of events.

As the night progressed, it became increasingly apparent the election was not going Clinton's way, and the atmosphere in the room shifted noticeably. Near the front, Joshua and the other students who had volunteered for the Clinton campaign now sat in stony silence. Across from them, on the other side of the aisle, Charlie was with the rest of Fed Soc, who were passing around a bottle of something or other.

On the screen, the coverage was continuing. Talking heads were consulted. An over-caffeinated CNN reporter was flicking between impressively digitalised maps of red and blue, zooming in on particular counties and districts of interest.

Wisconsin was slipping away when Dean Thompson announced she was going home to be with her family. 'I think I've seen enough,' she said, getting to her feet. She made a quick exit from the lecture hall, which was beginning to empty around us.

With the Dean gone, it was just me and Crane left in the row of seats. We were sitting very close together now, angled towards each other. Crane was muttering under his breath at the commentary on the screen. I could tell he was drunk, his words starting to slur.

Just before eleven, Trump won Florida, provoking a roar of outrage from the people left in the room, except the Fed Soc corner, where Reese Bryant was enthusiastically punching the air.

'Well, that's it, then.' Crane's head was in his hands, his body slumped low in his seat. 'That's fucking it. He has *actually* fucking won it. That man will be in the Oval Office.'

'Hard to believe,' I said softly, though this was not my first experience of world-shaking shock. 'You think life is predictable, but it's chaos.' I looked at him. 'It's all just chaos.' I meant what I said. Somewhere along the way, the world had tilted off its axis when I wasn't paying attention, and I wondered if tonight would make Crane feel that same sense of destabilisation. How reckless might it make him?

The fate of the broader world was something I couldn't influence, but, here in this room, with Crane, there was still something I could do. Why, then, was I hesitating? Why did I find myself wanting to offer comfort, instead of plunging the knife and twisting it?

For a moment, Crane said nothing. He just looked back at me. And in the brown irises and the dark tunnelled pupils, I saw my own face reflected, my own fear. It felt as if his hand would reach out for me, cup my cheek, and he would tell me it was all going to be OK, his voice certain and authoritative. And the horror I had felt each day of my life since Audrey died would ease, and I would be her, and she would be me, and together we would be OK again.

What was it about him that could make me feel this way? What weakness in me was drawn to the power he radiated?

Beside me, Crane turned away. 'I wish I could say something comforting.' He was staring down at his feet. 'But the truth is, Jessie, I think you're right. We're born in the dark, looking for something to light the way.' He was being unusually sincere and I realised, with a jolt, that he was much drunker than I had thought. 'I find that spark in my students, in people like you.' He paused. 'And it keeps me going, it keeps my feet on the ground. You need to find that spark for yourself. It will sustain you.' He looked at me again, his foot sending one of the empty bottles rattling across the floor. 'We begin in the dark and birth is the death of us.' He smiled at me. 'There's no point denying that, but there's not much point focusing on it either – it just is what it is.'

'I guess so . . .' I said, a little hopelessly. 'Maybe.'

'Don't give in to cynicism,' he said. 'You have your whole life ahead of you.'

I sort of laughed. 'Don't remind me.'

His expression was tender and I noticed that his knee was very close to mine. 'It won't always feel like this, Jess. You'll make your peace with it. You'll find consolations along the way. I can help you with that. If you want me to.'

Crane's hand was resting innocently on the brown corduroy material of his trousers, the fingers bent in towards his palm. It wasn't causing any trouble, not doing any harm. It was just there, waiting for me.

I reached out quickly, before I could stop myself, and gave that hand one quick squeeze. His eyes flashed my way, lit with surprise.

'Do you want to get out of here?' I said quietly.

Chapter Twenty

The city was on edge, the air charged, and in the eyes of the strangers we passed, I saw suspicion, and I saw fear. Crossing the river together, we walked down Walnut Street, where a man in a MAGA hat was roaring about victory, and another man told him to shut the fuck up from the other side of the road. They were advancing towards each other, shouts growing angrier, when Crane tugged urgently on my arm.

'Let's go this way,' he said, standing slightly in front of me, as if ready to protect me. My mind flashed to his wife. Where was she tonight?

I had been careful not to drink too much, and this caution was now paying dividends. Briefly, I wondered if this was how predators felt, walking next to their prey, with a belly full of ill intent and a heart of darkness.

We stepped into an off-licence on the corner of Walnut and 23rd. Every bar was blaring election coverage, and neither of us could stomach watching the advancing decline of the American republic live on a television screen. So, instead, we purchased a bottle of bourbon and shared it as we roamed the streets, past the shuttered shops, past apartments and townhouses, past churches and parks. My head felt light with the knowledge that we were doing something we shouldn't. Professor and student, overstepping the line dividing us into our publicly recognised roles.

Crane was animated, telling stories of his time as a student at Yale. The culture wars had been waging since then, decades of rancour, that seemed only a prelude now. I let him talk, listening, as he wanted me to, and answering when prompted. Outside City Hall, the mood was strained. Across the road, an argument was starting among a group of people outside a bar, voices elevated, tensions rising. We heard a glass smash, then shouting.

'I think it's time to call it a night,' Crane said, his hand on his head. He was swaying slightly. 'We should get you home.'

'Not yet,' I said, feeling opportunity begin to wane. My hand gripped his upper arm, pulling him into the central is-land on Broad Street, between the two lanes of traffic stopped at the lights on either side of us. Behind us, City Hall rose in all its baroque glory, its tower topped by the upright figure of William Penn, gazing out towards the Delaware River. 'We need to remember this night,' I said, removing my phone from my pocket.

As I took the selfie, I leaned my cheek right in against his. A timestamp, geolocated photograph would put us at this time, this place, together. I don't think he had awareness in the moment, of why that might not be a good thing for him. He seemed to have forgotten our relative positions in life, our disparate status. This didn't entirely shock me. Hadn't he done it all before?

He studied his phone as he took another swig of the bourbon. 'He's ahead in Pennsylvania too now,' he said, then threw his head back, his voice erupting into the air around us. 'FUCK IT!'

This sudden, booming exclamation caused a number of other people to look our way, which didn't seem like a positive de-velopment in the current environment. My eyes surveyed the possible dangers as I ushered him by the arm across the next set of traffic lights.

'Where are we going?' he said, his body tilted towards mine.

My resolve was slipping away. I didn't feel like the embodiment of justice. There was no righteous fury feeding my blood. Mostly, I was cold, and tired, and depressed at the state of the world, at the anger it created inside us, at our capacity to hurt each other. I looked at Crane, and I tried to hate him, but the killer instinct had faded inside me. In that moment, he was just a man, growing old, and a little pathetic.

'Home,' I said firmly. 'I'll call a car.'

Silent and compliant, he let me lead him towards a nearby building. Slowly, he crouched down, and then sat on the foot-path, his legs bent, his arms resting on his knees.

I sat down next to him while we waited for our car. It was a busy night for transportation, the city alive with movement, people swarming insect-like.

Crane let out a long sigh. 'There's still time for you,' he said. 'Maybe you'll still have a chance to see things get better, to fix all this.'

'Maybe,' I said, 'or maybe I'll end up making it worse.'

He turned towards me, shaking his head. 'Don't – don't talk like that, Jessie. You're too young and too smart to feel hopeless. There's nothing stopping you if you want to do it. No law, no morality. Just yourself and your choices.' He took another drink of bourbon. It dribbled on his chin. 'At the end of the day, it's just this. It's just power, and who gets to use it. The problem is the other side are pragmatists. They're focused on the end result. If you want to achieve something, you have to be as unprincipled as they are ... principles are useless in a fight. What good are principles when you're dead?'

My sister's face flashed before my eyes again. Dead and gone.

A twist of fate, an unlucky break, a mechanical failure, a driver's error. A man who killed her spirit, before her body followed. A man who was sitting next to me.

'You said once that we make our own justice,' I commented.

'Exactly,' he replied, nodding with a drunken solemnity. 'We make it for ourselves.'

'Even if justice requires us to punish the guilty?'

'Absolutely.'

'Even if it means breaking the law, breaking moral codes?'

'If that's what it takes.'

'But then who gets to punish us, Jay?'

He looked at me for a long moment. 'Whoever can.'

After what felt like an age, the car pulled up to the kerb in front of us. I held my arm out and Crane took it, letting me help him to his feet. He climbed in first.

For a moment, I hesitated, wavering, my eyes upturned to the sky, a thin layer of passing cloud and pollution obscuring the distant stars. 'What am I doing?' I whispered – to the sky or myself, I'm not sure – and when no answer came, I climbed into the car after him.

The driver asked us to confirm an address, so Crane gave his and then sat back in his seat. I yawned and slowly let my head come to rest on his shoulder, and then lower to his chest. We stayed like that in silence. I was so close to him now that I could hear the beat of his heart. His breath stirred the small strands of hair at my temples.

As we reached 218 Delancey Street, I sat up straight again while he unbuckled his seat belt.

'It was fun watching the world burn with you tonight,' I said to keep him engaged, and, when he looked at me, I gave a weak smile.

'Yeah,' he replied, rather stiffly now, as if proximity to his home was reminding him of who he was and, more importantly, who *I* was. 'Go straight home now, Jessica. The city isn't safe tonight.'

Carefully, I leaned forward across the seats and slowly, while he sat frozen before me, kissed his lips. As I drew away, his stubble scratched at the skin of my cheek. 'I will. Goodnight, Professor.'

He was initially startled, but then he grabbed the back of my head, and pulled me towards him, until our lips met again. The force had taken me by surprise, knocking the breath from my lungs, so that it felt as if I might suffocate.

My hair slipped free of his grasp as he let me go. He didn't smile, just climbed out of the car. He didn't say a word.

In the rear-view mirror, I saw the driver watching me, and I hoped he would remember what I had said – 'Goodnight, *Professor*' – if ever called upon in the future, if ever summoned to testify. He looked away from me when my eyes caught his. Yes: he would remember.

I took a screenshot of the app, with his name and the car make and model detailed, and then told him the address of my dorm. As we sailed back the way we had come – through a city still reeling from the stinging slap of reality – I tried to calm myself. This was fine – no, better than fine. It was triumph. And even though I had expected to feel a little better about it, in the face of the evening's crushing political defeat, I declared a first victory for Audrey.

Chapter Twenty-One

After that kiss, I had expected something to change in Crane's demeanour towards me, some hint of what had passed between us. In person and in emails, he was the same as he had been before, revealing no hint that anything had happened between us. His ability to behave as if it had never happened was almost impressive, our audience of students and faculty around the law school none the wiser.

Despite that, my inbox had started to become peppered with invitations – to talks, seminars, and even a drinks reception with the university president. Crane sent me postings about applications for internships, scholarships, international fellowships, offering to put in a kind word if I were interested in any of them.

On the surface, he seemed keen on advancing my career, but I knew he took joy in shaping me and my future, in possessing the ability to do it. He wanted to make me reliant on him. If I was overwhelmed by his generosity and dependent on his favour, it would weaken me, elevate his side of the power dynamic. Was this his game? Was this what he did to Audrey?

In the early days, I had been so focused on my own plan for Crane I had almost missed how easy he made it for me. But in writing down this account for you, in the process of remembering, I have found myself wondering if maybe he had *allowed* me to manipulate him, precisely because it suited him.

A week after election night, on a cold evening in mid-November, the Dean hosted a drinks reception in the Great Hall for a visiting judge from the European Court of Human Rights. Crane invited me and Charlie to meet the judge and network with any other people of prominence who might be there – one perk among many. It was not my kind of event, not my scene. Networking made my skin itch. But it was our first in-person interaction outside of the classroom since the kiss, and since his behaviour towards me had not changed overtly, I couldn't be sure how he would react to me in this setting. I needed to tread carefully, remain watchful, and try to gauge his mind so I could figure out what to do next.

Other students had been invited to the event as representatives of various organisations on campus and were present in recognition of their contribution to the law school. We were there solely because of Crane, and that dichotomy made me feel like an even bigger fraud.

But not Charlie. While I hung back, loitering near the refreshment table that had been set up under a very large baroque mirror, Charlie worked the room in his well-tailored suit and VMI tie, born for events like these.

Privilege like this attracted more privilege, success more success, like a stone gathering moss. It was easy to talk about human rights and equality in cushioned seats and panelled lecture halls, but one way or another, it was wealth that got us in the door, the hard work and the grades moot without the means to pay the hefty entrance fee. It didn't seem right that the people making, writing, and adjudicating our laws inevitably came from, or acquired, a privilege most people could only ever dream of.

I was sipping a glass of champagne when Crane came to find me. Standing just behind me, his hand rested on my back briefly, a pressure just below my ribs, he spoke into my ear. 'Jessie, let me introduce you to the judge.'

He didn't seem to have noticed the familiar way he had touched me, as if it had come naturally to him. It was exactly the sort of thing I wanted to happen. A slip here or there. A forgetfulness that might lead to recklessness. But my skin prickled, a minor revolt of my nervous system. There were times, in our game of cat and mouse, when I felt he was toying with me, a sharp claw catching at my tail, keeping me close.

And what of his wife? Did he think of her in moments like these? Did she cross his mind? How could he love her and behave like this? How could he be two people at once? Husband to her, villain to me.

Crane was in good form, talking enthusiastically, his fingers pressing lightly on my elbow. I drank some more champagne and buried my thoughts deep as he led me back to the judge, who was in the same spot, surrounded by the same group of people who seemed very keen to speak with him.

Crane, intent on making the connection, interrupted the chatter to introduce me as his 'brightest student'.

When I demurred from that title, not in the mood for flattery and fawning and pats on my back, the judge told me that young women shouldn't be modest and, somehow, I found the wherewithal not to reply that old men shouldn't tell young women what they should and should not be. Instead, I answered his questions about my academic interests, and my non-existent career plans. By the end of our chat, the judge said to email him if I was interested in applying for a traineeship at the court. I threw the business card he gave me in the bin on my way home. Whatever I did with my life, it would not be dependent on favours.

These cosy circles were anathema to me, these systems of reward exemplified by Crane's favouritism, his practice of plucking out the people he liked and putting them in rooms like this, so they'd be grateful to him when it came time to claim a return on investment. Favours passing back and forth, well-placed connections built like a scaffolding around their good fortune, making them too big to fail, too integral to fall, because if one should topple, so would the others.

I will admit, since I've promised you the truth, that there were moments when I did wonder, daydream, imagine myself in the sort of future Crane could offer, in mahogany-panelled rooms, by the plush seat of power, reaching out to take it for myself. But that's how it starts, a rot setting in, until you start to lose yourself, like so many others caught in a nepotistic system they once hated, in a constant round of *quid pro quo*.

I could tell from the atmosphere in the classroom these days, from the flickering of eyebrows and the flitting of eyes, that the other Law and Lit students had some sense of an unusual relationship developing between me and Crane. But my classmates only saw the very surface of it. An emotional affair of sorts was in full swing, hidden from prying eyes and curious minds. I seemed to have awoken a dormant itch, one he retained the presence of mind to fight when there was a real-world risk – witnesses, actions that could not be taken back. But words on a phone, the attention I gave to his thoughts, that was something he seemed unable to resist.

Late at night, or sometimes in the early hours when he couldn't sleep, he would send me written dispatches, snatches of ideas, the contents of his mind.

Jay Crane (05.56):

I envy you this time in your life. You're still so new and unformed. You can be anything right now, take any shape.

I'm lying here, unable to sleep because I'm a sad old man with a bad back. I hope you're out somewhere right now. I hope you're living. You get to a certain age, Jess, and you can't do these things anymore. You have responsibilities. People expect you to be predictable, respectable, consistent. They demand that you shut down the sides of yourself that long for freedom. You're supposed to stay home and out of trouble. Maybe I should fight that more often. Maybe I shouldn't have given up so easily.

My wish for you, Jess, is you never give up.

The longer we spoke and the more I saw the man behind the professor, the more my edges seemed to melt, and I would turn from a thing that is solid in the world into a pooling liquid of doubt, indecision, and misgiving. It wasn't all fake, you see. It wasn't all pretend. And in the face of his trust, when Crane was vulnerable with me, I would feel my resolve waver. It felt like my greatest failure, this inability to just hate him.

Once molten, I'd have to shut the laptop, or throw my phone to the other side of the bed, and stick headphones in my ears. Burning with shame, with frustration, with confusion, I would blare loud, rageful music into my ears, until I could neither hear, nor think about anything but the sound of drums, and guitar, until all other thoughts were drowned out. I would shut my eyes, and block the world out, until I was no longer thinking gentle thoughts about Crane, thinking of him as a man with a gamut of human emotions, as a human person, flawed and fallen.

I would harden myself again, because that is what it takes to fight back. I let my heart grow cold and dead inside me, because that was the price of my refusal to accept defeat. It required my anger to devour the soft emotions that might otherwise derail me from my mission. It was my anger that reminded me of all that Audrey had suffered, silently, and alone. My anger that would not bend, forgive, or forget. I didn't want to be here, doing any of this, but neither could I live in a world where Crane went unpunished.

That night, I would write all of it down in the diary, the sensation of Crane's hand on my back, the feel of his breath near my face as he spoke in my ear. I would add it to the evidence I had gathered so far. My plan was coming together and gaining ground and should have been cause for celebration. But, on my walk home, I couldn't shake the phantom presence of Crane's fingers on my skin, disgust making my limbs feel heavy, as if they had been tensed all night.

This quest for justice demanded a heavy price from me. It had taken over my life, my mind, and now, it was beginning to claim my body too. It would be worth it when Crane was exposed, his true face shown to the world, his true nature revealed. I clung to that idea and let it carry me back to my dorm.

Chapter Twenty-Two

The weekend before Thanksgiving, Crane invited me and Charlie to a pre-holiday dinner at his house. This time, the invitation was different.

> *Jay Crane (18.23):*
>
> *Dear Jessie and Charlie,*
>
> *My wife is very keen to meet the students I can't stop talking about and so I wondered if you might like to join us for some turkey and pies before we go our separate ways for Thanksgiving? Leyna is an excellent cook, and I might even open a good Margaux for the occasion, if you're lucky.*
>
> *Jay*

He mentioned her so casually, dropping the words *wife* and *Leyna* into the invitation as if nothing at all had occurred between us to make that a complicated matter. Why now? Why this moment? Was it, as his email seemed to suggest, at her insistence? Why did Leyna want to meet us?

Now that she had a name, Crane's wife came alive in my mind.

Not quite a wrinkle in my plans, but an unknown quantity, a cypher, and a source of niggling doubt. I didn't know how to account for her, or whether her existence should change my plan of action. It clearly hadn't changed things for Crane. His wife's absence from Audrey's records was unsettling. It felt deliberate, but I still didn't know why Audrey would have erased her like that. Was it guilt? Or something else? Did she have some role in the story? Either way, I needed to know who I would face at dinner.

Adding the name 'Leyna' to my internet trawl produced the answers I needed. The results turned up several photographs of them at the same university events. In one photo, she was clapping and smiling, reacting to something unseen in the frame, while he stood next to her, his hand in his pocket, smiling down at her from his superior height.

She was Professor Leyna King, an academic in the anthropology department at Franklin. A search of her name on the university database provided an image of a woman with a serious expression framed by long black hair. She was wearing a black silk blouse with her arms folded across her chest and her body angled diagonally away from the photographer in that unnatural way people pose when they're getting a photo taken for professional purposes.

Her bio said she was from Colorado and had received her PhD in anthropology from Stanford before moving to Philadelphia for a fellowship at Franklin. That was fifteen years ago. She seemed to value her privacy and had a lower public profile, though she appeared to be well-regarded in her field. It was just that Crane had the star power and enjoyed using it.

When Friday night came, I was still pondering the possible significance of Crane's wife as I made my way towards Center City. He had never mentioned her to me, and yet, she knew of me and Charlie. How would my plans for Crane affect her life? Would their marriage end? Would her reputation be damaged too? How would it impact her career? All she had worked for? What would happen to her when she – and the world – discovered the truth about him?

Or did she already know?

I was crossing the river at the Chestnut Street bridge when I bumped into Vera, Amanda, and Joshua. They were carrying placards under their arms, headed to Broad Street to join the protests that had been happening nightly outside City Hall since the election. I had been so wrapped up in Crane that I had almost forgotten about them. It felt like an occurrence underway in some other place, or on some other plane of reality, entirely separate from me.

'You should come with us, Jess,' Amanda said. 'I've got a spare placard—' She held it up, grinning broadly. It read: *'Tiny hands = tiny grasp on the Constitution.'*

'She's very proud of it.' Vera looked amused. 'I mean, I tried to tell her it was too long for anyone to read, but . . .'

'It's clever,' I said, with a smile. 'I like it.'

'Are you coming, Jessie?' Joshua asked, keeping one eye on the rest of the people streaming across the bridge towards the protest. 'There's a bunch of us heading there now.' He paused. 'You're welcome to join us?'

An olive branch extending towards me. I think he felt bad about goading Charlie that day on the courtyard and hoped to set things right with me.

I wanted to accept the fresh slate he offered. To disappear into a crowd and become just another protester, just another person chanting. But though we spoke the same language of dissatisfaction, they were a pack and right now I hunted alone.

'Unfortunately, I can't. I have plans already.' I offered a sad little shrug, hoping it would convey polite regret. 'Maybe next time?'

Joshua spun away, hurt, I supposed, by the disinterest I had shown in reconciling with him. I swallowed a sigh, and with it a mouthful of regret. If this were my real life and I was an ordinary student, I would have gone with them. If I weren't here solely for Crane, I might have found Joshua's interest in me flattering, instead of inconvenient. But I could not allow myself this distraction, not when I was getting close to Crane.

'What are your plans? Doing anything fun?' Amanda asked, convivially, or, at least, I didn't get the sense that she harboured any suspicions. She was like Audrey that way, trusting.

But Vera missed nothing. She caught my hesitation. 'Some secret rendezvous, is it?' An eyebrow arched. 'A boyfriend you're hiding from us?'

Amanda laughed. Joshua looked uncomfortable.

To my embarrassment, my cheeks flushed. 'No,' I said, quickly. 'God, no, it's ... it's a dinner with Professor Crane.'

None of them replied, the silence lasting long enough that I coughed awkwardly to break it.

'That sounds nice,' Amanda said eventually, but not convincingly, while Vera eyed me with concern.

Their reaction was exactly what would help me when I needed to call on witnesses. And yet, it made me squirm to know how I appeared to them now.

I checked the time on my phone. 'I, eh, I'm late actually, so ... I need to run.'

They said goodbye, and I strode away as fast as I could, weaving through the crowd until I reached Center City, leaving my classmates behind and pushing on towards Crane. It didn't feel like I had a choice, compulsion driving me down the city streets, as if some magnetised force were pulling me to him.

I so seldom left the environs of campus that the city had a way of feeling alien to me, the physical place but also the people whose lives weren't determined by grades on a piece of paper, by their rank among their classmates, or the high opinion of their professors. As I crossed at the far end of Broad Street, the sound of the protest met my ears, already underway outside City Hall. At a distance, the voices of the crowd rose, placards held high into the bitingly cold November evening.

Tonight, I needed to see how Crane would act towards me in the company of his wife. Could I spur him into doing something rash in her presence? To play with fire? Prelude to a final sin, for which he would soon be punished.

My footsteps quickened as I hurried on towards Delancey Street, forcing myself to focus on what I had lost, on the pain and the grief, feeding it with the memories that hurt the most.

We knew Audrey's route through Central America, mapping it from snippets in the occasional emails she sent to us. She had moved south from Mexico, to Belize, and onwards to Guatemala. On a road in the highlands, near the Mayan site at Tikal, the right-hand side of a bus had clipped a passing truck that was too large for the narrow dirt track. The smaller vehicle, with its bouncy axle, had slipped off the road and down the hillside, where it was crushed and chewed and swallowed whole by the jungle below.

Audrey was a passenger on that bus. She died, surrounded by strangers. There were no survivors. We only know what was recorded in the official report, compiled through external eyewitness accounts and the crash investigators. It contained only the cold facts: the angle at which the bus met the truck, its deadly trajectory down the slope, the speed at which it was travelling, the force with which it hit the trees. But I have sat inside that bus at night. In my dreams, I've seen the shards of glass, the bending metal, the bodies suspended in the air as the bus topples over, and takes me with it.

Nothing I could do to Crane would bring her back, but he was the reason my sister was on that bus, and I couldn't let that go, no matter what it cost me. There is a karmic consequence to a crime like Crane's. Not cause and effect so much as inevitability, a long, lingering tail, extending out into the unknowable future. Sometimes, the tail extends so far that the act and its karmic result might appear distinct. But everything I did to Crane was linked back to what he did to Audrey. It was the natural consequence of his crime – nothing more than that – and I was simply the conduit.

At number 218 Delancey Street, I reached forward and pressed the doorbell.

Chapter Twenty-Three

Leyna King sat at the table opposite Charlie, her dark hair at the nape of her neck in a neat chignon. She held a silver fork between the long fingers of her left hand, and, with her right, she played with the high collar of her dress. It was a deep blue colour, the same as the sapphire hanging from her neck.

We were on the dessert course, an array of pies on the table in front of us – pumpkin, blueberry, and pecan. With the side of his fork, Crane was cutting the last parcel of pastry on his plate, listening while Charlie told us about his time at the Virginia Military Institute as an undergraduate. Leyna was laughing at something Charlie said – a thin upper lip peeling back to reveal white teeth and pale pink gums – and I wondered again, for the thousandth time that night, if she knew about Audrey.

'You call each other rats?!' Leyna said, her head sitting in her cupped hand, her elbow resting on the table. 'Your friends?!' A thin silver bracelet slipped down from her wrist and settled further along her arm.

'Yeah, I mean, I know how it sounds, but it's this very old tradition,' Charlie replied. 'It's a whole part of the training – new cadets join the Rat Line and you have to learn your way out. We still call each other Brother Rat.' He glanced sideways at me, adding: 'Affectionately, obviously!'

'Obviously,' I said flatly. 'Sounds like a great place, Duke. I can see why you love it so much.'

'It is. They train you for life there – and I don't just mean physically. They teach you how to live.'

'They teach you to obey orders and worship a flag,' I said, falling into my usual pattern of bickering with him. 'Is that really living?'

'Right and you'd know, wouldn't you, Mooney? You'd understand how these things work from thousands of miles away in Ireland.'

'I've never been to Ireland,' Leyna said, to shift the conversation to a different topic, in the very fair assumption that Charlie and I were drifting towards squabble. She turned to her husband. 'You loved it there . . . didn't you, Jay?'

Up to this point in the evening, I had been absorbed in the eye-opening insight into their shared lives. They were sitting next to each other on one side of the oval table, husband and wife, and I had been quietly observing them from the other side, next to Charlie. The way they spoke to each other, the moments of silent communication that passed between them, in a dialect created by them, understood by them, unique to them - I parsed these interactions for signs of what Leyna knew or didn't know about her husband's behaviour.

Now that she had mentioned Crane's time in Ireland, the prospect of getting an answer had me on edge. We had just stepped onto dangerous ground.

Crane was nodding. 'I did.' He addressed Charlie: 'Jessie knows this already, but I taught for a semester in Trinity College, Dublin. It's some place. Beautiful campus.'

'You went to Trinity, didn't you?' Charlie said to me. 'Professor Crane could have taught you.'

I swallowed a mouthful of water. My elbow caught on my

plate, making the cutlery rattle against the ceramic. The sound seemed to echo through me. 'Yeah, but we, eh, didn't overlap,' I said quickly, then prompted Leyna, 'You didn't visit? While he was there? You didn't want to see Dublin?'

'No,' she replied. 'It was term time . . . I couldn't get away.'

All those months apart, away from each other, divided by an ocean—

'Leyna's a better professor than me.' Crane squeezed his wife's shoulder, pride coating his face. 'Her work comes first.'

'That's a shame. I'm sure you would have liked it.'

'I'd love to visit Ireland some time,' Leyna said. 'It seems like a beautiful country.' She was quiet then for a moment, those long fingers extending towards her wine glass. I watched them curl around the stem. 'My husband certainly had a whale of a time!' She glanced at him, his eyes briefly rising to meet hers. 'Seemed like he was out most nights of the week. Every time I rang him, he was in the pub.'

There was a smile on her face, but I thought I perceived a certain straining in the muscles around her mouth as she took a sip of wine.

Crane was smiling too. 'I was supposed to get some research work done, but I didn't do a thing. Like I said, my wife is the better scholar.' He laughed, as did Charlie and Leyna. But I knew exactly the distractions keeping him from his work, all the nights he had spent with Audrey, all the time he had spent pulling Audrey close to him, just as I was doing to him now, making her trust him, until—

'Sounds fun!' Charlie interrupted my thought. 'Mooney, you'll have to show me around when I come visit you.'

I shook my head firmly.

'Ah, don't pretend you won't miss me when we graduate, Mooney. You'll be begging me to visit.'

Leyna got up from the table to make a pot of coffee.

'You know, it's funny,' Crane said, once she was gone. His brown eyes pierced mine. They were lighter towards the middle of the iris, almost golden, ringed in a darker, nut brown. There was a peculiarity to the lamplight in the room making the effect more noticeable, or maybe it was just adrenaline heightening my senses. 'I'm surprised we didn't meet at all, not even around the law school.'

My fingers fidgeted with the spoon on the table in front of me. 'I don't know,' I said vaguely. 'Maybe you just didn't notice me.'

'No. No, that definitely wasn't it,' Crane said, glancing back at the door. 'You remind me of a student I met there.'

My heart stopped. There was a sensation, like falling, as if the ground had disappeared under me, as if I were hurtling through air.

'Audrey Mooney-Flynn.' Crane was still looking at me. 'Did you know her?'

My mouth was suddenly dry. Was this an ambush? Did he *know* I was Audrey's sister?

'No, I ... eh, don't know anyone called Audrey.' I was very conscious of the blood filling my cheeks, a fiery heat diffusing through my face and down my neck. I was conscious, also, of Charlie staring at me. I summoned my courage, then met Crane's eye, adding polite curiosity to my voice. 'Why do you ask? Who is she?'

'Oh, just a student I taught at Trinity,' Crane said, with a casual shrug. 'I can't really explain why, but you really remind me of her. You have the same smile, the same little gestures. When I first saw you in class, I thought you must be related.'

My glass was empty. I lifted the water jug, trying to hide the tremble in my hand. 'That's so weird,' I said. 'But, eh, no ... no relation. Unless my parents have been hiding her from me. It's a common name back home...'

It pained me to deny her like that, but what choice did I have? I had never had much of a presence on social media but, preparing for Philadelphia, I had deactivated any profile bearing my full name, just in case Crane went looking. I figured people who knew me would think it was part of my grieving process.

Crane picked some crumbs off his shirt, then smiled up at his wife as Leyna returned with the coffee. His body language was so relaxed, so easy, talking about my sister. I hated that. I hated that he was thinking of her and behaving so carelessly, his emotions so shallow. The words Audrey had written about him ran through my head. Squiggles of ink in a diary. Sans serif type on a phone screen. All those declarations of interest and then, abruptly, no more.

You know what you did.

Leyna was smiling down at me, offering coffee.

'Will you remember us the same way after we graduate, Professor?' Charlie asked, holding out his cup for Leyna. 'Do you remember all your favourites?'

Crane folded his arms across his chest. '*Et tu*, Charlie? You're accusing me of having favourites?'

Charlie smiled. 'No, I just ... some professors don't make the same sort of effort with students that you do.'

'My husband has such strong relationships with his students.' Leyna took her seat once more. 'I never have the same closeness. We tried to invite some of my students for dinner a few times, but it didn't work at all. It was just *awkward*. Not like this, not like it is with you two.' She turned to Crane. 'I don't know how you do it. The intimacy you create. It's wonderful.' Her eyes fell to her plate. 'I just don't have my husband's charm.'

'That's not true,' Crane said, his hand now over hers. 'It's just different teaching styles, different ways of doing things.' His hypocrisy was making me feel sick.

'Well—' She gave a small, tight laugh. 'I don't envy you the stalkers, Jay.'

Crane's spine hit the back of his chair. I could practically hear the crack of bone against wood. 'Leyna, that's ... Let's not talk about that,' he said, a careful eye stealing my way.

'Stalkers?' I said, bolt upright now. Had Crane noticed me behind him on campus? When they found that a rock had been thrown through their window, had they suspected a student?

Leyna was amused, as if it were something she found funny. I wondered if she resented us – me and Charlie sitting here in her home, wanting her husband for ourselves, his notoriety, his influence, his intellect, while she was reduced to the role of wife: superfluous, even an impediment.

She swatted the air in front of her face. 'I shouldn't have said anything. Don't listen to me.' Lifting the wine glass, she added, 'I've had too much of this.'

'Oh, come on,' I said, affecting ease. 'You can tell us!'

'No.' Crane's voice filled with sudden authority, the way it did in the classroom. 'We're not discussing it. It's not appropriate.' He pushed his chair back, on his feet now, and grabbed distract-edly at the empty plates. 'We're all finished with these, right?' he asked, stacking the plates with the remnants of pies on top of each other, clutching them to his chest as he headed towards the kitchen.

In his absence, Leyna let the air out of her lungs. 'He hates when I mention it,' she whispered to us, pinching her finger and thumb together and running them over her pink-painted lips as if she were closing a zip. 'I'll say no more.' She played with the bracelet on her wrist.

Rising to my feet, I gathered the cutlery, the spoons, the forks, the knives. I looked down at them in my hand: the knives.

'You can leave those, Jessie,' Leyna said. 'Don't worry about that. We'll clear up later.'

'It's no problem,' I replied, a thin smile slicing my face as I made my way to the kitchen, an opportunity finally presenting itself. 'I'll just be a minute.'

Crane was loading the dishwasher when I appeared at the kitchen door. He gripped the plates, the glasses, the empty bowls, his hands large, with thick fingers and a network of deep blue veins. From the dining room, we could hear Charlie and Leyna speaking again, laughing. But in the kitchen, it was silent, lit by the long, horizontal bulbs shining out from beneath the midnight-blue painted cabinets.

'She's really nice ... your wife,' I said, but I didn't like how it sounded. Disingenuous, maybe even mean.

Crane looked at me. 'She's brilliant,' he said. 'Don't know what she's doing with me.' The self-effacing act was tiring. He knew he had betrayed her, and that he was still betraying her.

'What was all that about stalkers?' I asked as I handed him the cutlery.

He took them from me, rinsing them under the tap. 'That piqued your interest, did it?'

'How could it not?'

'Look, I don't like to talk about it.' He dried his hands on the cloth thrown over his right shoulder. 'People go through a lot in college. Sometimes I get caught up in that. That's all it is, usually.'

'So ... your students regularly stalk you?'

He frowned at the scepticism in my voice. 'Not regularly. Very rarely, actually. But, yes, some students get a little fixated, a little intense. They see things that aren't there and attach to an idea of me. It has gotten me in trouble before when people get confused about the nature of these dinners ... they start to think we're friends, or ... or, well, sometimes more than friends.' His face was angled slightly away from me, as if he were avoiding my reaction. I couldn't tell if this was genuine. 'I don't like to think about all that.'

I didn't trust his self-serving account, but nor did I want to derail what I came to the kitchen to do, so I nodded, wet my lips with my tongue. 'Jay,' I said. 'We haven't talked about ... what happened ... you know, that kiss on election night.'

His voice was little more than a whisper when he stepped quickly towards me and spoke into my ear. 'Jesus Christ, Jessie ... what are you bringing that up for?' His eyes jumped to the empty doorway, through which we could still hear Leyna and Charlie chatting. 'This is my *home.*'

I didn't know what he meant by that exactly. Was there something sanctified about these four walls? Did it feel less real – less egregious – outside the boundaries of his shared life with his wife?

'I'm sorry, I just ... Don't you think about it? When you look at me? Because I can't get it out of my head.'

'Well, you have to get it out of your head, Jessie. Jesus *Christ.* It was a mistake. All right? We were drunk and I ... I just need to make clear ... I can't ... we *can't* ...'

This couldn't happen. I couldn't lose him. Not now. Not when I was so close. I dropped my gaze to his shoes. They were faded white tennis shoes, stained with a splash of the Margaux we had been drinking.

'What happens if we do?' I said, dipping my chin, eyes flicking up again, the picture of innocence.

'I could lose my job.' His voice was beseeching now, scratching out of his throat. 'My ... my wife. I love her.'

I looked at him and caught the fear cross his face. It brought about a tremendous calm in me. He was crumbling. Watching him now, I could sense the anxiety emanating off his body, from the tensed muscles in his shoulders and neck. He was scared of what I could do, what he might not be able to stop. The tables had turned.

I took a step forward, and he flinched slightly as I laid my hands on his chest. 'We'll be careful.'

His fingers closed around my wrists. He gently pushed me backwards from him, so I was at a safe distance again. 'It doesn't work . . . things go wrong. People find out.'

'You sound like this has happened to you before,' I said wryly. 'One of the stalkers?'

'No,' he said, panicked now. 'I'm just speaking generally.'

'Right.'

'Jess, *please* . . . this is hard for me. If I was your age . . . if I was free to . . .' He shook his head. 'If I was Charlie Duke sitting out there next to you . . . I would . . .' He sucked air into his mouth. 'The shit I would do to you.'

I felt a bolt of surprise at the strength behind those words. They sounded strange and lurid coming from his mouth, a sudden shift, from erudite professor to man with dick. Despite all that I knew, it was curiously alarming to see him revealed as he really was.

'But . . .' He swallowed, his Adam's apple rising and falling. 'We just can't.' There was mild terror in his eyes now. I wanted more of that. I wanted to see him quake. I wanted him to feel the way women feel. 'I can't . . . you must understand why . . .' He let my wrists go. They were slightly red where he had held them.

'You're always telling me to make my own rules,' I said, a slow smile lighting my face. And then, I sprang forward, filling the space between us and forcing my mouth against his so strenuously that my tooth caught his lower lip. From all that I had observed of him through Audrey's diary and messages, and my own character study since getting to know him in Philadelphia, I knew he liked a little spontaneity, a little danger, a little wildness, a bad streak in a good girl. But for a fleeting moment, for a fading instant, I'm not so sure that the wildness in me was pure pretence. Something slipped loose inside me, a flash of violence. He caught a handful of my hair and kissed me back, meeting my force with his own.

I stepped back and pulled myself firmly from his grasp, ignoring the tugging sensation before he released my hair from his fingers. Without a word, I walked out of the kitchen, back to the table, taking my seat next to Charlie, as peaceably as I could. The conversation continued, but all I heard was the pounding of heart against bone.

Chapter Twenty-Four

Beneath the tablecloth, my fingers twisted the fabric of my napkin tightly, as if it could help restrain the emotions storming through me. Charlie was sharing his plans for Thanksgiving. Family dinner at his grandmother's colonial estate outside Lexington, Virginia. Camp Duke, they liked to call it.

'And what about you?' Leyna asked, looking at me very steadily.

From the kitchen came the sound of running water, pots and pans being aggressively scrubbed. Sitting back in my chair with my wine glass in hand, I took a long, slow drink, trying to calm my heart rate.

There was a version of myself they expected to see at the table, someone who had not done anything noteworthy in the kitchen. I summoned her back into my body, fixing a smile to my face and dropping my shoulders. 'I don't really have any plans. I think there might be a dinner for the international students, but I'm not going. So, it'll probably just be me and my microwave.'

Quietly, Crane reappeared at the door. There was a drop of blood on his lip. It trembled at the edge, as if it might spill over.

'Oh! What happened to your lip, Jay?' Leyna asked, holding her linen napkin up to him. 'Here . . . use this.'

He dabbed at the blood, which seeped into the fabric, staining it a muddy brown. 'I . . . I bit my lip when I was eating some pie in the kitchen,' Crane said, then gave a shaky laugh. 'I suppose it's a sign I should stop picking at the leftovers.'

He sat down, then reached for the corkscrew, pulling the cork free and playing with it absently. He flipped it over and over in his hands, as if he were fascinated by it. He seemed determined not to look at me, but I knew that he wanted to, that I had captured his interest entirely.

'Well,' Charlie said, slapping his knees with both hands. 'On that note, I think it's time we said goodnight.' He fixed his fringe back from his forehead, before extending his hand to Leyna. 'Thank you both so much for a wonderful evening.'

My eyes were still on Crane, but his were on his thumb, which he kept dabbing at his lip and then inspecting for blood.

I pushed my chair back, rising to join Charlie. 'Yes, thank you. It was really memorable.' I turned to Leyna, with a breezy smile. 'It was lovely to meet you, Professor King.'

Her hand stretched towards me. 'And you, Jessie.'

'Dinner was wonderful,' I added, to this woman whose life I was invading and whose husband I had just kissed in her kitchen. Guilt lit through me, but only a flicker. Even if she was an innocent party in all this, it was ultimately irrelevant. This had to happen. There was no other way. Some things were more important.

Withdrawn, Crane followed us to the door. On the threshold, he shook Charlie's hand stiffly, then did the same to mine. 'Goodnight,' he said brusquely. 'And happy Thanksgiving.'

The door shut immediately and the night air swallowed us, cold against our cheeks. I zipped my jacket to my chin against the icy wind blowing concentrically in from the Delaware River and took off at speed down the cobblestone road, Charlie trailing behind me. The quiet residential streets of Old City sat on a planned grid, making me feel very far from the disorder of Dublin with its palimpsest nature. But it felt older than anywhere else I had visited on this side of the Atlantic, its past baked into the houses, the roads, the footpaths, down which revolutionary feet had once trod. They had taken great care to preserve a history that was, as yet, still young.

'He's funny, isn't he?' Charlie said, after a while. He had caught up and was walking close to me now. 'Like what was all that about stalkers?! That's crazy. I heard . . . I mean, there are rumours about him being a little too friendly with students sometimes . . . but stalking seems next level.'

He glanced my way, as if to check how I would react. I watched our feet moving, steadying myself through the rhythm of our steps.

'Professor King didn't quite say it, but – I don't know – it seemed like maybe she knows about all that . . . about his reputation. Don't you think? Don't you think she was hoping we might say something?' Charlie asked.

'I don't know,' I said, reluctant to delve into this topic. 'Maybe . . . but why would she put up with it?'

Charlie sniffled in the cold air. 'Who knows? Marriages are weird. Little locked boxes.'

'True.' I picked up the pace, the night too cold for dallying. 'Maybe you get used to it. You can get used to anything.'

'Do you think the rumours are true? Do you think he has ever slept with one of his current students?'

The streets were sleepy and it felt as if we were entirely alone in the world, nothing to distract Charlie from this line of questioning. I rubbed my fingers up and down the back of my neck, over the hilly topography of my spine, scratching at a non-existent itch. 'Why are you asking me that?'

'He can be a little loose, right? A little flirty?' I felt Charlie's eyes on my face. 'He's like that with you sometimes.'

'Do you think so?' I said limply, but then – I don't know if it was Charlie's comforting presence, or the lingering sharp contact of the kiss – the truth slipped free. 'I guess I know what you mean . . . sometimes it's like I get excited around him, because I think we see the world the same way – me and Crane – and that's, well, it's rare for me to find a kindred spirit, you know, because I'm not the most . . . the most *normal* person.' Charlie smiled but didn't interrupt me. 'I'm drawn to him because of that, I think. I learn so much from him . . . about, like, how to cope when you're wired the way I am . . .' Charlie's arms were folded, and he was scrutinizing me intensely, as if every word had to be remembered and filed away. 'And I like him. Honestly, I like his company.' I paused. 'But then, you know, there's this insurmountable thing between us . . . because, honestly, I also hate his interest in me.'

I stopped and turned to Charlie. 'Crane is like this sun, and when he's shining down on you, the world feels like a warm, golden place. But then he disappears again, and nothing else feels quite as interesting, or exciting, or worthwhile. When he's gone, all I want is the sun to shine some more.' The breath swept out of my mouth, clouding as it met the cold air. 'And it's not just that. It's worse than that, Duke. Much worse.' I met Charlie's eye. 'I know things about him. Other things.'

'What things?' Charlie asked. He was standing close, so that he had to crane his neck to look down at me, his height suddenly making me feel small. 'What things, Jess? What do you know? You can tell me. You know that, right?'

I stepped away from him, creating distance, shaking my head, moving on towards the lights and the noise of the city again, towards the cars and the sirens, the tall buildings and the people they towered over transforming us into a series of dots in motion, a colony of ants.

What the fuck was I doing? Confiding in Charlie Duke – of Camp Duke, of Fed Soc fame, of VMI combat training. How could he possibly understand? I wrapped my arms around my body, feeling the cold intensely. I shut my eyes and tried to reclaim control over my spiralling mind. The final hour approaching, the last step in my plan now imminent, the pressure getting to me.

'Jess? You OK?'

'Yeah . . . I'm fine. Sorry. I just . . . Let's talk about this another time, Charlie? Let's just . . . let's just go home now, OK?'

He hesitated and I could see him wondering whether to press the point, whether to squeeze it out of me. What would I have said? Would I have told him about Audrey? Would I have shown him the texts, the emails, the diary? Would I have told him what I was planning? Would I have told him why I was doing it? Would I have shown him the anger in my stomach, the rage in my blood, the grief in my heart?

But Charlie didn't push me. He allowed his question to hang in the space between us, unanswered, unresolved, as he walked behind me down the footpaths, down the sleepy roads, past the perfect houses, back to our imperfect lives.

He stayed with me past Rittenhouse Square, past his own apartment block, across the bridge, through the howling cold of the Schuylkill River, a silent presence, making sure I was safe, while my mind rumbled and roiled like a choppy sea.

At my dorm building, he pulled me into him, leaning his chin on the top of my head, waiting in the silence of a long, wordless pause.

'Goodnight, Duke,' I said eventually, drawing away from him abruptly and striding inside before I broke down completely.

'Goodnight, Mooney,' Charlie replied as I hurried away.

He was still standing there as I swiped my student card at the turnstile, as I said hello to the bored security guard at her podium, and headed towards the lift. I could see him through the frosted window while I waited. He gave a small wave before he turned and walked back towards his apartment. I think he was the greatest surprise of my life. Charlie Duke. Of all the men in the world who might give a shit about me, it seemed to be him.

Chapter Twenty-Five

With that kiss in his kitchen, we had reached the point of no return and I was ready to bring my plan to its conclusion.

At the beginning of December, the temperature plummeted in Philadelphia. One morning, abruptly and without warning, I opened the curtains across my rattling bedroom window to find the city rendered white. Opposite my dorm, the rooftop of the Franklin Bookstore was white, except for the round circles of melted snow where two pipes vented heat into the frozen air. In front of the building, tree branches bent and buckled with the weight now piled along their length, like heaps of powdered sugar.

By this point, I had assembled all the circumstantial evidence I could possibly need to prove a relationship with Crane. Photographs putting us together in the same place at the same time, a list of witnesses who could verify those key moments, and texts showing a growing intimacy between us. In piles next to my bed, in folders under the window, and pinned over my desk, I had written the story of my first term at Franklin, Crane at the heart of it. It closely resembled Audrey's experience, a careful reflection of the account in her diary, right down to the details, to the doodles she had scribbled in the margins, and the dog-eared corners. For my own peace of mind, I needed that echo, that direct connection from her life to mine, the mirroring of what had happened before. It was how I justified all this to myself, how I kept it square and steady in my head.

It began on the evening of the Law Ball at Trinity, the final year of her life. I have tried to remember that night, but it's dim in my mind, only taking on any significance afterwards. I almost didn't go that year. It wasn't my scene – fussy and elitist – but then Audrey told me to get over myself and come have some fun. She was good for me like that, knocking me off my high horse when I needed it. Besides, I never could say no to Audrey.

She lent me a dress – ankle-length, plain black, with some kind of bejewelled design at the neckline. I strapped a small bottle of vodka to my thigh with several layers of Sellotape, striding into the Shelbourne Hotel with it hidden beneath the folds of my dress.

While my sister was somewhere else – with Crane, as it transpired, though I didn't know that at the time – I was perched in the ladies' toilets offering shots of cheap vodka to everyone passing through. It was fun, actually, until a girl in my class, Roz Ferrity, started crying over a break-up with a boy who was very publicly dancing with another girl. The vodka I gave Roz only seemed to have intensified her feelings of loss, and so, I spent the rest of the night either consoling her, or holding back her hair while she puked. The role of protector had always come naturally to me, but I hadn't realised that it was my sister who needed me right then, my sister who was in danger.

With all the pieces in place and the relationship between me and Crane well established, I could have picked any night at the end of term to make my final move against him. But I chose the night of the Barrister's Ball because I liked the symmetry of it: what began at one ball would end at another. The Barrister's Ball was an annual formal event for students and staff of the

Franklin law school, right before the winter break, which meant I wouldn't have to face him in class afterwards.

To avoid raising suspicions, I still had to see the academic year through but, since the first term was now almost over, I was swiftly approaching a time when Crane would no longer fill my days. His classroom would no longer be the anchor of my weeks, his ideas no longer a constant ringing in my ears. For me, there was only one possible ending for us, only one resolution I could accept. Justice, if I could, or revenge, if I must.

Our final class was on *Crime and Punishment*. I was running late that Monday morning, struggling with a bad cold, and by the time I entered room 1.04B for the last time, everyone else was already seated around the table.

Crane hadn't arrived yet, late to his final performance. While we waited, Vera tapped a pen against the wooden table next to me, making an agitated knocking sound inside my skull. Amanda flicked through her copy of *Crime and Punishment*, scribbling down last-minute notes. Miserable, I held a tissue to my runny nose, while Ronald joked that maybe Crane had the same cold. I laughed awkwardly, as best I could, and opted not to look at Charlie. But though Ronald didn't seem to appreciate how close to the bone his joke had struck, I caught the irritated expression on Joshua's face before he could hide it.

In the end, Crane didn't show up. Instead, a rattled teaching assistant flew in, out of breath, at a quarter past eleven, to say that Professor Crane was sick. I was disappointed to miss Crane's take on *Crime and Punishment*, the story of a man who believes himself above the law and beyond the ordinary moral conventions of mere mortals. It was almost too fitting, and I wondered if he was avoiding me after that kiss in his kitchen.

The TA was not prepared to cover the class. There was some head scratching and then some perusing of Crane's handwritten notes, collected, I presumed, from the mess on his office desk. When these proved largely indecipherable, and with no idea what else to do with us, she decided to let us go.

Freed early, we trooped out of room 1.04B for the final time and moved through the silent library. Exams were approaching, a new tension invading the law school so that the slightest noise in the library would provoke loud hissing sounds of complaint from harried students. Some had made a rabbit's burrow of their carrells, bringing cushions or pillows, or, in one notable case, a sleeping bag. This was their world for the next few weeks.

'Seems kind of anti-climactic,' Ronald said, as we all stood in the corridor, unsure what to do next. 'I was ready for a big final episode of the Crane show.'

'I wanted to hear his take on Raskolnikov,' Joshua said.

Vera sniffed. 'I'm sure it would have been a masterpiece of amoral cynicism . . .'

'I'm just pissed that I actually read the book this week,' Charlie remarked.

'Coffee?' Amanda suggested, eyes roving around the group. 'End as we started?'

It did feel like an ending, like a circle meeting itself, a snake biting its tail.

My backpack was strapped to my shoulders, holding my books and notes, all the things I needed to study and internalise for my exams, but my cold was making my head heavy, and I couldn't imagine concentrating on anything for the rest of the day, not when my mind kept skipping back to Crane.

Together, we walked over to Joe's, grabbed cups of a Costa Rican blend, and then returned to the Ben. The place was empty, most people camped out at the library. We chose the couches opposite the marble statue, whose blank stare met the wall over our heads. I sat quietly near Ben Franklin's stony elbow, and let the conversation wash over me. Amanda and Charlie were arguing about something in the news. Ronald and Joshua were talking about Sunday night's NFL game. I was still thinking of Crane's absence, of what I had to do next, and what would be lost once I struck the final blow, the illusion of normality gone.

Ronald was the first to stand up. 'I've got another class,' he said, a sad smile on his face. 'But I'm going to miss this little Law and Lit group. It has been . . . really nice actually.'

'I've got to take off too.' Joshua raised his hand in a small wave. 'Keep it cool, kids.'

'Wait, guys. This feels really sad,' Amanda said from the couch. 'Like, I'm properly *sad* about this.'

'I'm not.' Vera snorted and met our insulted expressions with several blinks. 'Look, you guys are cool and all, and I'm sorry we won't be a little group anymore, or whatever, but I'm not sorry to see the back of Crane.'

'You really didn't like him?' Joshua asked.

Vera shook her head, her short, black hair moving with it.

'Still annoyed you weren't his favourite?' Ronald suggested.

A crooked eyebrow rose up towards Vera's hairline. 'You know I do not care about all of that. And it's . . . absolutely *not* why I don't like him.'

'Why, then?' Ronald asked. 'Come on, tell us. Why d'you hate him?'

Vera's eyes flicked my way, then back to Ronald, who was smiling, as if enjoying taunting her. Had he somehow missed the rumours about Crane? Or just dismissed them as untrue?

Vera folded her arms tightly. 'There are things you don't know, Ronald.'

'What things?' Joshua asked, before Ronald had a chance.

'I'm not getting into this,' she said with a sigh. 'It doesn't matter anyway. The class is over and maybe, now, we can all move on with our lives.' I had the distinct impression this was a comment meant for me.

'Stop dropping little cryptic clues,' Ronald urged. 'If you have something to say, just say it.'

Vera wrinkled her nose. 'There are . . . rumours about him.'

'Vera,' Charlie said, sharply. 'Stop it.'

I looked down at my phone, scrolling absently, hoping I might avoid being dragged into this.

'Rumours?' Ronald said, his interest piqued. 'About what?'

Vera tucked her hair behind her ear. 'Professor Grouse told me about a student who tried to make a complaint five years ago about Crane being inappropriate with her. It didn't get very far because she was stonewalled by faculty. She ended up withdrawing it, and he never faced any consequences.'

I was careful not to react, staring fixedly down at my phone. A prior complaint against Crane five years ago – that would have been before he left for Dublin, before he met Audrey, before he ruined my sister's life. If it had succeeded–

'Stonewalled by *which* faculty members?' Amanda said, cutting across my thoughts, her tone so icy it was polar. My professors' faces flashed into my mind like a police line-up. Which of them had let Crane off the hook? Who was complicit in this?

Vera adjusted the sleeves of her white shirt, unbuttoning the cuffs and rolling them to the elbow. 'Well, Professor Laurent was Dean at the time. She told the complainant there was no evidence and convinced her it would be better to withdraw the complaint than be called a liar.'

Amanda grumbled a word under her breath that I didn't catch but which I'm pretty sure was four letters long and not suitable for polite company.

'I bet she was one of his favourites,' Joshua muttered, and I knew, without checking, that he was staring at me. He was likely not the only one thinking it, but, by voicing the idea, Joshua triggered an immediate shift in the atmosphere around us. More particularly, around me.

Charlie's shoes squeaked on the polished tiles as he came to stand behind my right shoulder, as if readying himself to intervene. He couldn't have known how little I needed his protection, or how it suited my purposes that Joshua had set the idea free in my classmates – the thought of me and Crane, and an inappropriate relationship.

Vera shrugged Joshua's comment aside. 'What does it matter if she was a favourite? The point is Crane got away with it!'

I sipped my coffee and kept my thoughts to myself, observing the tension around me as if I had not been ratcheting it up since the moment I arrived at Franklin.

'The question now,' Vera added archly, 'is what *else* he gets away with.'

This was exactly why I was here, not only to answer Vera's question, but to bring an end to the impunity she had correctly identified. After all, what is justice if not this? What is justice if not the act of ensuring that people get what they deserve?

'Well, that's depressing,' Ronald said, hoisting his backpack onto his shoulder. 'I really liked Crane . . .' He checked the time on his phone, then made a face. 'I need to go . . . I'm late for my next lecture.'

'Same,' Joshua said. He shuffled his feet, as if he were reluctant to leave, and threw sidelong looks at me and Charlie.

It was over now, the Law and Lit spell broken, Crane's grip on my classmates wrenched open, thanks to Vera's revelation. They knew something of his real nature now, a small piece of the truth about him, and suspicion had been planted firmly in their minds. His halo was gone, our professor no longer deified, no longer a god.

We didn't stay together much longer. Those of us still left in the Ben began to drift away, each in a different direction. Not quite the ending I had expected, but a better one than I could have hoped for. We may have missed our last class, but I had done the reading and learned all that Crane could teach me. I knew that crime requires punishment.

Crane would get his.

Chapter Twenty-Six

The dress I wore to the Barrister's Ball was the same dress Audrey had worn to her final Law Ball. She had taken a selfie with Crane on the night of the ball and I had pinned the image to the corkboard over my desk that morning. I needed a strong reminder of why I was doing this, Audrey's smiling face giving me courage, Crane's brazen smile stoking my rage.

Standing in front of the mirror, I was a stranger to myself. The dress was metallic silver and fell from a deep V-neck to the floor, with layered pleats at the bust and thin straps around the shoulders. It had suited Audrey much better, but it was a comfort to me, making me feel more connected, as if I were now carrying the burden for Audrey, ensuring Crane's crime would not be forgotten, or go unpunished.

Her best friend, Chloe Desmond, had come to me months after Audrey's funeral, a horrible secret weighing her down. When she'd told Chloe what had happened at the Law Ball, Audrey had sworn her to silence. But Audrey was now dead, and Chloe's conscience was plagued. Was there something she could have done to keep Audrey from leaving? Could we have helped Audrey if we knew the truth?

Chloe didn't know the full details. She only knew what Audrey had told her the morning after the Law Ball, the moment branded into her memory, like a scar on her skin. Audrey was distraught, inconsolable, and barely intelligible. She had just spent the night with Crane. But it had not gone to plan. They had argued. He'd wanted to kiss and make up. She'd told him no, that she didn't want to sleep with him. But he didn't want to hear it. No wasn't an answer he was willing to accept. He knew best.

All those weeks and months watching my sister become a shell of herself, and this was why. She hadn't been running from me, or from my parents. She hadn't fled from her life because of something we had done. He had made it too painful for her to stay. Jay Crane had raped my sister.

You know what you did.

When I arrived at the law school that evening, the Great Hall was already filling up. The same people I saw every day in class were now dressed in tuxedos and long, swishing dresses, transformed by a little tailoring into their future selves. Future partners, executives, judges, and politicians, keeping the wheels of industry turning with that greasy lubricant we called the law.

My eyes scanned the room for Crane, but Amanda found me first.

'Jessie!' she called from the bar. 'Come here – we're doing Law and Lit shots!' Ronald was with her, she in a black minidress with feathers along the hem, and he in a tuxedo identical to all the other men's.

Amanda shoved a shot of something or other into my hand, and I raised it to my mouth, letting it touch my lips, before spilling it onto the floor while nobody was looking. Tonight required sobriety, laser focus, and a steady head.

'Let's go dance,' Ronald said, dragging us onto the dance floor, where we joined the other bodies, limbs writhing rhythmically in time to a Taylor Swift song – I can't remember which. I wasn't present, not really.

Dean Thompson was in the corner by the door, chatting to Hoffman and someone else I didn't recognise. She was dressed in a smart black suit with a white silk blouse, her hair tied up in a bright red head wrap. I couldn't see Charlie anywhere, but I would need to find him too at some point. He had become a pivotal part of all this.

Slipping away from the others, I hovered at the edge of the dance floor, scouring the room for sight of him.

'There you are,' said a voice at my ear.

I knew it was him before I turned around. 'Hello, Professor.' My confidence strengthened immediately with the realization that Crane must have been looking for me too. After his absence from class, I had wondered if maybe I had pushed him too far at dinner, but he was relaxed in front of me now, in good form, his face flushed, a very full glass of red wine in his hand. I could tell it wasn't the first.

'Hi, Professor Crane,' Amanda said, quickly at my shoulder, shouting to be heard over the music. Her greeting drew Crane's eyes briefly from me to her and he stepped back.

'Hello there,' Crane said, his manner immediately rigid. One hand was in his pocket. With the other, he raised his glass to his lips. 'Are you having a good night?' he asked her.

'Oh yes,' Amanda replied. 'We missed you in class the other day.'

Crane opened his mouth to respond, but Ronald was calling Amanda's name from the centre of the dance floor.

'All right, coming!' she yelled back, then said: 'Jessie, we're wanted. You coming?' She gave me a meaningful look, and I could feel her hoping I would walk away with her.

But I shook my head. 'You go ahead – I'll be over in a minute.'

Disappointment splashed across her face. Briefly, she hesitated, but when I did not change my mind, she slipped away into the crowd, leaving the two of us together at the edge of the moving mass of bodies. I watched one of the feathers from her dress drop slowly to the ground at my feet.

Crane's eyes fell on me again. He didn't say anything. I didn't either. But between us there passed a wave of knowledge. Secret knowledge. Knowledge of what could happen, what might very well happen, and, most pressing of all, what should definitely not happen. But Crane didn't know that betrayal lurked within the silky curling of my lips, between the batting flutter of my lashes.

'Are you having a good time?' I asked at last, because words needed to be spoken.

A small shrug of his shoulders. 'These things are mostly work for me, but, um ... my night is getting a little better now.' The song changed to Beyoncé and a roar of appreciation sounded from the dance floor. 'It's a bit awkward for me, you know. You feel very watched as a faculty member.' I nodded, as if in sympathy. 'You end up being an observer of other people's fun.'

'Right,' I said. 'That's not great.'

'Ah, it's fine.' He looked into his drink. 'It just makes me feel old. Redundant. Moving towards inevitable obscurity.'

'You're always saying that.'

He blanched. 'Am I?!'

Fuck. My tone was wrong. It was just all the self-pity, the *whining*. There were worse things than growing old. I could think of a few, Audrey flitting through my mind.

I twisted my hair around my finger, using the pain to keep me focused. 'I just mean you're not old.' I moderated my voice so that it was unthreatening, a little sexy. 'And you're anything but redundant.'

'That's kind of you to say.' Crane seemed cheered, having heard what he wanted to hear. God, he just drank it all down so easily. 'Sorry, I . . .' He sort of laughed. 'I shouldn't talk about myself. It isn't interesting for you.'

'Of course it is,' I said, leaning in and readying myself for the next step. 'But you don't need to worry. You're nowhere near obscurity. Honestly, we're all fascinated by you.' If my plan worked, Crane would not be forgotten. If my plan worked, he would beg for the peace of obscurity. My fingers reached for the bare skin between his silver watch strap and the cuff of his tuxedo. '*I* find you fascinating.'

'Jess—' he said, voice deep, before cutting himself off, his eyes springing upwards. I saw the warning in his face and snatched my hand back. My fingers closed around my glass instead.

From behind me, someone grabbed my shoulder. 'Jessie, are you coming?' It was Amanda again, her hand – inconveniently – gripping me, her tone firm. She turned to Crane: 'Mind if I steal her? I'll bring her back.'

'Of course, no theft necessary. Go dance . . .' he said, smiling casually, jostled slightly by the sea of students around him. It didn't matter. I knew I'd find him again, or he would find me.

'There was something about the way he was talking to you,' Amanda shouted in the direction of my ear. 'Everything OK? He's not being . . . inappropriate?'

'No, nothing like that,' I said. 'Nothing like that at all.'

I'm not sure she believed me, but it didn't matter. If Amanda came forward at some point in the future to speak about her suspicions on the night of the Barrister's Ball, then all to the good. I just couldn't have her intervening now, at this crucial moment.

I stood on the dance floor, shook my hips around for a while, and then, when a reasonable amount of time had passed, I said I was going to get a drink.

It was time.

Chapter Twenty-Seven

The DJ in the corner was playing 'Hot in Herre' by Nelly, and the Great Hall had, indeed, become very hot by then. The room was packed, more attendees arriving than the space could accommodate. I ran my hand through my frizzing hair and wondered where they could all be coming from.

Dancing and giggling and drinking around me, my fellow students appeared almost childlike now – impossibly innocent. They were experiencing the event exactly as it was presented, an evening to celebrate the end of term with classmates and professors. I had buried myself so deep within my ruse that I almost laughed at the simplicity of the scene, my world diverging bitterly from theirs as I moved past them, hunting for Crane.

To get to the other side of the room, I pressed further onto the dance floor, other people's sweat dripping down my arm. I stopped to orient myself and calm my nerves, while two students twerked against a marble pillar next to me, their friend recording the moment on her phone while she cheered them on.

As if out of nowhere, there was Charlie. His hand was extending through the crowd, pulling me towards him until my body was against his. 'Mooney, you fucking legend.' He was laughing into my ear. 'You're my hero, Mooney, you know that?'

I'm not sure what I had done to gain hero status in his eyes and, at the risk of stating the obvious, let me say that he was drunk. I looked him over, wondering if he could still be the reliable witness I needed. A ripple of nerves spread through the waters of my stomach.

I peeled his fingers from around my waist and watched his eyes. 'Charlie, how pissed are you?'

'Oh, man, Mooney, I'm so fucking wasted right now. Like, *really* wasted, I swear to God.' His mouth was against my cheek in what I can only describe as a sort of slobbering action. 'You look fucking hot, Mooney, you know that?'

'Ah, stop, Charlie. Don't get any ideas,' I said, slapping his arm. 'I need you to do something for me later. OK? Are you listening to me?'

'What?!' he shouted into my face. I winced as the sound barrelled my eardrum.

Leaning in closer, I spoke directly into his ear: 'Duke, this is *really* important.' His eyes were on me, a sudden seriousness entering them, as if he were trying hard to listen. 'Crane wants us to meet him, OK?'

He nodded slowly in the exaggerated manner of a drunk person attempting to seem sober.

'Crane wants to see us. He needs to tell us something important.' I gripped his arm tightly. 'Not now, Charlie, do you understand? I'll text you when he's ready, OK? Where's your phone? Do you have your phone?'

I had chosen Charlie as my witness for good reason. There was nobody else with his credibility, his family legacy, or his family's politics, who would also tell the truth when I asked him to. He had the unique advantage of being someone I thought I could trust, who people in positions of power would also believe. I had worked through all the possible outcomes, strategized every move, calculated the chances of failure. If I was going to succeed, it had to be Charlie Duke.

He looked at me, confused, as he rooted in his pocket. 'What's he want us for, Jess? I don't understand.' He produced his phone, holding it up for me.

I let a smile dance across my face, so that he wouldn't worry, so that he wouldn't try to follow me. It would be too soon. My fingers traced through his hair, the waves of soft blonde that gathered at the back of his head. My movements were gentle, soothing. Events needed to unfold exactly as I had planned them.

'He wants to see his favourites,' I said. 'Come when I text you, OK?'

Charlie nodded, and though he tried to ask more questions, I didn't let him, pushing the creeping doubt back down, and slipping away in search of Crane.

Dean Thompson was chatting to Professor Grouse by one of the exits. Vera was hovering near them, trying to insert herself into the conversation. She never did miss an opportunity.

I made my way towards the bar, and that's when he appeared through the mist of bodies. He didn't spot me at first, his eyes on the room, jumping from woman to woman, checking to see who might be watching him too.

'There you are,' I said as I reached him, speaking as if my heart was not in my throat.

'You were looking for me?' Crane replied. 'I was afraid you'd be sick of me by now. But seems we can't get enough of each other . . .' He smiled. 'Can we?'

'Oh, I'm not sure I could ever get enough of you,' I said. And it was true, just not in the way he meant it. It felt as if I could play this game forever, in a perpetual state of pregnant fervour, when victory could still be absolute, justice in the process of manifestation, like a liquid substance slowly crystallising around us, trapping him within it. But it was time for this to end.

He didn't seem to know how to respond, taking his time to drink his wine. Finally he shook his head, and stepped closer. 'Honestly, Jessica, what are we going to do with you?'

'What do you mean?' I asked coyly.

'You keep walking straight into danger.'

'Do I? Are you dangerous, Professor?'

'You know I am.'

I looked at him, feeling as if I might at any second hear the truth from his mouth.

Crane inched another step towards me so that I could feel the heat of his body through his tuxedo. 'You keep pushing me, Jessica. Testing me.'

'Testing you? No.'

'Then, what are you doing? What is all this?'

'You know what it is. You feel it too.'

He was straining against himself, against his instincts. 'I swear to God, Jess. You'll be the death of me.'

He was exactly where I needed him.

'Jay . . .' I let my voice drop, my breath rasping across my vocal cords. 'Can we go somewhere quiet? Somewhere we can talk? About all this?'

It was easy to make the suggestion because I knew he would agree.

'All right.' He set his glass down on the nearest surface, next to a marble bust of some judge or other. 'Where do you want to go? Outside? Some air, maybe?'

'No. Your office,' I said. My eyes spoke, making promises, possibility blooming. It was now or never: it had to be now.

Crane hesitated, his gaze flitting from my face to the spot where Dean Thompson, Professor Grouse, and the rest of the faculty had congregated. I took a final step forward, until my body was against his, until the fabric of Audrey's dress touched against Crane, as it had done the night he betrayed her.

I rose up towards his ear. 'Come on,' I whispered. 'Come with me. I need to show you something.'

Crane glanced back towards his colleagues, then followed me around the side of the dance floor, hugging the walls, skulking behind me, until we reached the stairs off the Great Hall.

It was beginning, this moment I had dreamed of, over the years of planning, justice about to unfold, the tables turning against Crane. From the instant Chloe had told me what she knew, I had wondered if I could find a way – if it were even possible – to strike back against this man who had violated my sister. Those who knew Audrey, those of us who had witnessed her pain, would not doubt what Chloe had to say. But, with Audrey gone, Chloe's word would never be enough to convince the broader world of what Crane had done. It was worse than a case of 'he said, she said', because *she* was dead and gone. Chloe's account was hearsay, and I was not willing to pin all my hopes on the opinions of strangers. Neither could I leave it open to public opinion, which was more likely to doubt than to believe. It's a hostile world for a woman who speaks out against a man. And who was I against someone of Crane's stature? Who was I, but a hysterical girl, wracked with grief for her sister?

To be believed, I would have to show proof, and I was on the stairs now with Crane, about to create the final, vital piece of it.

We climbed without looking back, and it felt as if I were walking him to his fate, as if three monstrous Furies were waiting in his office. I would make justice for Audrey, or have my revenge. I wasn't sure there was a difference anymore.

Chapter Twenty-Eight

A calm descended as the noise in the Great Hall faded behind us. We were moving slowly down the faculty corridor now, as if savouring the illegitimacy of what was about to happen, the great moral wrongs about to occur. A different wrong for each of us. But, if I pulled this off, the two wrongs would together make a right. I had no doubt about that.

Crane's office door was locked. While he fumbled in his pocket for the key, I sent a quick text to Charlie.

Jessica Mooney (23.44):

Come up to Crane's office! He wants a drink with his favourites. There's something he wants to tell us.

He would come. I had to believe that.

The key turned in the lock, and the door sprung open. I trailed Crane inside as he flicked on the light, then stretched over my head to shut the door behind me. Before he could close it, I pushed him forcefully towards his desk, my mouth on his. My hands were on the lapels of his tuxedo, turning around and dragging him down on top of me, so that my back was pressed against his desk.

'Wow, OK, wait.' He drew back and took a moment to catch his breath. His fingers were on my face, brushing my hair from my cheek as he looked me over, as if unsure that I were real.

Did he see Audrey? Did he recognise the dress, the ghost of another fateful night?

'What did you want to show me?' he asked.

I sensed that he was buying time, that he was trying to pull himself together, back from the brink. He had been so much more cautious with me than he had been with Audrey. Because here, in Philadelphia, he was living the life that he might lose, without the anonymity of a distant city. Here, he went home to his wife at night. I could understand his hesitancy, but it was obstructing me.

'Give me a second,' I said, grabbing my phone from my clutch again. I lifted it to take a selfie with him. 'Come here . . . I want something to remember this night.'

'Are you kidding me?' he asked, twisting away from the screen. 'No photos, Jess!'

'Right.' I glanced at my phone to check for a reply from Charlie. Still nothing. Where was he? 'You're right . . . you could get in trouble.'

'You forgot?' Crane said, a hand now on his face. It's possible I had misjudged his level of intoxication, or else I was causing him to sober up in a hurry. 'That's the kind of talk that worries me. I can't take *any* chances here. In fact, honestly, we really shouldn't be here. You can't . . . you can't be here.'

'Wait, Jay. Don't freak out.' I held his cheek in my hand. 'Look, it's just us. There's nothing to worry about. Nobody needs to know.'

He gave a weak laugh. 'You know, the thing that pisses me off about this whole situation is the idea that I'm the one with the power here. I mean, look at you. *Look* at you. You're the one with *all* the power – but *I* could get fired.' He shook his head, rueful. 'Can you imagine how that feels? You could literally make or break me right now – that's the power you have.' He turned away and I knew I was losing him. He was slipping out of my grasp, his reason – or maybe his fear – conquering his worst instincts. I couldn't allow that to happen.

On the desk next to me, my phone screen lit up. A text from Charlie. Finally. I couldn't read it, but I was pretty sure it meant he had seen my message and was hopefully on his way.

'What am I doing?! I *love* my wife. I really do,' Crane said, one hand on his hip, the other extended into the air. He kept saying it, as if repetition might help him to remember it, as if the thought of Leyna might rescue him from the parts of himself that had preyed on my sister. 'And yet, here I am ... with you ... unable to stop myself. I'm risking everything for you.'

I tried very hard not to scoff, not to laugh until I cried at the idea that I was the one with the power, that he was so weak, so enfeebled by attraction and lust that he was not capable of choice. The Furies flickered in my mind again, the ways the law failed women, the class where Crane had *agreed* with me. Where was that man now?

'I get it ... I do,' I said, mostly to shut him up, taking his hand in mine and holding it tentatively. If I was right, Charlie was due any minute. If this was going to happen – if the set-up was going to work – I needed Charlie to walk into the room and see me with Crane, in as compromising a position as possible. Then I would go to Charlie and fill in the blanks, telling him what he had seen was not consensual, just like the night of the Law Ball, when Crane had raped my sister. Good old dependable Charlie: a Duke, with a strong pedigree and a bright political future. He was no feminist, no ally, and he would be believed.

Crane's fingers tightened around mine as he closed the narrow space between our bodies. 'Jessie . . .' he breathed.

I looked from the door to my professor. 'I brought you here to show you something,' I said, taking hold of my sister's dress with my free hand and raising it up past my knee, past my thigh, until my hip was exposed to the light. On it was a curled snake. A tattoo. I had put it here for this moment. 'It's the serpent,' I said. 'From *Paradise Lost*. You . . . you inspired me, Jay.'

He bent down to get a good view and his hand gripped my upper thigh. I could hardly breathe. This was it. Now. All I needed was for Charlie to show up.

Crane's fingers pressed into the pinkish skin, making dents in the soft flesh of my leg while he studied the snake on my hip. 'Wow, this is . . . this is really something. I've had students say that I've inspired them before, but I don't think anyone has ever tattooed themselves. Truly, you are unique, Jessica Mooney.'

At last, his eyes met mine, and I observed a change in him, a shift. It wasn't exactly predatory, but I could see now what I hadn't been able to see before. How the Crane that I knew in the classroom could become the Crane who pursued my sister and wouldn't take no for an answer.

The next thing I knew, his hand had moved from my leg to my hip. I froze. I had thought about it so many times – when my trap would finally snap around him – but, somehow, I had forgotten that I would still have to live it. I had mistaken my thoughts for reality, my expectations for experience.

The sensation of his fingers approaching the fabric of my underwear sent a sharp bullet of regret through my insides. I hadn't realised until now how my whole self – mind, body, soul – would recoil, how my skin would feel as if it were peeling away from the flesh, and the flesh from the bone, while the knot in the very centre of my chest seemed to grow and tighten until it forced the breath from my lungs.

'Stop.'

My hand gripped Crane's arm, his eyes flashing upwards as I pushed him forcefully away before he could reach beneath the fabric.

I tugged my dress down, snatched my clutch and threw my phone into it.

'Wait, Jess – where are you going? What is this? What's happening here?' Crane said, panic beginning to rise. The change in me had caught him off guard, just as the change in him had done to me.

'Jessica!' he said, more loudly, and this time he grabbed at my arm. 'What happened? What did I do? You were all over me a minute ago – now, you're running away? You can't just *leave* like this.'

I pulled away, turning over on my ankle so that the heel of my shoe buckled and nearly snapped. I fell into the wall beside me and shrank from him again, making myself small.

'Jess, answer me!' The anger in his voice was nothing I had heard in him before. 'A minute ago it was fuck-me-eyes and snake tattoos. Now you're racing out of here as if I did something wrong?!'

'You did do something wrong,' I managed to say as I righted myself and grasped the door, my hand heavy on the handle. 'Just not to me.' The door swung open further and I ran through it.

Chapter Twenty-Nine

At the top of the stairs, I ran straight into Vera, my body slamming into hers with such force that I nearly sent us both toppling over.

'Wow, Jessie, Jesus . . . where are you going?!' she said, holding onto me so we both stayed upright. Charlie was coming up behind her. 'I ran into Charlie. He was mumbling something about you and Crane's office so I—' She stopped and examined me with fresh worry now.

I couldn't look at either of them, my eyes on the marble floor, my breath catching in my throat.

'Wait, hey . . .' Vera's voice softened. Her hands cupped my bare shoulders. 'Are you crying?'

I swiped under my eyes, a black streak of mascara smearing across my fingers. 'Can you just get me out of here? Quickly? Please?'

'Yes, Jessie, of course . . .' With her thumbs, she wiped away the tears and mascara, her touch so gentle that I almost cried again.

Charlie had just made it up the last few steps. 'What's going on?' he said. 'Where's Crane?'

There was a silence. I glanced back towards his office, hoping I wouldn't need to vocalise it. Vera's hair was pinned into a neat updo behind her head, her eyes beautifully dark, and in them, I found understanding. Comprehension.

I didn't need to say anything further. Vera switched, immediately, into action. 'Come on, Charlie,' she said, turning to him. 'We're going back downstairs.'

I knew from the way he was staring at me that he could tell something was up, but Charlie had the tact not to demand explanations. He trailed behind us, still a little drunk but sobering up fast, as Vera gripped me tight and walked me down the stairs.

As we reached the Great Hall, I dabbed at any lingering tears with the back of my hand. My plan had failed, all my work now in tatters around me, with no way of salvaging it. Now, Crane would have his guard up too. I had put him on alert.

The fastest way out of the building was through the crowd, the music, and the noise in the Great Hall. But the last thing I needed was for someone else to spot me now. Not like this.

With my head down, Vera leading the way, we moved towards the exit. At the cloakroom, I handed my ticket to the attendant. Faintly, I could hear someone calling our names. I pulled my coat on and pretended not to hear.

'Wait! Where are you guys going?' It was Amanda, heading towards us.

'Just go,' Vera said quietly to me, pointing towards the exit. 'I'll tell her you're feeling sick and meet you out there.' She stepped away, forming a human barrier between me and the rest of the law school as Charlie and I made for the door.

Out on 34th Street, we stood on the steps next to some smokers while I zipped my coat up over my dress. Mounds of snow lined the footpath, melting into sludge at the edges, white becoming muddy grey. Our breaths were wet on the cold air, and I watched the vapour cool and then dissipate, wishing I could do the same.

Charlie was unusually quiet, his arms wrapped around his body, but he was looking at me steadily.

'Please don't ask,' I said softly, refusing to meet his eye.

He considered me silently, seeing me as I never wanted to be seen, in a moment of pure vulnerability, but he didn't say a word.

The door opened, and Vera emerged. 'All right,' she said, shivering as the cold hit her. 'Do you want me to walk you home?'

'Charlie's going to take me,' I said, nodding towards him.

Charlie's company was simple. Anyone else would have probed for information, alive to the possibility of bad intent, of predation, of something rotten occurring inside that office. But though Charlie could tell that something was wrong, he didn't seem to need to confront it. It made his presence an easy, uncomplicated thing.

Vera's gaze travelled back and forth between us. In the end, she fixed on me. 'Jessie . . . I have to ask you. In Crane's office . . . Did anything—'

I knew what she was about to say, so I cut her off. 'It's not what you're thinking,' I said. 'You don't need to worry, Vera, I . . . I'll explain, I promise. Just not right now.' His crime was against my sister. I had stopped him before he got that far with me.

Vera's body relaxed. 'Oh thank God,' she whispered. 'I thought—'

'I know,' I said, the cold sharp against my skin, seeping in through the pores, making ice of my blood. 'Look, I'll fill you in tomorrow – I promise – I just . . . I just need to get home.'

'Sure, right,' Vera replied. 'Go home. We can speak tomorrow.'

She stayed on the top step while Charlie put his arm over my shoulders and led the way towards my dorm. I waved back at her as we turned out of sight, but I didn't see Vera go inside again. I'm not sure she did.

It was only a five-minute walk from the law school, though it felt longer that night. Audrey's shoes grated against the skin of my heels, my flesh raw and blistered.

It was stupid to come to Franklin, stupid to think I could somehow beat the odds, outwit the Fates, outmanoeuvre a man in power, change the meaningless nature of my sister's suffering and death and give it a purpose. Maybe I'd just leave. Maybe, in the morning, I'd just pack up my things and leave.

'You need your student card,' I said to Charlie as we reached the steps to my dorm. 'You need to show it to the security guard.'

He attempted to fish it out of his wallet, then dropped it on the ground, the alcohol still in his system making butter of his fingers. When finally he had it in hand, we both displayed our cards to the security guard, who pushed the button to give us entry. In the lift, Charlie leaned against the mirrored wall, observing me wordlessly, a thousand questions visible in his eyes. I rested my chin against my chest, burrowing myself deeper into my coat, revealing nothing.

At the kitchenette next to my room, I angled my head under the tap and let the water pour into my mouth. It dribbled along my chin and down my neck. Cupping my hands, I splashed more onto my face, cold against my skin.

Charlie was already lying on my bed when I went into my room, his tux jacket in a heap on the floor. 'Everything's spinning,' he said. 'I . . . don't feel so good.'

I unzipped my dress and draped it over the back of my desk chair, then pulled an old T-shirt over my head. Charlie's eyes were shut, his hair slipping across the smooth dome of his forehead. I hauled his shoes off his feet while he grunted a complaint, and tossed them onto the floor once I had leveraged the leather over the curve of his heel.

'Move over,' I said, as I climbed onto the bed next to him and covered us with the duvet. He was almost asleep, his mouth hanging open, his hot breath on my nose and cheeks.

I turned my back to him and stared at the dark wall. After a moment, his arm reached around me. I thought about batting it away but instead let my body relax, easing deeper into the bed until I was pressed up against him, his warmth becoming my warmth, his breath my breath, his slumbering peace slowly trickling into me.

I shut my eyes and the half-death of sleep quickly took me.

Chapter Thirty

Light pierced through the thin curtains and stung my dry eyes even before I opened them. I had slept very little, waking often throughout the night.

I sat up in bed and found Charlie staring at me, cross-legged at the other end, as if he had been waiting.

'What time is it?' I asked, throat raw and raspy. It felt early, much too early to be awake again.

'It's just after six,' Charlie said. He leaned his back against the wall, his expression that of the future politician again, a pensive, serious quality shining through his hangover. Only the circles under his eyes and the mess of his blonde hair gave him away.

'How are you feeling?' I said, shifting forward to rest on my elbow.

'I'm fine.' He scratched the dishevelled hair at the back of his head. 'You?'

'OK, I guess,' I replied. 'You need some water?'

'No.' His jaw tensed, and he squinted slightly. 'I just ... I need to ask. Are you going to start telling me the truth now, Jessie?'

My stomach did a tumble. And then another. 'Wh-what do you mean?'

He was staring straight ahead. I followed the path to the wall opposite, to the corkboard over my desk and, on it, directly at eye level, the photo of Audrey and Crane.

'It's the same dress,' he said, pointing at the silver dress hanging guiltily from the back of the chair, where I had left it the night before.

The photograph had been so far from my mind. It had never occurred to me, when I pinned it there, that Charlie – or anyone – would ever be here to see it. Next to it, my map of campus. On the desk, the black notebook.

'She's wearing the same dress,' Charlie continued. 'In the photo . . . the girl with Professor Crane.'

I shut my eyes tightly, letting my head fall into my hands.

'That's the girl he was talking about, right? The girl Crane knew in Dublin? That's the girl with your surname? It was something Mooney . . .'

'Audrey Mooney-Flynn,' I said quietly. There was no point lying to him now.

'Who is she?' he asked.

I lifted my face. 'My sister.'

He was still gazing at her image, Audrey smiling back at him. 'And you lied about knowing her because . . .?'

'Because if Crane knew why I was really here, I'd never be able to expose what he did. He'd get away with it.'

Charlie's tanned skin was now wan. 'Get away with *what?*'

I pulled my knees to my chest. 'They had an affair when he was in Dublin.' It felt so strange to say it aloud. 'And then, one night, they had an argument.' I met his eye. 'She was angry with him, and didn't want to sleep with him, but Crane told her she was being stubborn. He wouldn't take no for an answer. He said he knew her mind better than she did . . . And he, he, he . . .' I paused, taking a breath to stop my equivocations. 'He forced himself on her. Crane raped my sister.'

199

The word, its meaning, was so large, so grotesque, that it seemed to swell and fill the room.

I watched the information sink in slowly. 'No . . . he . . . Wait, seriously?! You *think* or . . .'

'I know he did,' I said. 'He raped my sister.'

My head rested against my knees as Charlie tried to make sense of what I had just told him. I wished it wasn't true, wished I had never come here, wished it hadn't been necessary, wished Audrey was alive in Dublin, was as she had been before.

'So, wait, last night . . .' Charlie asked, the mattress bending under him as he turned his body to face me. 'Did he . . . did Crane . . . Wait. What exactly happened? Did he *do* something to you?'

Unburdening myself to Charlie was, to my great surprise, not as hard as I would have thought. 'I had a plan. I was going to create the evidence that didn't exist for Audrey, all the pieces of the story that were lost when she died. I was going to set him up and say that he had done to me what he did to her. That way, I could report him, and he would be punished for that crime, for what I *know* he did to my sister. It's why I texted you to meet us at his office. I was going to make it look really bad for him, so that when you walked in, you'd think you caught him in the act. You were going to be my star witness. You were going to be the person who backed me up.' My voice broke. 'It was the only way, Charlie . . . it . . . it was the only option open to me.'

Charlie was completely still, not a whisper of a reaction in his face or body.

'But then . . . when Crane reached up my dress, I—' My lip was shaking. 'I thought I'd be able to just suck it up for a second and that you'd be there before anything could actually happen, but I . . .' I didn't finish the sentence. I couldn't describe the feeling to him. It didn't sound right when I tried to put it into words. He stayed quiet for a few beats longer, but I couldn't bear the silence. 'Charlie, do you think I'm a bad person?'

He was pensive. 'A bad person? No,' he said, then added in a low tone, 'not exactly.' He edged closer, his hand cupping my cheek, his thumb reaching upwards to dry the tears now falling. 'You're definitely a little bit terrifying,' he said, his blue eyes clear as water. 'But your sister, is she OK?' he asked gently. 'Audrey?'

'No. She—'The sound caught. I closed my eyes. 'She's dead.'

His hand fell from my face. 'Oh, I . . . I'm so sorry. Jessie, I . . . I don't know what to say.'

'You don't need to say anything.' I looked across at the image of Audrey pinned to the corkboard. 'I didn't know it happened until after she died – her and Crane. She kept it a secret. She carried it around with her all those months, trying to deal with it on her own. But she was never the same, Charlie. He broke her into pieces.'

'God, Jessie. I'm . . . I'm so sorry.' He gathered me into his arms, my head resting just under his chin. Despite the booze, and sweat, and yesterday's clothes, he smelled clean and fresh somehow, as if none of it could stick to his perfect skin.

I wished I could feel that clean.

'So, then,' Charlie said, pulling away and dangling his feet over the side of the bed. 'This whole time? You've been hiding this?'

I nodded slowly. With a glance upwards, I saw the contorted expression, the confusion making a mess of his handsome face.

'Are you angry with me?' I asked quietly, knowing the answer.

I could tell from his vacant stare, directed at the wall behind me, that Charlie's mind was racing ahead of him, calculating, adjusting, processing. 'Why lie to me? Why didn't you just tell me what you were planning?'

'I thought if . . .' I hesitated, a wave of shame knocking the breath from my lungs. 'If you'd thought you caught Crane in the act, you wouldn't have to lie. You could just . . . you could just honestly say what you saw.' I didn't tell him that I had kept my plan from him until now because I wasn't sure I could trust him with it.

He murmured something in response that I didn't quite catch.

'I'm sorry,' I said. 'I'm so sorry, Charlie, I . . . I thought it would be better if you really believed it, because then you . . . you . . . you wouldn't have to perjure yourself.'

'And now?' He was looking at the photo of Audrey and Crane again. 'What do you want me to do now?'

'Nothing. I mean . . . I can't ask you to . . . God, I've . . . I've made a mess of this. I'm sorry. I'm so sorry.' My fingernails clawed through my hair, raking at my scalp.

He tugged my hands away and held them. 'Stop,' he said. 'Just stop . . . Enough, Jess.'

He rocked me tenderly, and I sank into the deepest tiredness. All the months of duplicity, the years of rage and grief, carrying me to this point in time.

'What should we do with you, Jessie? What should we do now?' he whispered into my hair.

I tried to steady myself, wondering the same thing, but I had never planned for failure, never allowed the possibility to form in my mind.

'You know, you should tell Vera. She can help you.' Charlie sniffed, wiggling his nose. 'I mean, she knows there are rumours about Crane already and there was this thing that happened to her in our first year at Franklin. I don't know all the details, but Vera knows what she's doing. She'll be able to help you because I . . .'

'I understand,' I said, not making him say it out loud. 'I get it. I'll talk to Vera.'

But I couldn't imagine opening up to Vera like this. It was easier with Charlie because he didn't judge. Joshua had once described him as an agent of chaos, and I knew now what he meant by that: Charlie didn't abide by any creed or ideology, just his own self-interest. It made him a little unpredictable, sure, but also open-minded, and more tolerant of others than you might think when you first met him.

'I wish things were different. I mean, I wish I could help.' He paused, before a sharp burst of anger escaped. 'Fuck Crane, right? All that *Dead Poets Society* shit and the whole time he's a rapey fucking piece of shit?' His handsome face was a mask of anger, disappointment, and maybe even shame that he had once admired a man like that. 'But . . . I can't, I can't get wrapped up in this. I'm not *mad* at you exactly, Jess – you had your reasons, and I can respect them – but you did lie to me. You used me from the start. Our friendship was a means to an end for you.'

'No, I . . .' I shook my head. 'We *are* friends, Charlie.'

'Stop, Jessie, don't . . .' He shifted backwards from me. 'Friends don't use friends like this. You know that.'

He was right. Of course, he was right. But I still felt let down that he couldn't see beyond that to the bigger goal. Is that fair? I'm not sure, but it's how I felt.

'Look,' he said, his voice softer now. 'Whatever happens, Jessie, I'm rooting for you. But you know why I can't get involved in this.'

I did. Charlie would always put himself first. Then again, I was in no position to criticise him for that. My reasons might have been righteous, but since the moment I'd arrived in Philadelphia, I had done the same.

'I'm sorry I lied to you, Charlie,' I said again, studying the diamond-patterned duvet under me to avoid meeting his eye.

He released a small, tired laugh. 'You know, I really can't

believe you did this. The plotting, the lies ... you're doing a whole fucking *master's*, just to get to Crane.' He shook his head. 'It's brilliant, but, I mean ... completely terrifying, Mooney.'

'It's justice, Charlie.'

He was silent again, then pushed himself onto his feet and began hunting for his shoes. 'You know, in a way, I think Crane would be proud of you.'

I looked across at our professor's face in the photograph on the board, smiling next to Audrey.

'He taught you well,' Charlie said, as he shoved his feet into his shoes and searched for his tux jacket.

Charlie's observation reminded me of something Crane had said on election night. I had asked him about the boundary between right and wrong, asked who would punish us, if we were guilty.

'Whoever can,' came his reply.

Crane was guilty and deserved punishment for what he did to my sister. Audrey couldn't punish him, so I stepped forward to do it in her place. But when the moment finally arrived, when the idea became reality, I couldn't act.

My sister never told me what happened on the night of the Law Ball. She had deliberately chosen to keep me in the dark. When I asked Chloe why, she seemed to think it was Audrey's way of protecting me, as if knowledge of the crime were a virus that could infect me too.

But though there might have been some truth to that, I didn't find Chloe's explanation complete. It was a doubt I hadn't been able to shake, haunting my days at Franklin, lingering at the back of my mind, and at the edges of my thoughts. It came sneaking into my mind again now.

What if Audrey hadn't told me what happened precisely because she knew what I would do?

Chapter Thirty-One

After Charlie left, I tried to sleep again, bone-tired. But my mind would not rest, combing over all that had happened, as if answers might emerge for what I should do next. Through the thin curtains across my window, light shone, the day progressing, though I remained where I was, unable, or unwilling, to move.

Vera texted to say she was on campus if I wanted to talk. I needed to come clean, but the thought of admitting it all to Vera made me feel queasy.

I dragged myself into the shower and turned the valve until the water was so hot that it painted my skin a flaming red. I scrubbed the memory of the previous night off my body as best I could, then dressed quickly, tugging on a cable-knit jumper and black jeans, followed by thick-soled boots.

I sat on the edge of my bed, my finger tapping the metal bedframe. I couldn't prove Crane's guilt in a court of law, but all around me was evidence of a relationship between us. There was still a way I could hit him where it hurt. His reputation, his standing, his illustrious career.

Vera was waiting for me in the Franklin Bookstore opposite my building. I trudged along the pavement, newly cleared of snow, grit crunching underfoot. The sky remained entirely white, as if the clouds had sucked all colour from the world and trapped us in an empty space, a blank abyss.

Inside, the bookstore was warm and decorated for Christmas, garlands strung over bookshelves, tinsel wound around hand-rails. Carols played from the speakers and, on tables covered in Franklin University merchandise, there were prompts to remember the special people in your life with mugs, hats, and little flags bearing the Franklin crest.

The escalator carried me upwards to the café, where Vera sat at the window, one hand wrapped around a very large steaming mug of coffee. 'Jessie,' she said, looking up as I arrived at the table. 'How are you?'

I sat down across from her, eyes bloodshot, skin dry, expression grave. 'I'm fine,' I said. And then, before she could say anything, or I could shut down again, I opened up completely. I told Vera what had happened with Crane in his office, what I had done to bring us to that point, just as I had told Charlie. The full, ugly truth.

Vera listened carefully, her hands in her lap, while 'Jingle Bell Rock' played incongruously in the background. When, at length, I had finished, she took a breath, shook her head, and said: 'My goodness, Jessica.'

I watched the thoughts flash across her face, the pieces com-ing together, Jessica Mooney finally making some sense, even if it involved untangling a twisted knot of lies, of virtue and vice, angel and devil, to see me as I really was.

'I *knew* there was something up with you.' Vera paused. 'Now, I know.'

'Now, you know,' I echoed, nervous.

She seemed to teeter on the brink of words that wouldn't form, one thought overtaking another before she could voice it. I felt as if I sat before a jury of one.

'Well?' I eventually asked, prompting her when patience ran out. 'Go on. Tell me what you think of me.'

Her chin, which was a little pointed at the tip, jutted in my direction. 'Does it matter?' she asked. 'Does it matter what I – or anybody else – thinks of you, Jessie?'

It never used to matter to me, not when I was wrapped up tight within the comfort of my saviour complex. But I was exposed to the cold air now, and tired of being alone, tired of pushing everyone away, locking myself into perpetual loneliness.

'I guess it depends,' I said. 'Some opinions matter. Yours matters.' It was true, I realised, because I admired Vera's integrity and was, in that moment, questioning my own.

Vera raised her coffee, sipping cautiously so as not to burn her tongue. 'It shouldn't,' she said firmly. 'Your strength comes from your independence of thought, Jessica, and that is something I hope you never lose.'

I smiled sadly, not feeling so strong anymore.

'I'm sorry about your sister.' Vera took another sip.

'Thank you,' I replied, automatically, the thought of Audrey too raw.

'It's not the same, but I, um, I . . . I understand the impulse . . . the anger.' Vera pursed her lips, staring down at the black steaming surface of her coffee. 'I was dating this guy my first year at Franklin and he, um, he took a photo of me without my knowledge. You know, not entirely clothed.' She shifted in the chair to find a more comfortable position. 'He shared it with his friends . . . I don't know how many people. I didn't even know about it, not until a mutual acquaintance told me she had seen it.' She met my eye. 'I was just walking around campus obliviously and, all the while, total strangers were sharing that photo of me. And nobody mentioned it to me. Just this one girl I didn't even know that well.'

'Jesus Christ . . .'

'Right?'

'Scumbag.'

'Yeah.'

'Who was it?' I asked. 'Is he still in the law school?'

'He wasn't a law student.' The memory drew a frown across her brow. 'I reported him, and the university investigated. They suspended him in the end, but only because the girl who told me about it confirmed that she had seen the photo. It was the only corroborating evidence I could get. Nobody else would speak up and the university wasn't exactly issuing subpoenas, you know? So, I don't like what you've been doing, Jessie, but I can understand it.'

I nodded. 'They don't leave us much choice. It's fight back, or else live in a world where the bad guy constantly wins.'

'I hear you.'

'Do you?' My knee bobbed restlessly under the table, anxiety pulsing in the unseen space between us. 'The thing is, Vera, there's a reason I'm telling you this.'

She sat up a little straighter. 'Oh?'

'I may need your help.'

'Jessica . . .' She tutted – once, sharply – then turned to the window. 'I . . . I really don't know about that. I'm not . . . I'm not exactly *keen* on your plan.'

'I'm changing the plan.'

The second I had stopped Crane's advance, the old plan had dismantled around me, the structure cracking, breaking, falling apart, like pieces of old plaster. But it was more than that, more than just the bare logistics. When the time came, my hand around the knife, the blade at his throat, I couldn't strike. In the end, when it mattered, I was not as ruthless as I had imagined. In the end, I was not like Crane at all.

Vera sucked air in through her nose, nostrils widening. 'This new plan ... will it be legal?' she asked, in such a serious tone that, somehow, I found myself laughing.

I had purposefully maintained a low profile, but, at Franklin, Vera was queen. The thing is, you couldn't swing a cat at Franklin Law without hitting an overachieving, resumé-filling striver, but Vera was a different fish. She also managed to party with the best of them, rarely missing an opportunity to blow off a little steam. Never missed a night of Bar Review and attended every birthday party like a politician seeking votes.

All of this meant that Vera was in good standing with both of the important constituencies – those who tried hard and those who partied hard.

'Yes,' I said. 'Look, I can't ever prove what happened to Audrey, but maybe I can still show how he abuses his power over his students. There has already been at least one complaint before this, so we know there's a pattern. Maybe this time, if I tell Dean Thompson what Crane has been doing with me, it'll be different. I have evidence – loads of evidence – but it's no good if people don't know about it ... people have to know about the complaint this time so, no matter what else happens, Crane is exposed. I need you to help me get the word out about him.' I hesitated. It felt so small, not nearly the justice Audrey deserved. Yet there were few options left open to me, and this one was the most honest. A full attack on Crane's reputation and standing, the tool he used to create his favourites. 'It's not ... it's not enough, Vera, but I can still hurt him this way. And I can stop him doing it again.'

Vera remained unconvinced.

'If I go public, he'll fight me. I'm going to need pressure ... like, vocal public support.' I sighed, cocking my head to one side. 'Come on ... you can trust me.'

She gave me a beady eye. 'That remains to be seen, Jessie.'

A smile rose and quickly fell from my face. 'He can't get away with this, Vera.'

'On that, we can agree.' Her finger slid over the ceramic rim of her cup. 'But, to be clear, from now on, this is about prevention of future harm – not punishing past crimes with your sister.' Her stare was unyielding. 'Do you understand? You can't tell anyone else what you've just told me, about your . . . revenge quest. Nobody will believe you, for a start. They'll trust you even less if they know the truth of why you're here. So, if I help you, you have to leave what happened to Audrey in the past. I know that's asking a lot, but, from here on, it must be about what we can prove without lies – which is Crane's relationship with you.' She paused. 'Is that enough for you, Jessie? Because there won't be a big day in court, not this way. No handcuffs, no flashing lights. He won't be branded a rapist for what he did to your sister.' Again, she hesitated. 'His reputation will be tainted and the way he treats the women he teaches won't just be the stuff of rumour anymore. But we'll be focusing on protecting students in the future, not seeking revenge for what he did in the past.'

Such a loaded term – revenge. What did it even mean? How did it really differ from justice? Was it just a matter of perspective? Of whose side of the courtroom we sat on? In the end, what mattered more – principle or action?

Through the window, the naked branches of an oak tree stood stark against the white snow clouds. They seemed to me like fingers, pointing my way. I examined every word Vera said, turning it over, making it solid in my mind, trying to determine how I felt about it. She was right to question whether this would be enough. To move forward, I had to leave my sister behind, preserved in a permafrost of memory, lost in a time that was past and over, without the justice I had wanted for her. Could I really do it? Did I even have a choice anymore?

'Does this mean you'll help me?' I asked her.

Vera sat in silent contemplation Eventually, she looked up at me and exhaled. 'Yes. Fine. Fuck it, I'll help you.'

It wasn't exactly a ringing endorsement, more an acceptance that something had to be done. But I'd take it.

I thought of a quote by Ben Franklin that I had seen painted on the wall of the law school.

We must hang together, or surely we shall hang separately.

Chapter Thirty-Two

When you came to me, you were looking for answers and all I have given you is ever greater complexity, fractal as a fern or a snowflake. Justice, vengeance, it had all become warped. When grief lay thick around me, it was so much easier; the lines dividing right from wrong felt sharp. Light blazing on one side and darkness on the other. But now . . .

Now, I found myself flailing. I had been so *certain*, but certainty is, itself, not a solid thing. It is a cliff-face, battered by waves that chip away at the rock, assailed by a ravaging ocean of doubt.

The moment I went to Dean Thompson and made a complaint against Crane, the focus would fall on me, his crime against Audrey fading to nothingness, known only by a handful of people. Before I could do that, I needed to see Crane a final time and confront him about Audrey so I could hear his defence for myself. It is, you see, a principle of justice, the right to know the nature of the charges against you. And I was still aiming for justice. Or, as close as I could get to it.

As it happened, Crane had provided me with the perfect excuse. A big C on my final paper. It was clever, a thoroughly shrewd Crane move. He didn't fail me, because that would provoke me to appeal, at which point, the truth would emerge. Nor could he now be accused of favouritism on the basis of what had passed between us. An 'A+' could have raised eyebrows, even though, for the record, it was absolutely what I deserved.

But while the C was an attempt to cover his tracks, it was also, quite clearly, a warning shot. Our interests were no longer aligned. Crane could read the signs, and he would not go down without a fight. His entry into this next phase of the game was not unexpected, but it made things difficult to predict from that moment on. I wasn't in control of the situation anymore and my opponent was formidable.

Still, I had centuries of female rage on my side.

I doubt he was surprised to receive an email from me requesting a meeting to speak about the grade on my final paper. He replied formally, as professional with me now as when we had begun.

Jay Crane (09.36):

Dear Jessica,

Thank you for your email. My office hours are every Monday and Wednesday from 3–5 p.m. Please attend at a time of your convenience so we can discuss the matter of your grade.

Yours sincerely,

Jay Crane

Oh yes. He could see me coming now.

My insides were a knotted snake during that final week. It was a struggle to eat or sleep. I drifted through the days. At night, through the curtains of my dark room, I watched light flash from the beacon on the roof of the hospital in the distance. It was like a lighthouse, beaming a warning meant just for me. Rocks ahead.

When the time came to meet Crane, I found myself relieved more than anything. Whatever happened, at least I would no longer be locked in this state of dread, of wondering and fearing.

At the appointed hour, I made my way to his office, pausing outside to glance at my phone. The background image on the screen was a picture of me and Audrey. Staring down at my sister – trapped in an image, silent now – I considered what she might think of me.

I reached forward and knocked on the door.

'Come in,' Crane said, his voice elevating my heart rate immediately. This was it.

He was sitting at his desk when I walked in, typing on his laptop. The sight of me stilled his fingers.

'Ah, Jessie,' he said. 'You're finally going to face me.'

I slid into the seat opposite him, Crane ensconced sedately on the powerful side of the desk. How different the scene was from the night of the Barrister's Ball.

'I'm not here to talk about my grade,' I said at once, anxious to be back here again, in this room, with this man.

'I guessed.' Crane closed his laptop and pushed it to the side. 'So ... what are we going to talk about?' He straightened in his chair, his expression very fixed, very disciplined, observing me, as if I were on a witness stand.

'I have a question to ask you,' I said slowly, deliberately. 'And I have a confession to make.'

He paused. 'Oh?'

'Let me start with the question,' I said.

'All right.' He shifted into a more comfortable position, elbows resting on the arms of his chair, hands folded together. 'Go ahead.'

The words escaped on a single breath, finally released into the world. 'What happened between you and Audrey Mooney-Flynn?'

'Ah,' he said, his head falling forward, a slight shake of his shoulders as he laughed quietly. 'I knew it was too much of a coincidence.' He looked up at me again. 'Who is she to you?'

'My sister.'

'I *knew* there was something similar about you two ... but you had me doubting myself.' I waited while he processed this, surprised by his composure. 'And how is Audrey?'

'What do you mean?' I blinked several times.

His brow furrowed, as if sending back the same question. I couldn't believe he was going to make me say it.

'She's dead, Jay ...'

He gave a start. 'What?'

'Wait, you ... you didn't know?'

His shock was written in every line and crease on his face. 'No – I ... I ... I didn't know ... what happened to her?'

I hesitated, unsure if his reaction was genuine. Then again, who would have notified Crane of her death? It had been such an ever-present part of my life for the past two years that it hadn't occurred to me that the news wouldn't have made it back to him.

'It was an accident. A bus crash on a remote road in Guatemala.' I gave him the basics. It was all I could manage. 'The axel broke and the bus toppled down a hillside. Everyone died. Including my sister.' I leaned forward, shifting the conversation away from the source of my pain and towards the cause of my fury. 'The next question you should ask me is what was she doing there? And the answer to that is you, Jay. She was there because of what you did to her.'

He looked at me blankly, then frowned deeply. 'What? What are you saying? I don't . . . I don't understand.'

'You really don't know? She dropped out of university in January of her final year. She never told us why. It was just this sudden change in her. We couldn't get her out of her bedroom, even out of her bed most days. And then from nowhere she announced a plan to go travelling . . . to escape from us. She was going to Central America. Backpacking. Alone.' The memories flooded my mind. 'We got the news from the Guatemalan authorities, five months after she left Dublin. She had been dead days before we knew.'

My lower lip disappeared into my mouth and my jaw clenched. No matter how many times I told this story, no matter how many times life obliged me to recall it, it still felt like a knife to my chest.

'Jesus.' Crane's hand was in front of his face. 'Jessie – I—'

'We didn't understand why she had left . . . she was supposed to be at university, safe and sound, like all of her friends. *What* was she doing on a bus in Guatemala? How did she end up dead in a fucking morgue? She was fine . . . she was completely fine, and then *you* came along.'

I couldn't speak further, my voice breaking apart.

Crane reached for a box of tissues on a shelf behind him. He carried them around the desk and leaned down next to me to offer one.

'Jessie,' he said softly.

'Don't,' I replied, springing away from him. 'Don't try to be kind to me now.'

He stood at once to give me space. 'OK,' he said and moved back to the other side of his desk. 'Whatever you need.'

I took a moment to steady myself, gathering my strength, my anger. 'I need to hear you say what happened to her – what you did. Can you do that? Can you tell me the full truth, as you know it?'

His gaze was level. Slowly, quivering, he inhaled. 'Why would I do that?'

'Because you owe me, Jay. You owe me the truth.'

'I'd like to, Jessie, but you have a gun pointed at my head. How do I know you won't use it against me?'

'It's mutually assured destruction if I do, because I'll tell you the full truth too.'

He examined my face for signs of deception, for lies, though he wouldn't have recognised them if they were there. I knew how to hide from him.

I ran the tissue under my nose. 'This conversation is off the record,' I said. My disclosure was a risk, but one I had to take to get the truth out of him. It was necessary – for Audrey, for me. 'Whatever happens next, we owe each other the truth now. OK? I won't use it against you, and you won't use it against me.' He wouldn't use it against me because he'd have to admit what had happened with Audrey. Besides, the complaint I planned to file against him would be a separate thing. This, right now, was about forcing him to face what he did to my sister, to admit it. I was putting him on trial.

'I understand what you're offering.' He seemed very calm. I'm not sure I could have sat there and withstood the same anger I had seen in him on the night of the Barrister's Ball. 'But you're asking me to trust you when you've been lying to me from the moment we met.'

'You're a liar too . . . or did you tell Leyna about us?'

'Jesus . . .' It was a low, resigned mumble, more of a prayer than he might have realised. 'OK,' he said after a while. 'We can talk now, about Audrey, but I'll deny it later, if I have to, and, well, I don't like to put it like this, but . . . you know who they'll believe.'

'It won't come to that,' I said sniffing a couple of times.

'What do you want to know?' he asked.

'I read Audrey's emails to you,' I began.

'Yes.'

'And her diary entries.'

'OK.'

'She said she was in love with you.'

'She was.'

'Were you in love with her?'

'Maybe, for a while. But in a different way.'

'What does that mean?'

'Audrey was young. She had a very fixed idea of what love means. I think she wanted us to create a life together. Sometimes she'd talk that way . . . she'd say things about places we could go, or jobs she might apply for in New York, or DC, or even Philly. She talked a little about doing a master's here – like you're doing now.'

I squirmed in my seat, briefly imagining again that alternate timeline in which Audrey was here instead of me.

'I encouraged her when I thought they were opportunities that she'd really enjoy. I didn't think either of us *meant* it, but I wasn't exactly keen to confront her with the reality, you know? Because you don't do that in the early days. Do you? It's all plans and hopes and dreams and . . .' He glanced away. 'And I thought she knew that too . . . on some level. She must have, really, because I was always going to leave Dublin at the end of that term . . . and I just . . . I just thought that she *knew* – she must have known – that I was never going to leave my wife.'

Was this why Audrey had not mentioned Leyna in any of their correspondence or in her diary? A determined attempt to ignore her existence?

'I made a mistake with Audrey.' His gaze fell to his hands, the veins of which were prominent. 'It was stupid of me not to confront that difference between us earlier. I overlooked her age, her inexperience—'

'And Leyna?'

'What about her?'

'Does she know?'

He looked at me again. 'She does . . . Audrey wrote her a letter. After it ended.'

My heart began to beat harder.

'What did it say? The letter?'

'It said that Audrey and I were in love and having an affair. It said that I was betraying my wife.'

'That's it?'

'Pretty much.'

'And . . . and did Leyna reply?'

'No. Audrey was the least of her worries. What was there to say to her? She was focused on saving our marriage.' There was pain there, or regret, or perhaps both. He looked down at the desk in front of him.

I forged on. 'What happened on the night of the Law Ball?'

He sat back in his chair, a sigh escaping his lips, his face falling again. Falling and falling. 'Ah . . . the Law Ball.'

This was it. This was the moment of truth.

'You argued . . .' I prompted, knowing well that Crane would try to lead the narrative. He was used to being the teacher, the one in control, doing the talking, while I, the student, listened.

'Yes, we did, briefly. The night of the ball, she was upset about Leyna. She wanted to talk about me leaving my wife. Obviously, I told her I wouldn't do it.' He addressed me directly. 'In hindsight, that was the moment it ended. She was different the next day . . . changed. I tried to apologise afterwards for hurting her, but Audrey didn't want to speak to me.'

I took a breath, bringing to mind everything Chloe had told

me. 'Admit the rest of it, Jay. Confess.' He had moved past that night so completely, to the point that it might as well not have happened. But I needed to hear him admit what he had done. I needed to see him squirm.

He baulked. 'What are you talking about?'

'Audrey didn't want to sleep with you that night, but you weren't listening to her. She tried to say no, but you ignored her,' I said, pressing him, as if I were a lawyer questioning the accused. 'You forced yourself on my sister. You wouldn't stop when she told you to.'

'No! Jesus *Christ*, no! Jessie ... is ... is that what you've been thinking?' He pushed himself back from his desk, the chair rolling until it hit the bookshelves behind him, the spines of the books now atremble. 'Absolutely not, Jessica. How could you ... how could you *think* that of me?'

I didn't respond. I needed to hear how he answered the charge.

Crane ran his fingers over his cheeks, his stubble, then up through his greying hair. He used the edge of his desk to pull his chair towards me until his body met the wood again.

'On the night of the Law Ball, I ...' He stopped, breath catching. 'Well, she ... Audrey was drunk and a little hysterical.' He paused. 'I can't say it, Jessie – I—'

'Say it,' I demanded. 'Say the words. Admit them.'

'Listen, we did have sex that night, but it was *consensual*.' He couldn't look at me. I wished he would. He deserved to see the contempt on my face. 'I swear it was consensual.'

I let him sit in the silence of those words, watching him struggle to continue.

When, after several moments, he didn't speak, I prompted him again. 'And then?'

'And then ... the next morning, Audrey was ... well, I think the reality was dawning that we were over.' His eyes were glassy.

'She was very upset and I hurt her, terribly – I know that – but it wasn't like you're saying.'

I tried to control my anger, crossing my legs, my dangling foot twitching within the leather of my Doc Martens. 'There was no consent, Jay. She didn't want to sleep with you.'

'That's not *true*, Jess. You weren't there! You're making me into someone I'm not – I'm not that sort of guy! Audrey didn't ... She was ... she wasn't saying *no*. Maybe she regretted it afterwards – I don't know – it's not possible to read another person's mind. That's an absurd standard to impose. People aren't lawyers in bed and real life doesn't work like that.'

Somehow, though I knew what he was capable of, it stunned me to hear him spin the situation like that. It was revealing how he separated himself from his academic work, drawing a line between 'real life' and the feminist theory he wrote about. So quick to absent himself from the category of bad men who do bad things. Like so much else in his life, his vision of whether he was guilty turned on his own subjective experience. If he didn't see the nature of the problem, then it didn't exist. And if a definition of consent didn't suit him, then it must be unrealistic.

He was watching me now, misery on his face, overtaken every so often by defiance. My good opinion mattered to him. He still wanted it.

I looked down at my hands, shut my eyes, and saw her face, the sister who had once smiled so easily. He had buried her beneath a pain she carried alone, hoping to preserve us from the horror. And I had not protected her. I could not save her.

'You can keep denying it to yourself, keep telling yourself you're not a bad guy, really, but nothing will change what happened to Audrey. I saw her implode. She—' The words kept catching, but I forced them out. 'She collapsed inside, as if her whole sense of self, everything that made her Audrey – a living, breathing person – was taken from her.'

'No, I . . . I—' He was shaking now, a vein in his forehead pulsing. 'That's not true. Your sister was so unhappy, I—'

'Stop. Stop! *You're* the reason she was unhappy.'

'No, Jessie, I—' He took a breath and composed himself. 'You asked for the full truth, well . . . the reason I got to know your sister at all is that she came to me, early in the term, because she was thinking of dropping out of her law degree. She could talk to me about it because I like to help students find their path in life. I encourage them to consider the world more openly. You know that's true.'

'No.' I shook my head. 'No, that's not the case. She was never going to drop out.'

'Jess, I'm not lying to you. She was deeply unhappy. Her decision to leave wasn't about me.'

I couldn't stand the sight of him. I kept my eyes trained on my hands, picked compulsively at the loose skin around my nail, ripping at it until I felt a dull pain, saw blood bubble.

'You're . . . you're just trying to make yourself feel better.'

'I won't feel better about this. I promise you that. It'll haunt me. The knowledge that I hurt Audrey, and lied to her, when I should have helped her find her way in the world. That will never leave me.'

'Stop . . . I know what you're doing. You're going to say that you feel awful and that's punishment enough. But it's not enough. You need to be stopped. Because you barely even *resisted* when I came after you. You made it so easy. And that tells me that you'll do it again.'

Crane turned away, adjusting himself in his leather chair, folding his hands together over his chest again. 'So, we've reached the confession now: you came after me. You set me up.'

'Of course I did.'

'You came here *specifically* to set me up?'

'To set you up for something I know you did – to Audrey.'

His eyes widened. 'You were going to accuse me of rape.'

'A different victim, but the same crime exactly.'

He sat back, staring at me in wonder. 'I see it now,' he said. 'I see what you're up to … Clever, I'll give you that. If you were right about me, I'd even be impressed. But the trouble with your little scheme is that you don't have a guilty party. I didn't do what you're saying. Does that alter your calculations?'

In the lamplight, the yellow of his eyes shone.

'Are you saying she lied, Jay? Did Audrey lie when she said you wouldn't stop?'

'She was mistaken,' he said quietly. A silence followed. '… Or else I was.'

'Is that an admission of guilt?'

A beat passed, then another. His lip trembled. For a brief moment, I thought the truth might break out of him – Jay Crane crumbling before me – but steeliness crept into him again, a brazen confidence.

'You're not really interested in the truth of what happened. You came here to hurt me. It's just revenge now, Jessie. That's what this is.'

My mind flicked back to the conversation with Vera, to the promises I had made. 'My motivation doesn't matter. I'm stopping you abusing your position, once and for all, because you're clearly unable to stop yourself.' I paused. 'Honestly, I didn't think you'd make it so easy, Jay. I thought I'd have to try a lot harder.'

He threw his head back, his eyes on the ceiling. 'Well, shit,' he said. 'OK. You're really going there? Justice is on my side, Jessie. What you did was an attempt at entrapment.'

'Good luck proving it.'

'Right . . . so now it's about what we can prove? Is that what you're saying? That doesn't sound like justice to me.'

'It's not possible to immorally exploit a morally bankrupt system. You taught me that. You also taught me to make justice for myself.'

A slow smile spread across his face. 'So, that's it . . . that's the game? Using what I taught you against me?'

I leaned forward. 'You should be proud, Jay. You taught me so well.'

He shook his head, but he was still smiling. 'That's what the tattoo was about?'

'It was fake. Just a temporary kid's thing. I've already scrubbed it off.'

'Shiiiit,' he said, elongating the word as he sat deeper into his chair, the full extent of my actions slowly dawning on him.

'I'm giving you one last chance to do the right thing. Resign, Jay. Leave academia. If you don't, I'll go to Dean Thompson and tell her about your inappropriate behaviour with me.'

He shut his eyes. 'I have to say, Jessie, I'm really impressed. Truly, you are completely deranged.'

'Resign. Walk away. Accept you've been beaten. It's not too late to join the side of the angels.'

His eyes snapped open again. 'Now, Jessie,' he said. 'We both know you're no angel. This match is Satan versus Satan.'

I couldn't help but smile myself. 'You're a great teacher, but a terrible human, Jay.' I rose to my feet, Crane rising with me. 'Next time we meet, it'll all be on the record.'

'Next time we meet, I'll have a witness present.'

'Now you're catching on,' I said.

'May the best one win,' Crane said as I walked to the door.

'Whoever can, Jay. Whoever can.'

The door slammed firmly behind me.

The conversation had gone as I expected. Once I filed that complaint, there would not be another opportunity like this, but a very small part of me had hoped he might experience some spasm of remorse, some glimmer of guilt in the face of what he had done. If he had any decency, he would resign, seek redemption, and exile himself. But it wasn't in Crane to back down.

What he had said about my sister made me feel sick. His version of Audrey didn't chime with my own, a tale in which she was already unhappy, already on a road out of our lives before she ever met Crane. But if she had been as vulnerable as Crane said, Audrey would have been an easy target for his flattery and attention. Unhappiness was fertile ground in which he could sow the seeds of hope, making promises to his favourite of a bright future ahead. Hadn't he done the same with me? If Crane was right about my sister, my parents and I hadn't read the signs of her discontent until it was too late.

But I was the one who should have noticed. I was with her every day at Trinity, waiting for her after class, crossing campus at her side, sitting next to her on the train, listening while she recounted the events of her day.

If Crane was telling me the truth about her unhappiness, I had missed the warnings. I had failed her completely.

Chapter Thirty-Three

Now that Crane was on high alert, I needed to begin the Title IX process quickly. This was the procedure protecting against sex-based discrimination in education settings and would involve a formal complaint to Dean Thompson.

Sitting on the opposite side of her desk, I waited as her pen moved swiftly across a pad of yellow legal paper, the ink seeping out, while she recorded how Crane had used his status as my professor to pursue an inappropriate relationship with me. The bare facts, verifiable thanks to the evidence I had gathered throughout my first term, but nothing about Audrey at all.

The Dean's office was bright, the walls painted a warm cream. The shelves were covered in a variety of well-kept houseplants that made the air feel fresh. The room was tidy, the desk almost empty. There was little between us except the paper on which she was writing a set of facts that I had to hope might just be enough for Crane to lose the job he loved so much.

When I had finished my initial account, Dean Thompson stayed silent for a moment, watching my face, examining me for signs of danger, for the flash of a red flag in my eyes. I looked to a corner of the ceiling where an ornate cornice was peeling slightly, flaking plaster blowing gently in the current of warm air rising from the vent beneath it.

'I'm sorry to ask like this ... believe me,' the Dean began. 'It sounds very cold, but I hope you understand that this is my job. It's my legal responsibility.' I stared at the plaster, imagining a crack running through it, expanding across the ceiling, until it caved in. 'You see, it affects the seriousness of the complaint, so I need to ask.' She paused. 'Was there ever an absence of consent involved in the relationship?'

At the heart of Audrey's tragedy lay the question of consent, choice, agreement, which is to say, the very essence of what it is to be free. Freedom to decide, freedom to say no. It's what allows people to form boundaries between them and the external world, demarcating us from others, making us autonomous, capable of deciding what to allow into our world and into our bodies. We bolster and protect it with laws, with rules and social conventions, but there are people who break through anyway, and there are laws that protect the wrong cause. If you know how it feels to have someone cross that line, infiltrate your edges, violate that last boundary, that aching, wrenching pain like no other ... If you know that feeling, I am so sorry.

I sat forward on my chair. Abuse of power, taking advantage of position and prestige to attract the attention of young women – how did that impact a person's ability to freely choose? 'Consent isn't ... it isn't an easy thing.'

'Go on,' the Dean replied, her pen in her hand, poised, as if it were listening just as carefully as she. Its presence dried the words on my lips. 'It's just ... it's just consent isn't straightforward,' I said quietly. 'I don't know what I'm trying to say, really ...'

'I understand. I know what you're saying. It's anything but simple.'

'I just ...' I watched her pen flow again, the word upside down on the page, loopy 'c' and a sharp 't', followed by a question mark. *CONSENT?*

'Well, it's just, given his position, you know . . . and the impact he has on students, his personality, his charm, his success, his fame, his favouritism. It's just, like, in the absence of equality, is consent really possible? And what if he lied about loving you so that you would sleep with him? Or lied about leaving his wife for you? What if he made you think he knew your mind better than you did, and that thought wore you down, until you let him make the decision for you? Or what if you withdrew your consent and he didn't listen, because he thought he knew best? Because his will always triumphed? How can you have mean-ingful consent in those circumstances? When it was all untrue?'

Dean Thompson was completely still, unblinking, only her mouth moving as she spoke. 'Did . . . did that happen to you, Jessica? Is that why you're reporting him? Did Professor Crane lie to you like that?'

I was silent for one beat, then two, then three. 'No, not like that. No, he didn't do that . . .' To me.

The Dean edged forward, joining her two hands together on the table. 'Well, Jessica, from what you've told me, there has been a very serious lapse in our duty to you. The reason we have a system of rules governing the different types of relationships between faculty and students is precisely because consent is such a . . . a difficult area, as you say. It requires us to know our own minds, as if our minds are books we can read, as if our emotions are simple things you can describe in a single word.'

I was thinking about Audrey, about other women, about the way power silences us. 'Yes, that's . . . that's it exactly.'

She glanced down at her notes, at the words I had prompted her to write. 'There is a process I will follow pursuant to your complaint today and, if the university finds Professor Crane guilty of breaking the rules on a preponderance of the evidence, he will be sanctioned.'

'Sanctioned how? What will the punishment be?'

'I can't really discuss that with you, Jessica . . . I'm sure you'll understand.' She looked to the door, as if worried who might walk through it. After fighting herself for a moment, her voice fell, and she added: 'I need to make sure we follow the process so that the right outcome can prevail.' She met my eye. 'This time.'

Someone else had been down this road before me. But the law school had a different dean then, the complaint had been pulled before the faculty could fully review the case, and before the students could learn of it. This time, the charge had to stick.

'Are you OK, Jessica?'

I shrugged. 'I guess so. It's just exhausting . . . isn't it? All of it.'

'Yes,' she replied. 'Yes, it is.' She sat back again, the Dean seeming to leave the room, the woman behind the title taking her place. 'It's enough to make you tear your hair out sometimes, if I'm honest. But don't let them make you think that we aren't getting places. It's darkest before the dawn. And, like my mother used to say, the last shake of a rattlesnake is always the worst.'

I wanted to believe her, to put my faith in the vision of the world she offered, instead of Crane's version, where difference was irreducible, and conflict constant.

With a thin smile on my face, I thanked the Dean for her time and trudged out of her office. Someone had draped Christmas lights in the trees on the courtyard and they shone in through the window as I tucked my head down, hoping to escape the law school without encountering Crane.

In the Ben, a large red Santa hat covered Ben Franklin's marble head. My footsteps were loud in the empty space. The term was at an end, classes over, papers handed in, exams finished, and students were fleeing home for a couple of weeks, before it all began again next term. I was flying to Dublin in the morning, looking forward to putting an ocean between me and Crane so I could recharge before it all began in earnest.

Christmases weren't the same anymore, not with Audrey gone. Our loss sat stark against the merriment, the family reunions, the shared celebration, making us feel, more keenly, how we were separate from everyone else. We endured it as best we could, the three of us, and smiled politely when well-intentioned friends and relatives told us time would soothe our grief and make things easier. But we didn't want things to be easier. We wanted Audrey.

On Chestnut Walk, I caught the sound of carol singers on the quad to my left. I joined the group that had gathered to listen, the choir holding candles in one hand and sheets of music in the other, while they sang a harmonised 'Carol of the Bells', voices floating into the night. At the back of the small group, I stamped my feet for warmth, my gloved hands balled into fists at my side. There was a brief clap as the carollers finished, then launched into 'White Christmas'.

I almost didn't see him looking at me, his face half-obscured by a scarf, standing at the other side of the crowd. Crane. I stumbled back as I met his gaze, startled not only by his presence, but by the power of the anger directed my way. It felt explosive, burning through the frozen air between us.

His arm was around his wife, his hands encased in black gloves. In the fur-lined hood of her white ski jacket, Leyna's head bobbed in time to the singing, and I think it was her presence alone keeping Crane's temper in check.

Turning on my heel, I pushed through the throng and back onto Chestnut Walk, where I began to run. Something in the transformation of his face, in the ferocious anger, had sent adrenaline racing through me. It energised my feet as I sprinted past restaurants packed with diners, past shops open late for gift buyers, past a group of students wearing Christmas jumpers on their way into a bar, all the way to my dorm.

It wasn't over yet between us, me and Crane. As far as he was concerned, we were only getting started. And now, the hostility was out in the open. Now, he would fight back.

I could not let him win.

Chapter Thirty-Four

Returning to Philadelphia after a brief Christmas break in Dublin, I found myself caught up in an administrative process that was moving forward at a glacial pace. I handed over the evidence I could provide – the text messages, the photographs, details of the places we had been together, the invitations, the offers to help with job opportunities – after which there was nothing further I could do except sit and wait for an outcome. There were formal letters informing me of the next steps that would occur, of the Title IX coordinator they would appoint, of the test they would use in analysing the evidence, of the standards that would apply to such analysis. Rights of appeal, rights to be heard, rights to participate. But, ultimately, Crane's fate would be determined by the tenured faculty. His own colleagues.

For a week, I struggled against impatience and restlessness, trying not to let indiscipline derail me with bad habits, not when I had come this far. But by mid-January, despite my best efforts to keep things on track, control of the situation was slipping away. Crane's fate was undecided, his guilt still undefined by the powers that be, but public attention had quickly shifted off the conduct of the accused, and onto that of the accuser.

Me.

In classes, professors treated me differently. Some were hostile, some pointedly ignoring me, some falling over themselves to be sensitive towards me. A spotlight was beaming down on me, and I missed the anonymity I had taken for granted, fading in with the rest of the room, just another student, just like everyone else.

My name circulated freely around campus. When I left my dorm room now, a panopticon-type of surveillance began. In the canteen, the library, at the Ben, outside the Irish bar, walking down Chestnut Walk, passing through the Franklin Bookstore, in the queue for coffee at Joe's, down every corridor of the law school – no matter where I went, eyes followed. I was the girl who banged the professor, then snitched about it.

Posts had appeared online, threads discussing my supposed attack on Crane's reputation. Faceless trolls forming theories about me, creating grotesque versions of my character, moulded out of their misogyny. They said I had reported Crane because he dumped me. Predictable, right? Always the same – the archetype of the scorned woman coming to get them.

One commenter said I had probably made the whole thing up. Another said he was a student at Franklin Law and knew what I looked like. He called me an ugly slut and said he didn't think Crane would be bothered with me because I wasn't that hot.

I read the message again several times. This person was from the law school. He knew what I looked like. He could be any-where, at any time.

After that, when I left the law school at night, or when I was crossing campus from the library, a presence seemed to linger behind me. It was more than likely the work of my exhausted mind, the sense of constant observation casting a shadow behind me, like a Brocken spectre haunting my path. But it felt like a real solid thing.

I never saw anyone, no matter how often I peered into the

darkness behind me. Watching for any sudden movement, for the rustle of foliage, for the outline of a shadowed figure, my heart in my mouth, feeling as if I were being hunted.

On a run along the riverbank, early one morning before the sun had fully risen, I was so sure of footsteps behind me that I twisted around to check. The movement too quick, my foot slipped on a patch of ice, the fall heavy. I sliced the skin of my hands, though there was no other harm done, except to my confidence.

To avoid the scrutiny, and to keep away from Crane, I spent most of my time buried in a back corner of the Fine Arts library on the main campus. It was there that Vera found me with news, shortly before inauguration day. She was out of breath as she arrived, launching straight in without so much as a greeting. 'I've heard that Crane's going to get away with a warning,' she said, leaning against the desk so she could get a good look at me.

There were only a few other students up here beneath the vaulted ceilings, where the walls were as thick as the air. The windows bore messages, aphorisms to catch the eye when attention wandered from textbooks. One of those, in my line of sight, was a quote from *Othello*: *Men should be what they seem.*

Down below, flames crackled in the fireplace, the smell of burning logs mixing with that of old books. And up here, behind my desk, the cold winter light streamed in through a small round window. I had chosen this nook because it was hidden up a spiral staircase from the reading room, where nobody would have a reason to come.

'Grouse said the faculty have divided into two camps,' Vera said. 'Crane and Laurent are frightening all the old-timers, saying due process would require a full tribunal and full hearing of your complaint against Crane. He's saying he'll sue if they find against him without giving him a chance to speak in his own defence.'

'What is he going to say? That I'm just lying?'

'He's not denying that he gave you extra attention, but he says you're not emotionally stable and . . .' She paused. 'Are you sure you want to hear this?'

'Yes.'

'He's saying you're vulnerable, and he tried to help you, but you got the wrong idea.' Vera stopped again. 'He said it's something about . . . your sister.'

My fingers scraped the skin of my upper arm. 'Will there be a full hearing?'

'Unlikely.' Vera's shoulders dropped, fingertips brushing her hair. 'Dean Thompson told Grouse it's a dead-end. A full hearing would delay the process until after you've graduated and gone back to Ireland. The longer the delay, the less momentum. He's hoping it'll all just fizzle out and be forgotten.'

'He knows how to kill this, because he has done it before.' I frowned.

'Grouse says that Crane has been lobbying the tenured faculty very, *very* hard. He's tying your complaint to the petition against Laurent and categorising all of it as an attack on academic freedom.' She ran an impatient hand through her black hair. 'Because of *course* he is. Honestly, that man is . . .' She didn't finish the sentence.

There was a pattering sound against the roof as a heavy snow flurry passed over our heads. The glass was opaque, a series of matching panels with symmetrical geometric shapes arranged into ovals, divided by four criss-crossing lines in an art deco style. When I shut my eyes, I found the pattern waiting inside my eyelids.

'Crane doesn't even believe that,' I said, to myself as much as to Vera. 'He told me once that there's no such thing as free speech, just lines we draw around the things we like, and the things we don't.' I shook my head. 'God, he's so cynical.'

'I've been told Crane has the numbers,' Vera replied. 'They're talking about categorising your complaint as a minor breach of the code of conduct and giving him a formal warning – that's it. Basically nothing, not even a temporary suspension or loss of privileges. And this isn't the first time either . . . this is the *second* complaint in the last five years.'

I reached for my water bottle, taking a long drink, while I tried to sift through this information. 'What a shitty process. The jury is loaded with colleagues . . . friends, enemies . . . agendas. The outcome turns on a popularity contest. It's all just politics in the end.'

'The personal is political.'

'This is why you can't play fair. The game isn't fair,' I muttered.

My eyes drifted down to the reading room below, where a scattering of students sat at desks, headphones around ears, laptops opened, reading some text or other. Somewhere out of view, a librarian pushed a cart of books towards the shelves, the sound of a squeaking wheel breaking into the silence.

The world might shake and crumble outside these walls, but here, there was tradition, heritage, legacy – armour against the slashing knives of a hostile world, of budget cuts, and changing social standards.

Vera was watching me when I turned back to her. 'How are you holding up, Jessie? Is it getting to you? The attention?'

Yes.

'No,' I said hurriedly. 'It's fine . . . mostly . . . I just hate sitting around, doing nothing.'

She placed a hand on my shoulder, though it felt uneasy there, as if she wasn't quite sure what she was supposed to do now that she had made physical contact. 'I'm sorry,' she said limply, then added, unconvincingly: 'We'll get him. Whatever happens, we'll make sure people know what he's like.'

I didn't respond. Audrey used to say I cared too much about the things I couldn't change. She said that impulse would make me a good lawyer someday.

I think she was wrong about that. The law means playing by the rules. It means using the proper channels, the right process, the correct paperwork. And maybe we need a system like that – at least most of the time – to mark out the way forward. But systems that don't bend will break. And if your opponent is fighting dirty, then why would you fight clean?

Vera left, but I stayed a while longer, unable to concentrate on my work, listening to the snow and hail fall on the windows, my cheek resting on my arm. I would have to sit on my hands until the faculty decision was formally confirmed, and allow it to play out, but my mind was already whirring with fresh calculations, considering possible moves, accounting for new variables.

Crane said something on election night that kept echoing through my thoughts. *What good are principles when you're dead?* He was not a man of principles, so, despite my best efforts to play it straight through Title IX, I would have to take the fight back down to his level. I was beginning to think that the law needed people like me for the cases at the edge, the ones that don't fit neatly into the system as designed, where the bad guy makes a mockery of it, slipping through the net and walking free from the courtroom. Well, maybe someone needs to follow, slipping into the shadows after them, knife in hand.

Chapter Thirty-Five

By the time inauguration day came, I had been hiding in my dorm room for several days, skipping classes when I could, avoiding all contact with the outer world. I was still in bed that morning when my phone rang, the vibrations against the metal bedframe waking me involuntarily from a deep sleep. Amanda's name flashed on the screen. She was headed to tomorrow's Women's March with the American Constitution Society and had been trying to convince me to go with her. All I wanted to do was scramble beneath a duvet and block out the world, shield myself from its scrutiny.

Amanda only knew the official version of the story. I hadn't risked telling her the truth because, if I'm honest, I wasn't brave enough to see how she might react.

Bundling my coat over my pyjamas, I shoved my feet into boots and went down to meet her in the lobby. Her face fell immediately when she saw me walk out of the lift, undressed, and clearly not about to board a bus.

'There's still time, Jessie,' she said. 'Go get dressed and come with me. It'll be good for you! I promise, just ... please come with me.'

Next to us, the security guard was flicking through a newspaper, the next president and his wife gazing out at us from the front page.

'I don't feel well,' I mumbled. 'I'm sorry . . .'

A thin ripple of cold air was blowing in through a narrow crack between the swing doors, the hinges old and uncooperative. I wrapped my coat more tightly around me.

Amanda reached forward and ran a hand up and down my arm. 'Jess, I . . . I'm worried about you. You can't keep hiding away like this.'

'I'm fine. Really, I'm not hiding. I just don't feel well. You should go.'

Amanda's face held concern which tickled the guilt reflex in the pit of my stomach. I didn't deserve her care. I had concealed so much of myself from her, and she had so generously offered me friendship anyway.

'Are you still reading those comments online?' she asked. 'I told you to burn your phone.'

'I know.' I looked down at my feet, my boots scuffed with white salt stains from the grit used to keep the sidewalks clear of snow. 'It makes me feel better if I know what they're saying.'

'Well,' Amanda said, her lips set tightly together as she took in the shabby entrance space, painted a faded yellow and covered in notices identifying fire exits, directions not to use the lift in the event of an active shooter, and warnings not to spill hot drinks while carrying them through the turnstiles. Under our feet, the linoleum was a chessboard of dirty white and hospital green. 'I don't think you should spend all your time . . . *here.*'

'I won't,' I lied, 'but, look, you should go, or you'll miss your bus.'

Amanda hesitated, then threw her arms around me, squeezing me in a hug. 'Take care, Jess,' she said into my ear, and then, from the door, added: 'I'll send you photos from the march!'

I raised a hand and waved. 'Good luck!'

She smiled as she hurried away, the doors creaking to a slow close behind her.

As I turned, my eye met the security guard's. 'She going protesting?' she asked me, nodding towards the door.

'She is,' I said. 'The Women's March in DC.'

The guard rolled her eyes and snorted. I realised I didn't know her name, even though I had passed her several times a day for months now.

'Fat lot of good that's going to do,' she said, laughing, the pages of her newspaper crinkling. 'Doesn't matter who they put in power, nothing ever changes.'

I didn't reply, rubbing the back of my neck as I walked to the lift and pressed the button. But her words made my limbs feel heavy.

On the twelfth floor, my feet took me back to my dorm, where my face found my pillow once more. I lay in bed, thinking about the thin line between tragedy and comedy, wondering if society was slipping into a collective farce, until I drifted into sleep.

It was the rattle of my phone against the bedframe that woke me again.

Charlie Duke (09.05):

You in DC today?

It was the first time I had heard from him this term, and the sudden communication drove sleep from my mind. I lumbered into the kitchen and switched on the coffee pot, kneaded my face as I pondered the enormity of the effort required to shower.

Jessica Mooney (09.18):

No. Couldn't face it. I'm home.

Charlie Duke (09.19):

Want company?

Jessica Mooney (09.20):

No.

He came anyway, arriving twenty minutes later.

'You look like shit,' Charlie said in the lift as it rose towards my floor.

'Nice to see you too.'

He was examining me, but I didn't bother to hide from him now. He had always seen me anyway, no matter how hard I tried to conceal myself.

'What's going on with you?' he asked at last as we trudged to my room.

'What do you think?' I mumbled, letting him into the kitchenette. 'Do you want some coffee? There's some in the pot, but you might want to blast it in the microwave.'

'Tempting as that sounds, I'm good.'

I walked into my bedroom, wrapping myself in my duvet so that it sat over my head, like a particularly pathetic Virgin Mary.

Charlie eyed me from the door. 'Seriously, Mooney, you need to get out of this funk.'

'I'm fine. It's just the investigation ... Not good at waiting around.' This was partly true, but I didn't want to elaborate on the other ways that the process of filing the complaint had weighed on me, the burden of scrutiny, the intrusiveness of public interest. And beyond all that, there was the unresolved fear, still tormenting me, of whether this was something Audrey would have wanted me to do.

He sat down at my desk, pushing dirty laundry from the chair onto the floor. 'Listen, I, um . . . I wanted to let you know that, um . . .' His hand brushed his fringe. 'Well, there are some people talking . . .' One blonde eyebrow reached towards the other. 'About you.'

'OK.'

'There's a thread on Reddit.'

'Yeah, I know . . . I've seen it.' I scratched at my nose, then let my body slide onto the mattress so that I was horizontal again, the strain of being vertical too much.

'Do you know who's behind it?'

I turned onto my side so that I could look at him. 'Do *you*?'

'Unfortunately . . . yes.' One leg sat balanced on the other, one hand still combing through the part of his hair that flopped over from the right to the left. 'It's Reese Bryant. I overheard him talking with Kevin.' He looked at me. 'Are you . . .' He waved his hand in the air in front of his face. 'Mooney, you're not even blinking – are you alive?'

For a beat, I was silent.

'That little shit!' I shouted, sitting up, the duvet falling from my shoulders, familiar anger racing through me. 'Are you kidding me?'

'No, of course not.'

'*Reese* Bryant?! He couldn't even get into the fucking class!' I was so angry, so indignant, but it was also invigorating, energising, my blood flowing hot through my veins again. I caught my bottom lip between my fingers, pinching it tightly.

'They're nervous, I guess . . . some of the guys,' Charlie said.

'Vera's whipping up all this talk of demos on campus, about rape culture, or whatever. Some of them feel like they're targets.'

'Oh, come on. They're only targets if they're guilty.'

'Yeah, I know, I'm just trying to explain – not justifying it.'

I blinked, trying to restrain the flare of my temper. 'Charlie, honestly, I'm tired of excuses and I don't care for explanations. I just want action. I want this to stop. Do you understand?'

I watched the thoughts churn through his head. 'Yeah,' he said, after a while, nodding slowly. 'Yeah, I . . . I get it, Jessie. I'm going to handle this.'

The sharp edge of Charlie's profile, cast in shadow, was dramatic in the weak January light. 'What does that mean?' I couldn't imagine he would get involved – what was in it for him?

'I'll talk to him and, if that doesn't work, I'll do something else.'

'Something else . . .' I said, suddenly unsure that Charlie Duke was the person for the job. 'What do you mean?'

He laughed and sighed at the same time. 'What do you want me to say, Mooney? You want me to make some sort of insane plan involving aliases and an elaborate fake backstory?'

'Now you're talking . . .' I replied, fidgeting absently with a button on the duvet cover. Reese would listen to Charlie more than he'd listen to me or anyone else. 'You'll give him hell, Duke? Won't you? You won't go easy on him? Because he's your friend?'

He seemed almost insulted by the suggestion, then said: 'Honestly, I nearly punched Reese on the spot when I heard what he was doing.'

'Why didn't you?' I asked, provoking another short laugh from Charlie.

'I'm sorry . . . you know . . .' His face was turned towards the window. 'I know I haven't been there for you.' He moved from the chair to the bed, slipping his arm around my shoulder. 'I really am sorry, Mooney.'

'Ah, Duke . . .' A sad little laugh escaped from my mouth, the sound of strangled possibility. 'I'm sorry too.'

Charlie reached for my hand, and I gave it. We sat for a while on my bed, just like that, hand in hand, and we didn't say anything. And when it was time for the inauguration, we watched it on my laptop, and I said that this must be a big day for Charlie's people, and he told me to shut the fuck up, and then I texted Amanda asking if this could really be happening, and Charlie said his dad was in the crowd, and I called his dad a fascist, and Charlie said he was just a capitalist, and I asked if there was a difference, and then we started arguing, so we shut the laptop, went for coffee, and, before he left for class, I told Charlie that I was sorry I had lied to him, and used him, and ruined everything. Charlie said again that he was sorry he hadn't been there for me, kissed my cheek, and said I hadn't ruined a thing. We both knew it was a lie.

Chapter Thirty-Six

A week and a half after thousands of women had marched on DC to declare that Trump was not their president, I found myself back in the chair where I had made my initial complaint against Crane six weeks previously. The houseplants lining the shelves were verdant in the winter light, their soil wet, a petrichor scent filling the room. On the Dean's desk, next to her hand, coffee steamed from a ceramic cup with a large 'F' for Franklin on it. She was wearing a bright blue shift dress and a necklace of canary yellow acrylic beads that her fingers played with while she searched for the words to tell me of Crane's verdict. Her usual warmth was absent, making the light in the room feel colder, the exposure set too high. There was anger simmering beneath her skin: we were all angry these days.

Instinctively, my hands crossed in front of me, rubbing opposite arms for warmth. It wasn't good news. The tenured faculty had voted to give Professor Crane what amounted to a slap on the wrist – a private letter of reprimand, some restrictions around employing students in a research capacity, and a loss of access to his research funding for the rest of the year. That was it.

There were differing opinions on the nature of the relationship. Since I was a graduate student and an adult, some of the faculty felt it would be inappropriate to harshly punish what had been a consensual relationship. The abuse of power, the conflict of interest, the fact that he would be grading me – these were things that did not seem to concern them. It might have felt different if they had just disbelieved me, if they had accepted Crane's word that there had been no relationship at all and ignored the evidence. Instead, they had believed me, and chosen to do nothing about it.

Like a pin pricking a balloon, my heart withered. After my conversation with Vera, I couldn't be surprised by the outcome. Still, it was a gut punch to hear the Dean say it. I had blinked at the last moment and Crane had not. I should have stuck to the original plan to recreate the evidence and accuse Crane of doing to me what he did to my sister. But I had stopped short in the face of that lie, tripped up by a combination of fear and moral compunction. Why had I doubted myself? Why hadn't I just gone for the jugular while I had the chance that night in Crane's office? Or, I could have told the Dean what she needed to hear for the process to work, that there was no consent. Crane would not have hesitated if he were in my shoes, but I did. This is how he won, how he would keep on winning. And I *knew* that. But I had bowed to the pressure of conscience.

Outside on Sansom Street, I thought about screaming. But the day was bright, the snow was starting to melt, and the scene too ordinary to disturb.

I shouldn't have been the centre of this story, and yet, I had put myself there anyway. I had read Audrey's diaries, her texts, her emails. I had taken her clothes, her shoes. I had made her pain my pain, her dreams my dreams. I had tried to make her trauma my trauma so I could make justice for the dead. Instead, I'd made a mess.

On my phone, a text from Vera.

Vera Lin (09.23):

What's the verdict?

I texted back.

Jessica Mooney (09.37):

Minor breach of conduct. Minimal punishment.

I watched the three ellipses on my screen while Vera typed her reply.

Vera Lin (09.38):

Fucking predictable. Ghouls. What do you want us to do? I can get the student organisations on it? Maybe circulate a student petition?

Jessica Mooney (09.40):

If you want, but it won't make any difference . . . I should have trusted my own methods.

The tips of my fingers were numb in the cold, my breath a cloud in front of my face.

Vera Lin (09.50):

What does that mean? What will you do?

I thought of that night in the crowd of carollers, the way his eyes

247

landed on mine, the rage radiating from him. The figure of his wife at his side, unaware of my presence. There was one obvious weakness I could still exploit.

Jessica Mooney (09.51):

The less you know, the better.

Chapter Thirty-Seven

After the Title IX verdict, there was a clear target for protest, and Vera began coalition building with the student organisations against the result. We were already riled up after the election, already angry, and the Title IX result gave fresh energy to the students who had been out protesting the new administration. A slap on the wrist for Crane, a slap in the face for students. Someone even fixed a banner to the railings along Chestnut Walk, calling for an investigation into campus rape culture. I don't know if it was a direct response to the faculty's decision on Crane, or a sign of the wider atmosphere of female anger, but it gave me a small boost.

Journalists from the outside world, beyond the campus bubble, were beginning to sniff around the story. I waited for the day they would find me – when you would find me – and wondered how I could possibly explain what had happened between me and Crane, and what was happening still. Would you have even believed me if I tried?

With the snow thawing rapidly into the gutters and the cold dwindling out of the air, I started to run again more regularly. My blood was hot and restless. Crane was still in his job and his tenure meant he could remain there for decades to come. The current crop of students, the ones who knew about me, would graduate and move on, a fresh crop arriving to replace us, then another to replace them, again and again, year after year. In time, rumours might fade, whispers could fall silent, and then it could happen again.

Altruism was only part of my reasoning. After all I had been through, I wanted to see him suffer properly, and a slap on the wrist wasn't nearly enough. We weren't finished yet.

My running route was different now. Instead of towards the Schuylkill River, I ran south to the Woodlands, weaving through the graves of the cemetery there. The winter had made a wasteland of the vegetation, so that the headstones appeared like stone teeth in a rotten mouth. Among them, the first shoots of spring were bursting through the dead ground, occasional brushstrokes of colour revealing a lone crocus, here or there. The cemetery was laid out concentrically and, once I had run around each layer and found its heart, I would leave, heading in the direction of the Franklin Museum.

My route was specifically planned – not to enjoy the fresh air, or the movement of my muscles, or the quiet birdsong sounding from some hidden place within the tangle of bare branches lining the road – but to see Leyna King.

I timed my runs so that I would pass by the museum just as she arrived for work each morning. From the other side of the road, I would slow to a jog, or stretch against the wall of the stadium, and watch for her upright posture as she crossed from the bus stop.

Her wool coat was a deep shade of burgundy and, most days, she wore a navy beret over her dark hair. When it rained, she held a large black umbrella. When the sun shone, however faintly, she wore cat's eye sunglasses. There was nothing out of the ordinary in her manner, nothing to suggest that the investigation of her husband had caused any strain, or changed anything about her life.

One morning, I didn't spot Leyna at all. For weeks, I had been waiting, vacillating, hoping that I would know when the moment was right to confront her. But her absence made me feel a flush of panic. What if she had finally noticed me?

I could understand why Audrey needed to write that letter to Leyna. I felt the same urge in me now, to see Crane's wife acknowledge what had happened. It was all less real otherwise, as if Crane could, by sheer force of will, erase his sins and misdeeds, rewriting things as they were and making them as he wanted them to be. He had placed himself beyond the law and beyond the university disciplinary procedure, but maybe – *maybe* – his wife could get through to him. Maybe she could push him to face who he was, and even resign. Surely, she didn't believe his stories of students turned stalkers? Surely, she *knew* the man she had married?

Crane had looked me in the eye and said he loved Leyna, and I believed him. It was not even contradictory, or difficult to accept, because we always hurt the ones we love. At the core of every tragedy sits this uncomfortable truth.

I made a snap decision. From the Franklin Museum, I ran east, my feet beating the footpath harder now, down to the end of South Street, and across the bridge towards the other side of the city. When I arrived on Delancey Street, my throat was raw, my chest heaving.

I slowed at the window of number 218. For just the briefest of moments, as I peeked inside, I could see their interior world again. The table was laid with a new tablecloth, the candelabra unlit, some discarded books lying open on their spines. The house seemed empty. No evidence of Leyna, or Crane.

I was catching my breath, still gazing inside, when she saw me. Framed by the window, arms crossed over her chest, expression one of fear – no, that's not right. It was terror.

Look, I know what you're thinking. In my defence, I hadn't meant to *stalk* her like this, but her face left me with no illusions that this was precisely what I had done. She was scared of me.

Recognising this, I wanted to run away, but I made myself walk to the door and ring the doorbell. I made myself lay his wrongdoing before the feet of the woman he loved the most.

The door opened. Leyna did not invite me in.

'What are you doing here?' Her gaze darted back and forth. 'What do you want from me?'

I tried to steady my breath. 'Surely you must know?'

Her lips were pale. 'You've come to break my family apart,' she said.

'No ...' I replied. 'I've come to understand you.' This wasn't entirely true. I still didn't know where Leyna stood in all this. She remained a mystery to me, unpredictable, unfathomable. But I was there because she was also Crane's weak spot.

'To understand me?' Her jaw was carefully set, teeth clenched, but I could see the wavering in her eye, the uncertainty. 'What makes you think you could?'

I didn't want to be this woman's enemy. We always blame the women. 'I'd like to try.'

Leyna's hand remained on the door, poised and ready to shut it in my face. My time was short, my opportunity scant.

'My sister sent you a letter.'

'Your sister, Audrey.'

'Yes.'

'Jay told me she ... she died.'

'She did.'

Leyna sighed, her hand sliding off the door and onto her neck. A crack ran through her resolution, humanity seeping through. 'I'm sorry,' she said quietly, looking so tired, so completely spent, that I found myself pitying her. Stepping out of the way with a flick of her head, she added: 'You'd better come in.'

For the last time, I entered Crane's home. The light was warm at this time of day, shining off the portraits, off the bookshelves, catching on the gold foil lettering on the cloth spines of his books. Leyna had been burning patchouli, the fragrance curling into the air from incense sticks near the front door.

'You want to know about your sister?' Leyna asked in the foyer, disturbing my thought. 'You want to know what she said in her letter?'

'She told you about the affair, about the two of them.'

'Yes.'

'Did she tell you the rest?' I held her eye. 'Did she tell you what he did to her?'

Leyna did not look away. 'No. But Jay . . . he told me what you accused him of.'

'All of it?'

'Oh yes. I heard it all.' I watched her lips part, then close, then part again. 'You allege that your sister withdrew consent and Jay ignored this.'

Such clinical terms for a crime of such enduring horror. I supposed this was how she protected herself from its full burden, wringing the emotion out of it, so that it appeared to her devoid of real significance. They felt more like *his* words, covered in a gloss of legality, the sort of words that take a person and make them a complainant, an accuser, a victim, a survivor. Not Audrey any longer, but a party to a proceeding.

I felt hope slip away. '*Allege* . . .' I said. 'So, you don't believe it.'

'It's only one side of a complicated story.'

'And you're taking his side? Just like that?'

'I know my husband,' she replied, folding her arms carefully, her right hand resting delicately on the crook of her left. 'Jay likes to be adored – that is his weakness. That is how we find ourselves in these little messes. It's how we end up with women, like you, stalking him ... finding their way to his door.'

My cheeks grew hot.

Her eyes narrowed briefly. 'Did you throw that rock through our window?' Having asked the question, she seemed to change her mind about wanting an answer. 'You know what, it doesn't matter now ...' Leyna took a step towards me. 'Jessica, I know that this must have caused you a great deal of pain, but you're imagining that my husband is a monster – he's not. I promise you that. Your sister was mistaken. I would not be here if I thought him capable of this.'

Could she possibly believe what she was saying?

'You're *sure* of that?' I asked her, her blind loyalty to Crane something I could not quite accept. 'There's no doubt? No un-certainty? You really know that?'

She nodded once, a tight bobbing movement.

I turned away briefly, focusing on the curl of scented smoke from the incense sticks, before trying a different tack. 'Leyna, he betrays you ... again and again. That doesn't bother you?'

She looked at me then with a mixture of such raw anger and raw pain that she seemed to me a woman stuck in a prison, and I wondered if she knew that she could leave. Was something keeping her from pushing open the door and walking out?

'I won't answer that,' she said. 'Frankly, Jessica, it's none of your business.' She stepped over to the door, her hand now on the lock. 'I've given you enough of my time. I've answered your questions ... I did that for your sister, for Audrey, out of respect for the dead.' She paused, eyes piercing me. 'We're finished now. I want you to go, and I don't want to see you again. You're not welcome here.'

The door swung open. As I left, I spun around to ask my final question. It was a long a shot, but I had to try. 'Do you still have it, Leyna? The letter? Jay told me about it.'

For one brief second, it was possible she would say yes. Something in her expression, a slight glance to the side, as if she were looking in its direction.

'The letter is gone,' Leyna said firmly. 'Long gone. I didn't keep it.'

I nodded, unsurprised by her answer. I didn't know if she was telling me the truth, about both the contents of the letter and whether it still existed. But she had chosen to stand by her husband. She had chosen Crane.

As I left Delancey Street for the final time, there was one last play left open to me. I had tried to circumvent the law's barriers, then tried the formal processes, tried public pressure to destroy Crane's reputation, and, lastly, tried an appeal to his wife. I had tried everything you might care to tell me would bring justice. But nothing did. The deck was stacked against me. In the eyes of most right-minded members of society, this was the point where I should walk away. I should give up, accept defeat, resign myself to the limits and constraints, to the assertion that, sometimes, life isn't fair and justice doesn't always follow.

But you should know by now that I couldn't do that. In life, sometimes all that's left is your refusal. And I refused. Despite it all, I refused to let him win.

Perhaps this is where I lose you. Perhaps this is where you draw the line. I'm not sure I should tell you what comes next, not even off the record, not even deep background. If I had bothered with a lawyer, they would tell me to delete this, to hold the backspace down and wipe the page clean. But we've come this far together. Why stop now?

Chapter Thirty-Eight

I had been avoiding Crane in the months since the night I saw him in the crowd. His teaching schedule had changed this term, but his daily habits had not and my detailed notes of his usual movements around campus still allowed me to keep track him.

Wednesdays:
Crane buys a coffee at Joe's around 8.15

He's in his office between 8.30 and 10
Office hours 3–5

Thursdays:
Starts late, usually after 10
Lunch at his desk, or else he goes to food truck – usually 2ish for falafel.
Stays late in office. No dinner.

My knowledge of his movements had given me a fighting chance of keeping away from him. Now I needed to do the opposite.

I needed to face Crane again.

He tended to spend midweek evenings working late in his office, especially Thursdays, which is how I knew he'd be there.

The first time I tried to go to his office, I didn't quite make it to the door before his voice came wafting out to meet me on the corridor. He was on the phone – with Leyna, I think – talking about when to expect him home. The sound of an ordinary conversation, a domestic closeness, stopped me in my tracks. From where I stood, back against the wall, I could see that he had propped the door open with a stack of books. It was a fire door, heavy and supported by a springy hinge at the top. Cautiously, I extended my foot towards the books, aiming a careful kick, so that they scattered onto the ground, freeing the door and causing it to swing shut with a loud bang. I didn't wait around for him to come and investigate, but I like to think he knew I had been there.

The second time, as I approached his office, Crane's shadow was visible on the wall, cast by the dim light of his desk lamp. A shift occurred inside the room, followed by the wheels of his chair moving rapidly backward. He could feel my presence, and I could feel his too. His footsteps were heavy against the old carpet. 'Jessie?'

I don't know what would have happened if he found me there.

After that, I didn't return for a few days. The prospect of facing him frightened me, which raised the question of *why* I was still persevering. Why wasn't I able to leave things be? What was really motivating me? Was it still justice? Still Audrey? Still future students? Or had I let it get personal? Was this now Jessie versus Crane?

I tried to distract myself, attending one of the many protests that had been organised in Philadelphia since the election, this one a march against discrimination. With Vera and Amanda, I stood with a placard over my head, chanting along with the others. But it didn't make me feel better to stand in a crowd. I couldn't shake the sense that we were screaming into a void, our voices rising into an unfeeling sky, swallowed up by the vacuum of space.

Online, Reese Bryant's Reddit thread had been shut down thanks to Charlie. I don't know what he did, but I hadn't seen my name online in weeks, interest dwindling as time went on, the news cycle with it. I still saw Reese every so often around the law school, usually on the corridor between classes, but he ducked whenever he spotted me.

We were still not as we had been, me and Charlie, our friendship a faded thing, like ink on the pages of a book left too long in the sun. The revelation about Crane, the story of what had happened to Audrey, and the truth about me – it had changed something in Charlie, shaking, to some degree, the foundations of his perfect world, and the assumptions of a privileged youth. He had never really questioned his trust in authority, or his faith in the legal system, because he had never had a reason to until he met me. Now, he was keeping his head down, distancing himself, and working towards graduation. I was still working to bring down Crane.

One night, working late in the library, I spotted a quote in an article I was reading for my Criminal Procedure class. '*The requirement in criminal trials to prove a guilty mind stands in opposition to the unresolvable reality that human beings are perspectival creatures and conflicting truths are unavoidable.*'

I scanned down to the citation, his name printed in black ink: Jay Crane. *Conflicting truths are unavoidable.* It felt as if he were saying it directly to me, referring to what had happened with my sister. The words rankled me, familiar anger curdling in my stomach.

Instead of heading home, I turned back towards the faculty offices, down the silent corridor once more. I couldn't keep avoiding this moment and my rage at his words was the kick I needed. Between the investigation, the damage to his reputation, and my confrontation with Leyna, I had heaped as much pressure on him as possible. Now I could exploit that pressure and strike one final time.

Crane must have heard me because he was on me within seconds. I would not describe Crane as a large man, but the force of his anger made him huge as he came barrelling at me through the door, pushing me backwards several steps, and pinning me against the other side of the corridor. I felt my back hit the panelled wall, as if the wood had teeth to bite me. The pain was intense, but my shock diminished the impact. He was looking at me with a hatred I can barely describe. It's different: hatred and anger. Audre Lorde once said that *hatred is the fury of those who do not share our goals*. In Crane, I saw it in pure form.

'Why won't you go *away*?! Why won't you leave me alone? My *wife*, Jessie?! You harassed my wife? You followed her? She saw you. She saw you watching her at the museum. Then you show up at our house? You had the *gall* to drag her into this!' He expectorated as he shouted, a venomous spit coating my face. 'Why are you doing this to us?!'

I shut my eyes.

'Answer me, Jessie! *When* will it stop? When will it be enough for you?!'

His hand was around my neck, which he held with a force that scared me. 'I don't know,' I whispered.

'What? *What?* You don't know? What does that mean? What the *hell* does that mean? You don't *know*? You attacked Leyna at our home. Our *home*, Jessie. Do you know how that made her feel? She's not part of this. Do you understand me? Attack me if you must, but you stay away from my wife.'

His wife. How precious she was now. Had he thought of her when he was with my sister, when he was with me?

'Jay – please let me go.' His large hand clenched my neck, relying on the last, remaining power he had over me. Physical strength. I could feel myself begin to panic, my breath growing laboured. My eyes met his and, for a moment, I wondered how far he might go. It was possible I had messed with his head so much that he had finally flipped. Maybe this was it. Maybe I had driven him too far. And now, all he had to do was squeeze.

I think, perhaps, it was this realization that stopped him, the fear in my eyes reflecting how he appeared to me now. For me, in the body of a small woman, he would always be a threat, even if he saw himself as one of the good ones.

His grip on my throat slackened. He took a step away, gazing at me then, in awe, or horror, while I took mouthfuls of air into my lungs again. Wordless, I looked back at Crane as the hatred drained from his face, replaced now by a disturbed shock at what he had just done.

'Oh God . . . Jesus . . .' He stepped back further, as if it were proximity to me that had caused the violence to flare in him. 'I'm . . . sorry.' He turned away. 'I'm sorry. I shouldn't have . . . Jess, I'm sorry . . . I can't . . .'

The end of his sentence disappeared into his office along with him. The door slammed solidly and definitively, leaving me alone in the empty corridor. I checked for any witnesses, anyone who might have heard him shouting, who might have seen his hand around my neck. But there wasn't a sound, not a guard, or a member of the janitorial staff.

Shaking, I walked away, the pain in my neck the only sensation I could feel.

It was the last time I ever saw Professor Crane.

A purple bruise rose around my spine the next morning and, when I lifted my hair back, in the mirror, I found round red marks on my neck. I placed my fingers against those marks, one by one, to fill where his fingertips had pressed down.

Pulling my T-shirt off, I held my phone over my shoulder and photographed the bruises on my back, then did the same with the ones on my neck.

It was with reluctance that I downloaded them onto my laptop and then saved them onto the USB key, along with all the other evidence I had collected against Crane. I studied the images on my screen, zooming in and out to get a better view. None of this was my fault. The system should have worked. The rules should have applied. There should have been another way.

But there was not. Nobody to save us, except ourselves.

That night, sitting at my desk in my dorm room, I typed out an email and attached copies of the photographs.

Jessica Mooney (21.34):

Jay,

You know what you did. See attached.

J

Maybe the moment had come when he would finally face consequences for his behaviour. I like to think I was giving him a choice, rather than blackmailing him, but I know what a lawyer on the other side might say.

It took twenty minutes for him to reply, during which time I imagined what might be happening at 218 Delagny Street Street. Did he show the photos to Leyna? Were they deciding together what they would do? Were they calling a lawyer? Or busily plotting a way to outmanoeuvre me – again?

Jay Crane (21.57):

What do you want?

I replied immediately.

Jessica Mooney (21.58):

Resign. Go away. It's time. You lost. Resign or I'll tell Dean Thompson you attacked me and then I'll go to the police. If you resign, this stays between us.

I hit send, then waited, my hand tapping against my chest, where the knot usually formed. I refreshed my inbox. Refreshed again.

Nothing.

An hour passed with no response.

I laid my head on my arm and tried to determine what I would do if he refused me, blaring Wolf Alice to keep me company. I would have to take myself down to a police station and tell them what had happened. *My professor put his hand around my throat and pinned me to a wall.* These marks are where his fingers throttled me. This mark on my back is where the wall panelling struck my spine. Here are the injuries. The law might doubt my word, but not the bruising on my body. The faculty couldn't ignore an assault that was visible. But did I trust them? Did I trust the police? The lawyers? The courts?

Crane's number flashed on my phone.

I sat up straight, swallowing hard, then reached for it.

'There's only one thing I want to hear from you.'

'Jess, can we please talk about this?'

'You lost, Jay. Please just make this easy for everyone and accept my terms.'

'This isn't a game, Jessica. It's my life.'

'I'm not playing.'

He was silent, reconsidering his line of attack. 'You're right to be angry with me. I understand.' He paused. 'I need you to know, I'm very sorry. I am . . . I . . . I don't know what happened to me. It was . . . it was very wrong.'

'If you are truly sorry, as you say, you know what to do. Resign. Leave academia. Stay away from students.'

'Jesus, Jessica, come *on*. You're asking too much. You're messing with my life here!'

My fingers drummed my bruised neck. 'Jay, I'm not doing this to you. You did it to yourself.'

I could feel the panic in him, rising out of the place he kept hidden, the side of himself that did all the things of which he was ashamed, the side he liked to pretend didn't really exist, the side that had reached out and choked me. 'You . . . you little *bitch*.'

There it was. 'Is that wise, Jay? Cursing at me right now?'

'Jesus,' he said quietly, and then his voice broke. 'Please . . . Jess. Don't do this to me.'

'Learn this lesson. Learn to listen when a woman says no. Learn to fucking *care*.' My head rolled back on my spine, my eyes on the ceiling, exasperated. When would he stop fighting me? When would he *finally* accept that he was wrong? 'You need to accept this new reality. Make it easy for yourself. Maintain what reputation you have left. Go quietly. If you fight your fate, things will get much worse for you.'

A strangled groan sounded from the back of his throat. 'Please . . .' he said again. 'Is there anything else I can do? I can pay you?'

'Don't make this pathetic . . .'

'I'm not a bad guy, Jessie! It's not like I killed someone—' He stopped himself, realising his error too late, the spectre of my dead sister appearing between us. 'You know, after Audrey died, before I came to Philadelphia, I headed to Central America,' I said finally. 'I wanted to see what she had seen during her last few days of life. So, I sat on the white sand in Belize, looking out at the Caribbean Sea. It was turquoise, and teal, and silver when the sunlight hit the waves – really, it was beautiful, Jay.' I took a deep breath, steadying myself. 'You can still go there . . . you can take some time this summer and see that water. You and I – we still have opportunities like that. We can make better choices, maybe even learn to live more quietly. But Audrey will never have that. She's gone. That's what your actions caused. Because you didn't listen when she said no.'

I could hear Crane's breathing.

'I really liked your class, you know. You were my favourite teacher. I learned a lot from you. You told me that justice has to be made. Well, this is me making it.'

I waited, but he didn't speak.

'I've offered you a good deal. You still get to live a good life. Take this chance. There won't be another.'

I hung up. He needed to know that I wasn't negotiating any-more. Losing his career, his access to students, it felt like the right punishment. The other route, the police, a courtroom, did not. To rely on the unpredictability of a criminal justice system meant losing control of the outcome. I wouldn't make that mis-take again.

Pushing my chair back, I walked to the window and opened the thin curtains a crack. I pressed my hot face to the cold glass and looked over the roofs of the buildings opposite, the bookstore in the foreground and, behind it, the hospital with its flashing beacon. To my left, I could just make out the main campus, the classrooms, lecture halls and libraries of Franklin University, peaceful at this time of night.

Five minutes later, Crane's reply popped into my inbox.

Jay Crane (23.24):

OK.

Chapter Thirty-Nine

It took a while, but, eventually, news filtered through to the students that Crane had resigned from Franklin. It was obvious why. Rumours spread that he had secured a private sector job at a law firm in DC. There were no stories about him in the newspapers yet, but maybe you'll be the one to change that.

The last time I checked, before writing this, Leyna was still listed as an active faculty member on the Franklin website, which makes me wonder if their marriage survived after all.

Crane didn't lose everything. It was not perfect justice for what he did to Audrey. But I've never been a believer in the idea of 'perfect' anyway. It was probably never a possibility, not for a man like Crane. I will admit to you that there was a small sense of victory, a weak glow of triumph that I had caused *some* consequence – for Audrey, for his other victims, and for myself.

When I graduated in May, I didn't think of Crane at all. Beneath the bright lights of the auditorium, dressed in my graduation gown, I lined up with the other students to receive my degree from Dean Thompson, with distinction. She shook my hand vigorously as she handed me my diploma. 'Thank you, Jessica,' she said, her eyes shining. I hadn't told anyone what happened with Crane on that corridor, yet something in the way she spoke made me feel as if she knew I was responsible for his departure.

While polite clapping sounded, I smiled out at the dark auditorium beyond. My family weren't there to cheer me on, my parents still in Dublin, but I waved and smiled as if they had been present nonetheless. As I took my seat again, I slipped past Vera at the start of the row, who nodded knowingly. Behind her, three rows back, I spotted Joshua, but he wasn't looking at me, instead watching the next student receive her degree. Ronald, beside Joshua, clapped hard as I met his eye, and then let out a loud cheer. As I passed her, Amanda leaned forward from the row behind me, embracing me tightly. 'Congratulations!' she breathed into my ear before I moved on. And, finally, as I took my seat next to him, Charlie reached over, and squeezed my knee. Though we had all drifted apart outside the walls of 1.04B, graduation had brought us back together one last time.

They were still calling out the names of other graduates, more cheers for each, and while I sat clapping dutifully, I let my thoughts fall to Audrey. There were no graduation photos of her because she never had that chance. Now, I had done it twice.

There was breath in my lungs, blood beating through my heart. I was alive, with a future ahead of me to figure out – both the gift and the punishment I deserved.

Now, all that is left of this story is you.

From the moment you approached me outside the law school, and slipped your card into my hand, I have contemplated what to do with you. That summer, a movement exploded, a push to topple the autocracy of male power over female bodies. You were investigating Crane and the story behind the protests at Franklin. You saw my name online. You heard it on the lips of other students. You spoke to Vera. You found me. You asked if I wanted to tell my story. I said I didn't know. So, you told me to write it all down, and see how it felt.

I can't say that it feels good.

I've thought countless times of deleting this account and sparing myself the stress of its existence. Instead, I could tell you a simple story, one where Crane is a villain and I am a hero. You could publish that story in your newspaper and seal his fate for good.

Do we need our stories of heroes and villains, of angels and demons? Do we need good on one side, evil on the other? Clear motives. Unimpeachable character. Or does the world need to know the ugly truth of how everything occurred?

Crane gave me some advice once, at a dinner in his house. *Know thyself,* he said, and I took that lesson to heart. I stared hard at who I am and didn't blink. I know my failings, and yet, I keep going.

Let me finish how I began. Let me give these closing words to my sister. I have wondered what she would say to me now, what she would advise. Antigone was buried alive in her pursuit of justice – my sister would not want that for me. I think of that now, as I try to move forward.

Every day, without fail, I see her face. I still listen for her voice, but not in the records she left behind. Not in the emails, the diaries, or the texts. Not in the things she had lost, or the ways she had suffered. I let her speak, now, where she is still to be found. High in the treetops, in the whistle of wind at my ear, in the silence of a clear night beneath a pearly moon.

Let me tell you how she was, in the days before Crane, walking with me, Mum and Dad on Portmarnock Beach on a sunny day. The wind sweeping her blonde hair into a set of antlers on her head, the sun turning her nose red. I called her Rudolph and she told me to feck off, snorting with laughter, freckles spread across her skin, a scattering across her cheeks. I have tried to draw their pattern, to remember them on paper, but the way they fell, like specks of paint across her face, is lost to me now. I can't get them right.

With grief comes regret. There are words you wish you had spoken, feelings you wish you had expressed, secrets you wish you had known. In the end, I could not heal Audrey's wounds, or soothe her pain, but I had done what I could to find a form of justice.

Eventually, you let go. You change or you die. You turn from the past and face forward. But not alone. You bring them with you, the ones you love. Never truly gone. Always with me.

Always, my favourite.

Dear readers,

The Favourite is a story that first began to form when I was living in Philadelphia in 2016. I arrived into a city in the grips of a historic presidential election campaign, when it seemed as if the first woman president was on her way to the White House. Just like Jessie in the book, I watched the election results in a lecture hall at my university, witnessed the protests that followed, and felt the fury of the women who marched on Inauguration Day. The experience had an indelible effect on me.

After graduating, I returned home to Dublin in the summer of 2017, just as the Me Too movement was kicking off in earnest. Back in Ireland, a high-profile rape trial was taking place and I found myself drawn into countless conversations about consent, the prosecution of sexual crimes, and the ordeal that victims of such crimes face going to court. So often, verdicts depend solely on whether or not a woman is believed. When it comes to sexual crimes, the absence of evidence quickly becomes an absence of justice.

That summer, I began writing a first draft of this book, sketching out ideas for a character who was as angry and frustrated at the legal system as I was, someone who knew the law and could interrogate it, but who was also not afraid to work around it. I placed the story in a law school so I could bring you, the reader, into a lecture hall, and pose a central question for you to consider: what do you do if you know a man is guilty of a crime but can't prove it?

As a lawyer, these are the sorts of knotty ethical questions that I've always been drawn to, the holes and the gaps between the law's promise of justice and its ability to deliver it. There is something about sexual crimes against women which cause our legal system to crumble, exposing a rot in the patriarchal root system. As a writer, I wanted to interrogate the human impact of that failure, as well as exploring my own feelings of anger about it. Writing this story, I wanted Jessie's anger to feel raw because, in the face of injustice, anger is not only reasonable, but necessary.

I'm very glad to say that *The Favourite* is a work of fiction, as are all of the characters. None of the events in the book happened to me, anyone I know, or anyone I am personally aware of. But versions of this story have occurred over and over again and so I know they may resonate with readers. The character of Jay Crane is pure fiction but, for some readers, he may feel familiar, as might Audrey's trauma. To readers who have had such an experience, I would like to take this opportunity to say that I am so very sorry, and I stand with you.

With very best wishes,

Rosemary

Acknowledgements

I would like to begin with a heartfelt thanks to my publishers, Orion Fiction and Graydon House, for their support and dedication to this story. A book begins with a spark of imagination in the mind of the writer but it takes a team to bring it into the world. In particular, I am deeply grateful for the rigour and commitment of my editors, Leodora Darlington and Melanie Fried. Their attention, guidance, and care for this story helped it to grow and strengthen, and I am hugely grateful to have had the benefit of their talent and expertise. Thanks also to Sahil Javed for his work and support, and Charlotte Mursell for her edits on an early draft.

I would also like to thank my incredible agent Hayley Steed for always being in my corner, as well as for her keen editorial eye, which helped craft and steer this story from its very earliest, tentative days. I'd also like to thank Georgia McVeigh for her editorial support, Elinor Davies, and all the team at the Madeleine Milburn Literary Agency. I am also enormously grateful to Kermit Roosevelt whose fiction workshop gave me the confidence to pursue novel writing seriously and whose support of my career over the years is much appreciated.

I was very lucky to have hugely enjoyed my time at the universities where I have studied, and I'm indebted to a great many teachers and law professors who have inspired me and supported my career, both as a lawyer and writer. In a very real way, they have taught me how to think, and I am so grateful to have had an opportunity to learn so much from them.

I don't have a sister, but Jessie's love for her family is based on my own, as are her experiences of grief. To my family — Anne Marie, Brian, Bobby, and my father, Brendan, whom I miss every day — thank you from the bottom of my heart for the love and support you have always given me.

Finally, the idea for this book began with a series of excited text messages between me and my husband, David Kenny, where we talked about the idea of a student who takes a professor's scholarship to heart and uses it against him. From those initial texts, the characters of Jessica Mooney and Jay Crane were born and, at every step since, David has helped me to craft their class-room interactions and thoughts on the law. His insight and ideas provided the intellectual heart of the book and our conversations gave me endless inspiration. This story would not be the same without his enormous talents as a teacher and scholar, nor would I be the same without the strength of our bond and the depth of our love. Dave, you are a wonder and I adore you.

Credits

Rosemary Hennigan and Orion Fiction would like to thank everyone at Orion who worked on the publication of *The Favourite* in the UK.

Editorial
Leodora Darlington
Sahil Javed

Copy editor
Laura Gerrard
Jade Craddock

Proof reader
Marian Reid

Audio
Paul Stark
Jake Alderson

Contracts
Dan Herron
Ellie Bowker
Alyx Hurst

Design
Charlotte Abrams-Simpson
Tomás Almeida
Joanna Ridley

Editorial Management
Charlie Panayiotou
Jane Hughes
Bartley Shaw

Finance
Jasdip Nandra
Nick Gibson
Sue Baker

Production
Ruth Sharvell

Publicity and Marketing
Sharina Smith

Sales
Jen Wilson
Esther Waters
Victoria Laws
Toluwalope Ayo-Ajala
Rachael Hum
Ellie Kyrke-Smith
Sinead White
Georgina Cutler

Operations
Jo Jacobs
Dan Stevens

**If you loved *The Favourite*, don't miss
Rosemary Hennigan's tense and utterly gripping debut . . .**

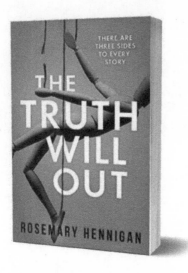

*'Maybe I've told that version of the story so often,
that I can't remember the truth of it anymore.'*

Dara Gaffney is fresh out of drama school when she lands the
leading role in the revival of Eabha de Lacey's hugely successful
yet controversial play.

Based on the true story of the death of Cillian Butler, many
claim that Eabha had an ulterior motive when she penned it.
Cillian's death remains a mystery to this day, and Eabha and
her brother, Austin, the only witnesses.

As the media storm builds and the opening night draws closer,
the cast find it harder and harder to separate themselves from
the characters.

As the truth of Cillian's fate becomes clear, Dara's loyalty to
her role will be irrevocably questioned as the terrible history
starts to repeat itself . . .

Reader's Guide

1. Do you feel like Crane got the right punishment in the end? Why or why not?

2. Discuss how systems of power — legal, academic — protect certain groups of people over others in the novel. How does this play out in real life as well? Do you feel like there's been progress since the #metoo movement launched?

3. Jessie herself admits that her plan is morally ambiguous but feels it's the only way to get justice for her sister. Did you ultimately understand her rationale?

4. Did any of Crane's lectures in particular resonate with you? Discuss the way literature can reflect, perpetuate, and challenge power inequity. How should one today evaluate the social themes of a novel or story written decades or centuries ago?

5. What do you envision Jessie's future will be like? How will she use her degree, if at all?

6. Did you have a favourite student in the Law and Literature cohort? Where do you think each of them will end up?

7. Can justice and revenge ever be one and the same? Why or why not?

8. Do you think Leyna knew the truth about Crane's behaviour? Why do you think she stuck by him?